Text Classics

LOUIS STONE was born in Leicester, England, in 1871. He and his family migrated to Brisbane in 1884, and soon moved to Redfern, then Waterloo, neighbouring inner suburbs of Sydney.

With the aid of a scholarship Stone attended Fort Street Training School and studied arts at the University of Sydney. He qualified as a teacher in 1895. Intermittent work in Sydney primary schools led to country postings from 1900. Stone returned to the city in 1904, where he married and began writing. Health problems, the result of anxiety, plagued his teaching career.

Jonah was published in London in 1911. The novel painstakingly describes the conditions and distinctive characters—larrikins—of the working-class inner city. Norman Lindsay, A. G. Stephens and Nettie Palmer admired its realistic depiction of Sydney life.

Stone subsequently wrote, without success, the novel *Betty Wayside* (1915). He began writing for the stage and went to London in 1920 to try his luck. On his return to Australia his plays *The Lap of the Gods* (1923) and *The Watch that Wouldn't Go* (1926) were published.

In 1933 *Jonah* was published in the United States and in Australia, where it stayed in print for many years. It was eventually adapted for television by the ABC and performed as a stage play.

Louis Stone died in 1935, having retired from teaching four years earlier.

FRANK MOORHOUSE has written fiction, non-fiction, screenplays and essays, and edited many collections of writing. His books include the three Edith Campbell Berry novels: *Grand Days*, which won a South Australian Premier's Award; *Dark Palace*, which won the Miles Franklin Literary Award; and *Cold Light*, which won a Queensland Literary Award.

ALSO BY LOUIS STONE

Betty Wayside

Jonah
Louis Stone

Text Publishing Melbourne Australia

textclassics.com.au
textpublishing.com.au

The Text Publishing Company
Swann House
22 William Street
Melbourne Victoria 3000
Australia

First published in the United Kingdom by Methuen 1911
This edition published by The Text Publishing Company 2013

Cover design by WH Chong
Page design by Text
Typeset by Midland Typesetters

Printed in Australia by Griffin Press, an Accredited ISO AS/NZS 14001:2004
Environmental Management System printer

Primary print ISBN: 9781922147448
Ebook ISBN: 9781922148490
Author: Stone, Louis, 1871–1935.
Title: Jonah / by Louis Stone; introduced by Frank Moorhouse.
Series: Text classics.
Dewey Number: A823.2

CONTENTS

Gangland
by Frank Moorhouse

ONE of the pleasures of reading *Jonah*, first published in 1911 in London, is that it gives us rare and vivid access to urban life at the beginning of the twentieth century in Australia—or more particularly inner Sydney, although I suspect that Louis Stone's novel describes life in many of our cities one hundred years ago.

Another of the pleasures is that some of the houses of the period still exist in Waterloo—just. One of my friends lives in one of these buildings in a street in neighbouring Redfern very like the one where Jonah is set: a terrace house which opens straight onto a step to the footpath—no front garden—and has three rooms downstairs, two rooms upstairs, one with a small balcony overhanging the street. In *Jonah*'s time there would have been an outdoor toilet and almost certainly no bathroom. Lanes run behind these old streets, from which the outside toilet was emptied into dunny carts which called during the early hours.

The houses are cramped—my friend's has three people living in it. In the days of *Jonah* a family of six or seven would have crowded into the space. Ceilings are about three metres high and the gas light fittings still remain. In the time of the novel the houses were lit by kerosene lamps and candles.

The central street of Stone's book is called Cardigan—a name taken from other suburbs which I suspect Stone transferred into Waterloo to protect identities.

It is possible to see the historical demographic divisions of *Jonah* in a direct lineage from the first European settlement, with its strictly demarcated society of convicts, free settlers, soldiers and administrators. The convicts' place was taken in the mid-nineteenth century by poorly paid unskilled workers who lived in tight inner-city communities but had the same attitudes as the convicts—non-cooperation with the authorities, with the police and 'government'.

This fierce demarcation continued in Waterloo and adjoining suburbs, especially Redfern, well into the twentieth century. It is characterised by a vigilant hostile insularity—that is, a community akin to an island surrounded by dangerous seas. Strangers who wandered into the neighbourhood could expect to be insulted or jostled or robbed. These were no-go areas.

The first part of *Jonah* describes the life of a 'push'—the gangs which operated in these neighbourhoods were usually named after the street which was central to their lives, so we have the Cardigan Street Push and the Ivy Street Push. (Ivy Street is in nearby Darlington.) They policed their turf brutally and recklessly, punishing those who transgressed the gang or who were suspected of co-operating with the authorities. They did not place much value on marriage as a rite or contract, were not fussed about illegitimate children and ignored religious morals—'people who spoke about love were either fools or liars.' They had their own argot, and were to varying degrees illiterate. There was an ethic of mutual aid among neighbours.

The interiors of their houses were sparsely decorated with calendars and almanacs which contained astronomical data, ecclesiastical and other anniversaries, and sometimes astrological and meteorological forecasts, public holidays and other miscellaneous information, as well as advertising the businesses which gave them out. One character in *Jonah* brings home two undescribed prints he has come across, which he and his young wife hang with careful consideration. Furniture was second-hand or homemade.

A delicacy on Saturday nights was provided by the Pieman, whose cart came around selling pie and gravy, or pie and mashed peas, or mashed peas on their own, or saveloys: fat, red-skinned smoked sausages of seasoned pork. Beer was the drink of choice for both men and women, with the women sometimes drinking brandy or gin and water, and often becoming staggering drunk. Cigarette smoking and gambling, especially two-up, were acceptable habits.

The arts enjoyed by these communities were mouth-organ music and singing, street hymns sung by the band of the Salvation Army, and occasional visits to the Tivoli for pantomimes and music-hall theatre. There was no radio or film, and the only books for those who could read were novelettes—short, light or sentimental novels. Upward mobility was symbolised by having a piano.

In the novel there is a church nearby, Trinity, which sounds like a Methodist-leaning Anglicanism. The new rector

> had brought some strange ideas from London,
> where he had worked in the slums. He had
> founded a workman's club, and smoked his
> pipe with the members; formed a brigade
> of newsboys and riff-raff, and taught them
> elementary morality with the aid of boxing-
> gloves; and offended his congregation by
> treating the poor with the same consideration
> as themselves. And then, astonished by the
> number of mothers who were not wives, that
> he discovered on his rounds, he had announced
> that he would open the church on the first

Saturday night in every month to marry any couples without needless questions. They could pay, if they chose, but nothing was expected.

Louis Stone was born in Leicester in 1871 and was in his late thirties when he wrote *Jonah*. His description of inner-Sydney life was based in part on his own experiences of growing up in Waterloo. The *Oxford Companion to Australian Literature* refers to Stone 'painstakingly gathering material for his representation of city life'.

It also says that Stone was the first Australian writer to make the larrikin popular—though C. J. Dennis's 'Sentimental Bloke' poems had started to appear in the *Bulletin* a couple of years earlier. *Jonah* was later published in the US under the title *Larrikin*.

The Australian intelligentsia has for some time held a romantic idea of the 'larrikin spirit' which conveniently forgets the brutal gang life while enjoying the slang and the anti-authoritarianism, insofar as it is an expression of egalitarianism and a rebellion against capitalism and its attendant state structure of courts and police. This aspect of Australian identity is often described nostalgically, yet it seems to glorify antisocial attitudes and behaviour at odds with contemporary values.

Slipping in and out of realism, Stone's novel follows the rise of two Push members—Jonah, a violent leader, and Chook, his loyal mate and offsider—into the shopkeeper class, towards bourgeois married respectability. Jonah marks his eventual ascension by buying a piano for his son.

Stone captures the language of this subculture with some success, although he is tripped up by history as words change or lose their meanings—one example is his rendering of the word 'come' as 'cum'. I am unsure how 'come' was pronounced by, say, the university educated at that time, but Stone's phonetic spelling seems to imply that there is some distance between their 'come' and that of the working class, and, of course, the word has since picked up another meaning. (I recently read George Eliot's *Scenes of Clerical Life*, where she tries very hard accurately to render dialect but like Stone does not realise that the other classes— the university educated and the upper class—also speak a dialect, 'proper English'.)

Jonah's publication history tells us that the book has nevertheless enjoyed a near-constant readership. Published in the UK by Methuen in 1911, and praised by John Galsworthy and Norman Lindsay as well as the Sydney press, it had an Australian edition in 1933, with subsequent republications in the 1940s, '60s, '70s and '80s, and an Angus & Robertson Classics edition in 1991. Dorothy Green, in her introduction to the 1991 publication, says that Stone continued to make changes to the book in the early editions. There was a stage version and the ABC adapted the novel for a television series in 1982. It was also made into a musical with the title *Jonah Jones* by the Sydney Theatre Company in 1985.

Stone, a school teacher, suffered debilitating nervous illnesses, and despite a pilgrimage to London to seek success—something which quite a few of the promising young Australian writers of the nineteenth and twentieth centuries, including Henry Lawson, did—and despite having his first novel published in the UK, US and Australia, he did not create a body of accomplished work. Only *Jonah* lives on. Stone died in 1935, aged sixty-four.

Within a few decades most inner-Sydney housing had passed from the white working class, who moved to the outer suburbs after being forced out of their homes or selling them to young, well-off people who saw that the houses could be renovated and that inner-city living could become fashionable.

But Redfern, next door to Waterloo, continued to be a holdout, especially after the white working class there had been replaced by Aboriginal tenants in and around the precinct called The Block. During the wave of gentrification they refused to leave and resisted with violent protests. Over the past thirty years the Aboriginal Housing Company gradually purchased houses for use as an Aboriginal-managed housing project.

Some of the Aboriginal dwellers had shown many of the characteristics of poor white renters. Until recently the suburb was still considered a no-go area by taxi drivers and outsiders, continuing its two-hundred-year reputation as a hostile enclave.

Jonah is an enduring and very readable novel which throws up curious and fearful connections with the places we have come from and the stories that brought us along.

(Thanks to Professor Brian Kiernan for his portrait of Louis Stone in the *Australian Dictionary of Biography* and for a conversation about Stone.)

Jonah

PART ONE

LARRIKINS ALL

One side of the street glittered like a brilliant eruption with the light from a row of shops; the other, lined with houses, was almost deserted, for the people, drawn like moths by the glare, crowded and jostled under the lights.

It was Saturday night, and Waterloo, by immemorial habit, had flung itself on the shops, bent on plunder. For an hour past a stream of people had flowed from the back streets into Botany Road, where the shops stood in shining rows, awaiting the conflict.

The butcher's caught the eye with a flare of colour as the light played on the pink and white flesh of sheep, gutted and skewered like victims for sacrifice; the saffron and red quarters of beef, hanging like the limbs of a dismembered Colossus; and the carcasses of pigs, the unclean beast of the Jews, pallid as a corpse. The butchers passed in and out, sweating and greasy, hoarsely crying the prices as they cut and hacked the meat. The people crowded about, sniffing the odour of dead flesh, hungry and brutal—carnivora seeking their prey.

At the grocer's the light was reflected from the gay labels on tins and packages and bottles, and the air was heavy with the confused odour of tea, coffee and spices.

Cabbages, piled in heaps against the door-posts of the greengrocer's, threw a rank smell of vegetables on the air; the fruit within, built in pyramids for display, filled the nostrils with the fragrant, wholesome scents of the orchard.

The buyers surged against the barricade of counters, shouting their orders, contesting the ground inch by inch as they fought for the value of a penny. And they emerged staggering under the weight of their plunder, laden like ants with food for hungry mouths—the insatiable maw of the people.

The Push was gathered under the veranda at the corner of Cardigan Street, smoking cigarettes and discussing the weightier matters of life—horses and women. They were all young—from eighteen to twenty-five—for the larrikin never grows old. They leaned against the veranda posts, or squatted below the windows of the shop, which had been to let for months.

Here they met nightly, as men meet at their club—a terror to the neighbourhood. Their chief diversion was to guy the pedestrians, leaping from insult to swift retaliation if one resented their foul comments.

6

"Gar!" one was saying, "I tell yer some 'orses know more'n a man. I remember old Joe Riley goin' inter the stable one day to a brown mare as 'ad a derry on 'im 'cause 'e flogged 'er crool. Well, wot does she do? She squeezes 'im up agin the side o' the stable, an' nearly stiffens 'im afore 'e cud git out. My oath, she did!"

"That's nuthin' ter wot a mare as was runnin' leader in Daly's 'bus used ter do," began another, stirred by that rivalry which makes talkers magnify and invent to cap a story; but he stopped suddenly as two girls approached.

One was short and fat, a nugget, with square, sullen features; the other, thin as a rake, with a mass of red hair that fell to her waist in a thick coil.

"'Ello, Ada, w'ere you goin'?" he inquired, with a facetious grin. "Cum 'ere, I want ter talk ter yer."

The fat girl stopped and laughed.

"Can't—I'm in a 'urry," she replied.

"Well, kin I cum wid yer?" he asked, with another grin.

"Not wi' that face, Chook," she answered, laughing.

"None o' yer lip, now, or I'll tell Jonah wot yer were doin' last night," said Chook.

"W'ere is Joe?" asked the girl, suddenly serious. "Tell 'im I want ter see 'im."

"Gone ter buy a smoke; 'e'll be back in a minit."

"Right-oh, tell 'im wot I said," replied Ada, moving away.

"'Ere, 'old 'ard, ain't yer goin' ter interdooce yer cobber?" cried Chook, staring at the red-headed girl.

"An' 'er ginger 'air was scorchin' all 'er back," he sang in parody, suddenly cutting a caper and snapping his fingers.

7

The girl's white skin flushed pink with anger, her eyes sparkled with hate.

"Ugly swine! I'll smack yer jaw, if yer talk ter me," she cried.

"Blimey, 'ot stuff, ain't it?" inquired Chook.

"Cum on, Pinkey. Never mind 'im," cried Ada, moving off.

"Yah, go 'ome an' wash yer neck!" shouted Chook, with sudden venom.

The red-headed girl stood silent, searching her mind for a stinging retort.

"Yer'd catch yer death o' cold if yer washed yer own," she cried; and the two passed out of sight, tittering.

Chook turned to his mates.

"She kin give it lip, can't she?" said he, in admiration.

A moment later the leader of the Push crossed the street, and took his place in silence under the veranda. A first glance surprised the eye, for he was a hunchback, with the uncanny look of the deformed—the head, large and powerful, wedged between the shoulders as if a giant's hand had pressed it down, the hump projecting behind, monstrous and inhuman. His face held you with a pair of restless grey eyes, the colour and temper of steel, deep with malicious intelligence. His nose was large and thin, curved like the beak of an eagle. Chook, whose acquaintance he had made years ago when selling newspapers, was his mate. Both carried nicknames, corrupted from Jones and Fowles, with the rude wit of the streets.

"Ada's lookin' fer yous, Jonah," said Chook.

"Yer don't say so?" replied the hunchback, raising his leg to strike a match. "Was Pinkey with 'er?" he added.

"D'ye mean a little moll wi' ginger hair?" asked Chook. Jonah nodded.

"My oath, she was! Gi' me a knockout in one act," said Chook; and the others laughed.

"Ginger fer pluck!" cried someone.

And they began to argue whether you could tell a woman's character from the colour of her hair; whether red-haired women were more deceitful than others.

Suddenly, up the road, appeared a detachment of the Salvation Army, stepping in time to the muffled beat of a drum. The procession halted at the street corner, stepped out of the way of traffic, and formed a circle. The Push moved to the kerbstone, and, with a derisive grin, awaited the performance.

The wavering flame of the kerosene torches, topped with thick smoke, shone yellow against the whiter light of the gas-jets in the shops. The men, in red jerseys and flat caps, held the poles of the torches in rest. When a gust of air blew the thick black smoke into their eyes, they patiently turned their heads. The sisters, conscious of the public gaze, stood with downcast eyes, their faces framed in grotesque poke-bonnets.

The Captain, a man of fifty, with the knotty, misshapen hands of a workman, stepped into the centre of the ring, took off his cap, and began to speak.

"Oh friends, we 'ave met 'ere again tonight to inquire after the safety of yer everlastin' souls. Yer pass by, thinkin' only of yer idle pleasures, w'en at any moment yer might be

9

called to judgment by 'Im Who made us all equal in 'Is eyes. Yer pass by without 'earin' the sweet voice of Jesus callin' on yer to be saved this very minit. For 'E is callin' yer to come an' be saved an' find salvation, as 'E called me many years ago. I was then like yerselves, full of wickedness, an' gloryin' in sin. But I 'eard the voice of 'Im Who died on the Cross, an' saw I was rushin' 'eadlong to 'ell. An' 'Is blood washed all my sins away, an' made me whiter than snow. Whiter than snow, friends—whiter than snow! An' 'E'll do the same fer you if yer will only come an' be saved. Oh, can't yer 'ear the voice of Jesus callin' to yer to come an' live with 'Im in 'Is blessed mansions in the sky? Oh, come tonight an' find salvation!"

His arms were outstretched in a passionate gesture of appeal, his rough voice vibrated with emotion, the common face flamed with the ecstasy of the fanatic. When he stopped for breath or wiped the sweat from his face, the Army spurred him on with cries of "Hallelujah! Amen!" as one pokes a dying fire.

The Lieutenant, who was the comedian of the company, met with a grin of approval as he faced the ring of torches like an actor facing the footlights, posing before the crowd that had gathered, flashing his vulgar conceit in the public eye. And he praised God in a song and dance, fitting his words to the latest craze of the music-hall:

> "Oh! won't you come and join us?
> Jesus leads the throng,"

snapping his fingers, grimacing, cutting capers that would have delighted the gallery of a theatre.

"Encore!" yelled the Push as he danced himself to a standstill, hot and breathless.

The rank and file came forward to testify. The men stammered in confusion, terrified by the noise they made, shrinking from the crowd as a timid bather shrinks from icy water, driven to this performance by an unseen power. But the women were shrill and self-possessed, scolding their hearers, demanding an instant surrender to the Army, whose advantages they pointed out with a glib fluency as if it were a Benefit Lodge.

Then the men knelt in the dust, the women covered their faces, and the Captain began to pray. His voice rose in shrill entreaty, mixed with the cries of the shopmen and the noise of the streets.

The spectators, familiar with the sight, listened in nonchalance, stopping to watch the group for a minute as they would look into a shop window. The exhibition stirred no religious feeling in them, for their minds, with the tenacity of childhood, associated religion with churches, parsons and hymn-books.

The Push grew restless, divided between a desire to upset the meeting and fear of the police.

"Well I used ter think a funeral was slow," remarked Chook, losing patience; and he stepped behind Jonah.

"'Ere, look out!" yelled Jonah the next minute, as, with a push from Chook, he collided violently with one of the soldiers and fell into the centre of the ring.

"'E shoved me," cried Jonah as he got up, pointing with an injured air to the grinning Chook. "I'll gi' yer a kick in the neck, if yer git me lumbered," he added, scowling with counterfeit anger at his mate.

11

"If yer was my son…" said the Captain severely. "If yer was my son…" he repeated, halting for words.

"I should 'ave trotters as big as yer own," cried Jonah, pointing to the man's feet, cased in enormous bluchers. The Push yelled with derision as Jonah edged out of the circle, ready for flight.

The Captain flushed angrily, and then his face cleared.

"Well, friends," he cried, "God gave me big feet to tramp the streets and preach the Gospel to my fellow men." And the interrupted service went on.

Jonah, who carried the brains of the Push, devised a fresh attack, involving Chook, a broken bottle, and the big drum.

"It'll cut it like butter," he was explaining; when suddenly there was a cry of "Nit! 'Ere's a cop!" and the Push bolted like rabbits.

Jonah and Chook alone stood their ground, with reluctant valour, for the policeman was already beside them. Chook shoved the broken bottle into his pocket, and listened with unusual interest to the last hymn of the Army. Jonah, with one eye on the policeman, looked worried, as if he were struggling with a desire to join the Army and lead a pure life. The policeman looked hard at them and turned away.

The pair were making a strategic movement to the rear, when the two girls who had exchanged shots with Chook at the corner passed them. The fat girl tapped Jonah on the back. He turned with a start.

"Nit yer larks!" he cried. "I thought it was the cop."

"Cum 'ere Joe; I want yer," said the girl.

12

"Wot's up now?" he cried, following her along the street.

They stood in earnest talk for some minutes, while Chook complimented the red-headed girl on her wit.

"Yer knocked me sky-'igh," he confessed, with a leer.

"Did I?"

"Yer did. Gi' me one straight on the point," he admitted.

"Yous keep a civil tongue in yer head," she cried, and the curious pink flush spread over her white skin.

"Orl right, wot are yer narked about?" inquired Chook.

He noticed, with surprise, that she was pretty, with small regular features; her eyes quick and bright, like a bird's. Under the gaslight her hair was the colour of a new penny.

"W'y, I don't believe yer 'air is red," said Chook, coming nearer.

"Now then, keep yer 'ands to yerself," cried the girl, giving him a vigorous push. Before he could repeat his attack, she walked away to join Ada, who hailed her shrilly.

Jonah rejoined his mate in gloomy silence. The Push had scattered—some to the two-up school, some to the dance-room. The butcher's flare of lights shone with a desolate air on piles of bones and scraps of meat—the debris of battle. The greengrocer's was stripped bare to the shelves, as if an army of locusts had marched through with ravenous tooth.

"Comin' down the street?" asked Chook, feeling absently in his pockets.

"No," said Jonah.

"W'y, wot's up now?" inquired Chook in surprise.

13

"Oh, nuthin'; but I'm goin' ter sleep at Ada's tonight," replied Jonah, staring at the shops.

"'Strewth!" cried Chook, looking at him in wonder. "Wot's the game now?"

"Oh! the old woman wants me ter put in the night there. Says some blokes 'ave bin after 'er fowls," replied Jonah, hesitating like a boy inventing an excuse.

"Fowls!" cried Chook, with infinite scorn. "Wants yer to nuss the bloomin' kid."

"My oath, she don't," replied Jonah, with great heartiness.

"Well, gimme a smoke," said Chook, feeling again in his pockets.

Jonah took out a packet of cigarettes, counted how many were left, and gave him one.

"Kin yer spare it?" asked Chook, derisively. "Lucky I've only got one mouth."

"Mouth? More like a hole in a wall," grinned Jonah.

"Well, so long. See yer tomorrer," said Chook, moving off. "'Ere, gimme a match," he added.

"Better tell yer old woman I'm sleepin' out," said Jonah.

He was boarding with Chook's family, paying what he could spare out of fifteen shillings or a pound a week.

"Oh, I don't suppose you'll be missed," replied Chook, graciously.

"Rye buck!" cried Jonah.

14

2

JONAH EATS GREEN PEAS

Eighteen months past, Jonah had met Ada, who worked at Packard's boot factory, at a dance. Struck by her skill in dancing, he courted her in the larrikin fashion. At night he stood in front of the house, and whistled till she came out. Then they went to the park, where they sprawled on the grass in obscure corners.

At intervals the quick spurt of a match lit up their faces, followed by the red glow of Jonah's everlasting cigarette. Their talk ran incessantly on their acquaintances, whose sayings and doings they discussed with monotonous detail. If it rained, they stood under a veranda in the conventional attitude—Jonah leaning against the wall, Ada standing in front of him. The etiquette of Cardigan Street considered any other position scandalous.

On Saturday night they went to Bob Fenner's dance-room, or strolled down to Paddy's Market. When Jonah was flush, he took her to the "Tiv.", where they sat in the gallery, packed like sardines. If it were hot, Jonah sat in his shirtsleeves, and went out for a drink at the intermission. When they reached home, they stood in the lane bordering the cottage where Ada lived, and talked for an hour in the dim light of the lamp opposite, before she went in.

Sometimes, in a gay humour, she knocked off Jonah's hat, and he retaliated with a punch in the ribs. Then a scuffle followed, with slaps, blows and stifled yells, till Ada's mother, awakened by the noise, knocked on the wall with her slipper. And this was their romance of love.

Mrs Yabsley was a widow; for Ada's father, scorning old age, had preferred to die of drink in his prime. The publicans lost a good customer, but his widow found life easier.

"Talk about payin' ter see men swaller knives an' swords!" she exclaimed. "My old man could swaller tables an' chairs faster than I could buy 'em."

So she opened a laundry, and washed and ironed for the neighbourhood. Cardigan Street was proud of her. Her eyes twinkled in a big, humorous face; her arm was like a leg of mutton; the floors creaked beneath her as she walked. She laughed as a bull roars; her face turned purple; she fought for air; the veins rose like cords on her forehead. She was pointed out to strangers like a public building as she sat on her veranda, gossiping with the neighbours in a voice that shook the windows. There was no tongue like hers within a mile. Her sayings were quoted like the newspaper. Draymen laughed at her jokes.

16

Yet the women took their secret troubles to her. For this unwieldy jester, with the jolly red face and rough tongue, could touch the heart with a word when she was in the humour. Then she spoke so wisely and kindly that the tears gathered in stubborn eyes, and the poor fools went home comforted.

Ever since her daughter was a child she had speculated on her marriage. There was to be no nonsense about love. That was all very well in novelettes, but in Cardigan Street love-matches were a failure. Generally the first few months saw the divine spark drowned in beer. She would pick a steady man with his two pounds a week; he would jump at the chance, and the whole street would turn out to the wedding. But, as is common, her far-seeing eyes had neglected the things that lay under her nose. Ada, in open revolt, had chosen Jonah the larrikin, a hunchback, crafty as the devil, and monstrous to the sight. In six months the inevitable had happened.

She was dismayed, but unshaken; and set to work to repair the damage with the craft and strategy of an old general. She made no fuss when the child was born, and Jonah, who meditated flight, in fear of maintenance, was assured he had nothing to worry about. Mrs Yabsley had a brief interview with him at the street corner.

"As fer puttin yous inter court; I'll wait till y'earn enough ter keep yerself, an' Gawd knows w'en that'll 'appen," she remarked pleasantly.

As she spoke she earnestly considered the large head, wedged between the shoulders as if a giant's hand had pressed it down, the masterful nose, the keen grey eyes, and the cynical lips; and in that moment determined to make him Ada's husband. Yet he was the last man she would have chosen for a son-in-law. A loafer and a vagabond, he spoke of marriage with a grin. Half his time was spent under the veranda at the corner with the Push. He worked at his trade by fits and starts, earning enough to keep himself in cigarettes.

That was six months ago, and Ada had returned to the factory, where her disaster created no stir. Such accidents were common.

Mrs Yabsley reared the child as she had reared her daughter, in a box-cradle near the wash-tub or ironing-board, for Ada proved an indifferent mother.

Then, with a sudden change of front, she encouraged Jonah's intimacy with Ada. She invited him to the house, which he avoided with an animal craft and suspicion, meeting Ada in the streets. It was her scheme to get him to live in the house; the rest, she thought, would be easy. But Jonah feared dimly that if he ventured inside the house he would bring himself under the law. So he grinned, and kept his distance, like an animal that fears a trap.

But at last, his resistance worn to a thread by constant coaxing, he had agreed to spend the night there on account of the fowls. He was interested in these, for one pair was his gift to Ada, the fruit of some midnight raid.

Jonah stood alone at the corner watching the crowd. Chook's reference to the baby had shaken his resolution, and he decided to think it over. And as he watched the moving procession with the pleasure of a spectator at the play, he thought uneasily of women and marriage.

As he nodded from time to time to an acquaintance, a young man passed him carrying a child in his arms. His wife, a slip of a girl, loaded with bundles, gave Jonah a quick look of fear and scorn. The man stared Jonah full in the face without a sign of recognition, and bent his head over the child with a caressing movement. Jonah noted the look of humble pride in his eyes, and marvelled. Twelve months ago he was Jonah's rival in the Push, famous for his strength and audacity, and now butter wouldn't melt in his mouth. Jonah called to mind other cases, with a sudden fear in his heart at this mysterious ceremony before a parson that affected men like a disease, robbing them of all a man desired, and leaving them contented, and happy. He turned into Cardigan Street with the air of a man who is putting his neck in the noose, resolving secretly to cut and run at the least hint of danger.

As he walked slowly up the street he became aware of a commotion at the corner of George Street. He saw that a crowd had gathered, and quickened his pace, for a crowd in Cardigan Street generally meant a fight. Jonah elbowed his way through the ring, and found a young policeman, new to this beat, struggling with an undersized man with the face of a ferret. Jonah's first thought was to effect a rescue, as his practised eye took in the details of the scene. Let them get away from the light of the street lamp, and with a sudden rush the thing would be done. He looked round for the Push, and remembered that they were scattered. Then he saw that the captive was a stranger, and decided to look on quietly and note the policeman's methods for future use.

On finding that he was overmatched in strength, the prisoner had dropped to the ground, and, with silent, cat-like movements baulked the policeman's efforts. As Jonah looked on, the constable straightened his back, wiped the sweat from his face, and then, suddenly desperate, called on the nearest to help him. The men slipped behind the women, who laughed in his face. It was his first arrest, and he looked in astonishment at the grinning, hostile faces, too nervous to use his strength, harassed by the hatred of the people.

"Take 'im yerself; do yer own dirty work."

"Wot's the poor bloke done?"

"Nuthin', yer may be sure."

"These Johns run a man in, an' swear his life away ter git a stripe on their sleeve."

"They think they kin knock a man about as they like 'cause 'e's poor."

"They'd find plenty to do if they took the scoundrels that walk the streets in a top 'at."

"It don't pay. They know which side their bread's buttered, don't yous fergit."

Chiefly by his own efforts the prisoner had become a disreputable wreck. Hatless, with torn collar, his clothes covered with the dirt he was rolling in, ten minutes' struggle with the policeman had transformed him into a scarecrow.

"If there was any men about, they wouldn't see a decent young man turned into a criminal under their very eyes," cried a virago, looking round for a champion.

"If I was a man, I'd…"

She stopped as Sergeant Carmody arrived with a brisk air, and the crowd fell back, silent before the official who knew every face in the ring. In an instant the captive was lifted to his feet, his arms were twisted behind his back till the sinews cracked, and the procession moved off to the station.

When Jonah reached the cottage, he stood irresolute on the other side of the street. Already regretting his promise, he turned to go, when Ada came to the door and saw him under the gas lamp. He crossed the street, trying to show by his walk that his presence was a mere accident.

"Cum in," cried Ada. "Mum won't eat yer."

Mrs Yabsley, who was ironing among a pile of shirts and collars, looked up, with the iron in her hand.

"W'y, Joe, ye're quite a stranger!" she cried. "Sit down an' make yerself at 'ome."

"'Ow do, missus?" said Jonah, looking round nervously for the child, but it was not visible.

"I knowed yer wouldn't let them take the old woman's fowls," she continued. "'Ere, Ada, go an' git a jug o' beer."

The room, which served for a laundry, was dimly lit with a candle. The pile of white linen brought into relief the dirt and poverty of the interior. The walls were stained with grease and patches of dirt, added slowly through the years as a face gathers wrinkles. But Jonah saw nothing of this. He was used to dirt.

He sat down, and, with a sudden attack of politeness, decided to take off his hat, but, uncertain of his footing, pushed it on the back of his head as a compromise. He lit a cigarette, and felt more at ease.

A faint odour of scorching reached his nostrils as Mrs Yabsley passed the hot iron over the white fronts. The

21

small black iron ran swiftly over the clean surface, leaving a smooth, shining track behind it. And he watched, with an idler's pleasure, the swift, mechanical movements.

When the beer came, Jonah gallantly offered it to Mrs Yabsley, whose face was hot and red.

"Just leave a drop in the jug, an' I'll be thankful for it when I'm done," she replied, wiping her forehead on her sleeve. Jonah had risen in her esteem.

After some awkward attempts at conversation, Jonah relapsed into silence. He was glad that he had brought his mouth-organ, won in a shilling raffle. He would give them a tune later on.

When she had finished the last shirt, Mrs Yabsley looked at the clock with an exclamation. It was nearly ten. She had to deliver the shirts, and then buy the week's supplies. For she did her shopping at the last minute, in a panic. It had been her mother's way—to dash into the butcher's as he swept the last bones together, to hammer at the grocer's door as he turned out the lights. And she always forgot something, which she got on Sunday morning from the little shop at the corner.

As she was tying the shirts into bundles, she heard the tinkle of a bell in the street, and a hoarse voice that cried: "Peas an' pies, all 'ot, all 'ot!"

"'Ow'd yer like some peas, Joe?" she cried, dropping the shirts and seizing a basin.

"I wouldn't mind," said Jonah.

"'Ere, Ada, run an' git threepenn'orth," she cried.

In a minute Ada returned with the basin full of green peas, boiled into a squashy mass.

Mrs Yabsley went out with the shirts, and Jonah and Ada sat down to the peas, which they ate with keen relish, after sprinkling them with pepper and vinegar.

After the green peas, Ada noticed that Jonah was looking furtively about the room and listening, as if he expected to hear something. She guessed the cause, and decided to change his thoughts.

"Give us a tune, Joe," she cried.

Jonah took the mouth-organ from his pocket, and rubbed it carefully on his sleeve. He was a famous performer on this instrument, and on holiday nights the Push marched through the streets, with Jonah in the lead, playing tunes that he learned at the Tiv. He breathed slowly into the tubes, running up and down the scale, as a pianist runs his fingers over the keyboard before playing, and then struck into a sentimental ballad.

In five minutes he had warmed up to his work, changing from one tune to another with barely a pause, revelling in the simple rhythm and facile phrases of the popular songs. Ada listened spellbound, amazed by this talent for music, carried back to the gallery of the music-hall where she had heard these very tunes. At last he struck into a waltz, marking the time with his foot, drawing his breath in rapid jerks to accentuate the bass.

"Must 'ave a turn, if I die fer it," cried Ada, springing to her feet, and, with her arms extended to embrace an imaginary partner, she began to spin round on her toes. Ada's only talent lay in her feet, and, conscious of her skill, she danced before the hunchback with the lightness of a feather, revolving smoothly on one spot, reversing, advancing and retreating in a straight line, displaying every intricacy of the waltz. The sight was too much for Jonah, and, dropping the mouth-organ, he seized her in his arms.

"Wot did yer stop for?" cried Ada. "We carn't darnce without a tune."

"Carn't we?" said Jonah, in derision, and began to hum the words of the waltz that he had been playing:

> *"White Wings, they never grow weary,*
> *They carry me cheerily over the sea;*
> *Night comes, I long for my dearie—*
> *I'll spread out my White Wings and sail home to thee."*

The pair had no equals in the true larrikin style, called "cass dancing", and they revolved slowly on a space the size of a dinner-plate, Ada's head on Jonah's breast, their bodies pressed together, rigid as the pasteboard figures in a peep-show. They were interrupted by a cry from Mrs Yabsley's bedroom. Jonah stopped instantly, with a look of dismay on his face. Ada looked at him with a curious smile, and burst out laughing.

"I'll 'ave ter put 'im to sleep now. Cum an' ave a look at 'im, Joe—'e won't eat yer."

"No fear," cried Jonah, recoiling with anger. "Wot did yer promise before I agreed to come down?"

Chook's words flashed across his mind. This was a trap, and he had been a fool to come.

"I'll cum tomorrow, an' fix up the fowls," he cried, and, grabbing his mouth-organ, turned to go—to find his way blocked by Mrs Yabsley, carrying a shoulder of mutton and a bag of groceries.

24

3

CARDIGAN STREET AT HOME

Mrs Yabsley came to the door for a breath of fresh air, and surveyed Cardigan Street with a loving eye. She had lived there since her marriage twenty years ago, and to her it was the pick of Sydney, the centre of the habitable globe. She gave her opinion to every newcomer in her tremendous voice, that broke on their unaccustomed ears like thunder:

"I've lived 'ere ever since I was a young married woman, an' I know wot I'm talkin' about. My 'usband used ter take me to the play before we was married, but I never see any play equal ter wot 'appens in this street, if yer only keeps yer eyes open. I see people as wears spectacles readin' books. I don't wonder. If their eyesight was good, they'd be able ter see fer themselves instead of readin' about it in a book. I can't read myself, bein' no scholar, but I can see that books an' plays is fer them as ain't got no eyes in their 'eads."

The street, which Mrs Yabsley loved, was a street of poor folk—people to whom poverty clung like their shirt. It tumbled over the ridge opposite the church, fell rapidly for a hundred yards, and then, recovering its balance, sauntered easily down the slope till it met Botany Road on level ground. It was a street of small houses and large families, and struck the eye as mean and dingy, for most of the houses were standing on their last legs, and paint was scarce. The children used to kick and scrape it off the fences, and their parents rub it off the walls by leaning against them in a tired way for hours at a stretch. On hot summer nights the houses emptied their inhabitants on to the verandas and footpaths. The children, swarming like rabbits, played in the middle of the road. With clasped hands they formed a ring, and circled joyously to a song of childland, the immemorial rhymes handed down from one generation to another as savages preserve tribal rites. The fresh, shrill voices broke on the air, mingled with silvery peals of laughter.

> *"What will you give to know her name,*
> *Know her name, know her name?*
> *What will you give to know her name,*
> *On a cold and frosty morning?"*

Across the street would come a burst of coarse laughter, and a string of foul, obscene words on the heels of a jest. And again the childish trebles would ring on the tainted air:

> *"Green gravel, green gravel,*
> *Your true love is dead;*

26

They were ragged and dirty, true children of the gutter, but Romance, with the cloudy hair and starry eyes, held them captive for a few merciful years. Their parents lolled against the walls, or squatted on the kerbstone, devouring with infinite relish petty scandals about their neighbours, or shaking with laughter at some spicy yarn.

About ten o'clock the children would be driven indoors with threats and blows, and put to bed. By eleven the street was quiet, and only gave a last flicker of life when a drunken man came swearing down the street, full of beer, and offering to fight anyone for the pleasure of the thing. By twelve the street was dead, and the tread of the policeman echoed with a forlorn sound as if he were walking through a cemetery.

As Mrs Yabsley leaned over the gate, Mrs Swadling caught sight of her, and, throwing her apron over her head, crossed the street, bent on gossip. Then Mrs Jones, who had been watching her through the window, dropped her mending and hurried out.

The three women stood and talked of the weather, talking for talking's sake as men smoke a pipe in the intervals of work. Presently Mrs Yabsley looked hard at Mrs Swadling, who was shading her head from the sun with her apron.

"Wot's the matter with yer eye?" she said, abruptly.

"Nuthin'," said Mrs Swadling, and coloured.

The eye she was shading was black from a recent blow,

27

a present from her husband, Sam the carter, who came home for his tea, fighting drunk, as regular as clockwork.

"I thought I 'eard Sam snorin' after tea," said Mrs Jones.

"Yes, 'e was; but 'e woke up about twelve, an' give me beans 'cause I'd let 'im sleep till the pubs was shut."

"An' yer laid 'im out wi' the broom-handle, I s'pose?"

"No fear," said Mrs Swadling. "I ran down the yard, an' 'ollered blue murder."

"Well," said Mrs Yabsley, reflectively, "an 'usband is like the weather, or a wart on yer nose. It's no use quarrelling with it. If yer don't like it, yer've got ter lump it. An' if yer believe all yer 'ear, everybody else 'as got a worse."

She looked down the street, and saw Jonah and Chook, with a few others of the Push, sunning themselves in the morning air. Her face darkened.

"I see the Push 'ave got Jimmy Sinclair at last. Only six months ago 'e went ter Sunday school reg'lar, an' butter wouldn't melt in 'is mouth. Well, if smokin' cigarettes, an' spittin', and swearin' was 'ard work, they'd all die rich men. There's Waxy Collins. Last week 'e told 'is father 'e'd 'ave ter keep 'im till 'e was twenty-one 'cause of the law, an' the old fool believed 'im. An' little Joe Crutch, as used ter come 'ere beggin' a spoonful of drippin' fer 'is mother, come 'ome drunk the other night so natural, that 'is mother mistook 'im fer 'is father, an' landed 'im on the ear with 'er fist. An 'im the apple of 'er eye, as the sayin' is. It's 'ard ter be a mother in Cardigan Street. Yer girls are mothers before their bones are set, an' yer sons are dodgin' the p'liceman round the corner before they're in long trousers."

It was rare for Mrs Yabsley to touch on her private sorrows, and there was an embarrassing silence. But suddenly, from the corner of Pitt Street, appeared a strange figure of a man, roaring out a song in the voice of one selling fish. Every head turned.

"'Ello," said Mrs Jones, "Froggy's on the job today."

The singer was a Frenchman with a wooden leg, dressed as a sailor. As he hopped slowly down the street with the aid of a crutch, his grizzled beard and scowling face turned mechanically to right and left, sweeping the street with threatening eyes that gave him the look of a retired pirate, begging the tribute that he had taken by force in better days. The song ended abruptly, and he wiped the sweat from his face with an enormous handkerchief. Then he began another.

The women were silent, greedily drinking in the strange, foreign sounds, touched for a moment with the sense of things forlorn and far away. The singer still roared, though the tune was caressing, languishing, a love song. But his eyes rolled fiercely, and his moustache seemed to bristle with anger.

> "*Le pinson et la fauvette*
>   *Chantaient nos chastes amours,*
>   *Que les oiseaux chantent toujours,*
> *Pauvre Colinette, pauvre Colinette.*"

When he reached the women he hopped to the pavement, holding out his hat like a collection plate, with a beseeching air. The women were embarrassed, grudging

29

the pennies, but afraid of being thought mean. Mrs Yabsley broke the silence.

"I don't know wot ye're singin' about, an' I shouldn't like ter meet yer on a dark night, but I'm always willin' ter patronize the opera, as they say."

She fumbled in her pocket till she found tuppence. The sailor took the money, rolled his eyes, gave her a magnificent bow, and continued on his way with a fresh stanza:

> "Lorsque nous allions tous deux
>   Dans la verdoyante allée,
>   Comme elle était essoufflée,
> Et comme j'étais radieux."

"The more fool you," said Mrs Jones, who was ashamed of having nothing to give. "I've 'eard 'e's got a terrace of 'ouses, an' thousands in the bank. My cousin told me 'e sees 'im bankin' 'is money reg'lar in George Street every week."

And then a conversation followed, with instances of immense fortunes made by organ-grinders, German bands, and street-singers—men who cadged in rags for a living, and could drive their carriage if they chose. The women lent a greedy ear to these romances, like a page out of their favourite novelettes.

They were interrupted by an extraordinary noise from the French singer, who seemed suddenly to have gone mad. The Push had watched in ominous silence the approach of the Frenchman. But, as he passed them and finished a verse, a blood-curdling cry rose from the group. It was a perfect imitation of a dog baying the moon in agony. The singer stopped and scowled at the group, but the Push seemed to be unaware of his existence. He moved on, and began another verse. As he stopped to take breath the cry went up again, the agonized wail of a cur whose feelings are harrowed by music. The singer stopped, choking with rage, bewildered by the novelty of the attack. The Push seemed lost in thought. Again he turned to go, when a stone, jerked as if from a catapult, struck him on the shoulder. As he turned, roaring like a bull, a piece of blue metal struck him above the eye, cutting the flesh to the bone. The blood began to trickle slowly down his cheek.

Still roaring, he hopped on his crutch with incredible speed towards the Push, who stood their ground for a minute and then, with the instinct of the cur, bolted. The sailor stopped, and shook his fist at their retreating forms, showering strange, foreign maledictions on the fleeing enemy. It was evident that he could swear better than he could sing.

"Them wretches is givin' Froggy beans," said Mrs Swadling.

'Lucky fer 'im it's daylight, or they'd tickle 'is ribs with their boots," said Mrs Jones.

"Jonah and Chooks at the bottom o' that," said Mrs Swadling, looking hard at Mrs Yabsley.

"Ah, the devil an' is 'oof!" said Mrs Yabsley grimly, and was silent.

The sailor disappeared round the corner, and five minutes later the Push had slipped back, one by one, to their places under the veranda. Mrs Jones was in the middle of a story:

"'Er breath was that strong, it nearly knocked me down, an' so I sez to 'er, 'Mark my words, I'll pocket yer insults no longer, an' you in a temperance lodge. I'll make it my bizness to go to the sekertary this very day, an' tell 'im of yer goin's on.' An' she sez...w'y, there she is again," cried Mrs Jones, as she caught the sound of a shrill voice, high-pitched and quarrelsome. The women craned their necks to look.

A woman of about forty, drunken, bedraggled, dressed in dingy black, was pacing up and down the pavement in front of the barber's. She blinked like a drunken owl, and stepped high on the level footpath as if it were mountainous. And without looking at anything, she threw a string of insults at the barber, hiding behind the partition in his shop. For seven years she had passed as his wife, and then, one day, sick of her drunken bouts, he had turned her out, and married Flash Kate, the ragpicker's daughter. Sloppy Mary had accepted her lot with resignation, and went out charring for a living; but whenever she had a drop too much she made for the barber's, forgetting by a curious lapse of memory that it was no longer her home. And as usual the barber's new wife had pushed her into the street, staggering, and now stood on guard at the door, her coarse, handsome features alive with contempt.

"Wotcher doin' in my 'ouse?" suddenly inquired Sloppy, blinking with suspicion at Flash Kate. "Yous go 'ome, me fine lady, afore yer git yerself talked about."

The woman at the door laughed loudly, and pretended to examine with keen interest a new wedding ring on her finger.

"Cum 'ere, an' I'll tear yer blasted eyes out," cried the drunkard, turning on her furiously.

The ragpicker's daughter leaned forward, and inquired, "'Ow d'ye like yer eggs done?"

At this simple inquiry the drunkard stamped her foot with rage, calling on her enemy to prepare for instant death. And the two women bombarded one another with insults, raking the gutter for adjectives, spitting like angry cats across the width of the pavement.

The Push gathered round, grinning from ear to ear, sooling the women on as if they were dogs. But just as a shove from behind threw Sloppy nearly into the arms of her enemy, the Push caught sight of a policeman, and walked away with an air of extreme nonchalance. At the same moment the drunkard saw the dreaded uniform, and, obeying the laws of Cardigan Street, pulled herself together and walked away, mumbling to herself.

The three women watched the performance without a word, critical as spectators at a play. When they saw there would be no scratching, they resumed their conversation.

"W'en a woman takes to drink, she's found a short cut to 'ell, an' lets everybody know it," said Mrs Yabsley, briefly. "But this won't git my work done," and she tucked up her sleeves and went in.

The Push, bent on killing time, and despairing of any fresh diversion in the street, dispersed slowly, one by one, to meet again at night.

The Cardigan Street Push, composed of twenty or thirty young men of the neighbourhood, was a social wart of a kind familiar to the streets of Sydney. Originally banded together to amuse themselves at other people's expenses, the Push found new cares and duties thrust upon them, the chief of which was chastising anyone who interfered with their pleasures. Their feats ranged from kicking an enemy senseless, and leaving him for dead, to wrecking hotel windows with blue metal, if the landlord had contrived to offend them. Another of their duties was to check ungodly pride in the rival Pushes by battering them out of shape with fists and blue metal at regular intervals.

They were the scum of the streets. How they lived was a mystery, except to people who kept fowls, or forgot to lock their doors at night. A few were vicious idlers, sponging on their parents for a living at twenty years of age; others simply mischievous lads, with a trade at their fingers' ends, if they chose to work. A few were honest, unless temptation stared them too hard in the face. On such occasions their views were simple as A B C. "Well, if yer lost a chance, somebody else collared it, an' w'ere were yer?"

The police, variously named "Johns", "cops" and "traps", were their natural enemies. If one of the Push got into trouble, the others clubbed together and paid his fine; and if that failed, they made it hot for the prosecutors. Generally their offences were disorderly conduct, bashing their enemies, and resisting the police.

Both Jonah and Chook worked for a living—Chook by crying fish and vegetables in the streets, Jonah by making and mending for Hans Paasch, the German shoemaker on Botany Road. But Chook often lacked the few shillings to buy his stock-in-trade, and Jonah never felt inclined for work till Wednesday. Then he would stroll languidly down to the shop. The old German would thrust out his chin, and blink at him over his glasses. And he always greeted Jonah with one of two set phrases:

"Ah, you haf come, haf you? I vas choost going to advertise for a man." This meant that work was plentiful. When trade was slack, he would shake his head sadly as if he were standing over the grave of his last sixpence, and say:

"Ah, it vas no use; dere is not enough work to fill one mouth."

Jonah always listened to either speech with utter indifference, took off his coat, put on his leather apron, and set to work silently and swiftly like a man in anger.

Although he always grumbled, Paasch was quite satisfied. He had too much work for one, and not enough for two. So Jonah, who was a good workman, and content to make three or four days in a week, suited him exactly. Besides, Jonah had started with him as an errand-boy at five shillings a week, years ago, and was used to his odd ways.

Hans Paasch was born in Bavaria, in the town of Hassloch. His father was a shoemaker, and destined Hans for the same trade. The boy preferred to be a fiddler, but his father taught him his trade thoroughly with the end of a strap.

In his eighteenth year Hans suddenly ended the dispute by running away from home with his beloved fiddle. He made his way to the coast, and got passage on a cargo tramp to England. There he heard of the wonderful land called Australia, where gold was to be had for the picking up. The fever took him, and he worked his passage out to Melbourne on a sailing ship. He reached the goldfields, dug without success, and would have starved but for his fiddle.

A year found him back in Melbourne, penniless. Here he met another German in the same condition. They decided to work their way overland to Sydney, Hans playing the fiddle and his mate singing. Then began a Bohemian life of music by the wayside inns, sleep in the open air, and meals when it pleased God to send them.

This had proved to be the solitary sunlit passage in his life, for when he reached Sydney he found that his music had no money value, and, under the goad of hunger, took to the trade that he had learned so unwillingly. Twenty years ago he had opened his small shop on the Botany Road, and today it remained unchanged, dwarfed by larger buildings on either side. He lived by himself in the room over the shop, where he spent his time reading the newspaper as a child spells out a lesson, or playing his beloved violin. He was a good player, but his music was a puzzle and a derision to Jonah, for his tastes were classical, and sometimes he spent as much as a shilling on a back seat at a concert in the Town Hall. Jonah scratched his ear and listened, amazed that a man could play for hours without finding a tune. The neighbours said that Paasch lived on the smell of an oil rag; but that was untrue, for he spent hours cooking strange messes soaked in vinegar, the sight of which turned Jonah's stomach.

Bob Fenner's dance-room, three doors away, was a thorn in his side. Three nights in the week a brazen cornet struck into a set of lancers, drowning the metallic thud of the piano, and compelling his ear to follow the latest popular air to the last bar.

His solitary life, his fiddling, and his singular mixture of gruffness and politeness had bred legends among the women of the neighbourhood. He was a German baron, who had forfeited his title and estates through killing a man in a duel; and never a milder pair of eyes looked timidly through spectacles. He was a famous musician, who had chosen to blot himself out of the world for love of a high-born lady; and, in his opinion, women were useful to cook and sew, nothing more.

4

JONAH DISCOVERS THE BABY

Joey the pieman had scented a new customer in Mrs Yabsley, and on the following Saturday night he stopped in front of the house and rattled the lids of his cans to attract her attention. His voice, thin and cracked with the wear of the streets, chanted his familiar cry to an accompaniment faintly suggestive of clashing cymbals:

"Peas an' pies, all 'ot, all 'ot!"

His cart, a kitchen on wheels, sent out a column of smoke from its stovepipe chimney; and when he raised the lids of the shining cans, a fragrant steam rose on the air. The cart, painted modestly in red, bore a strange legend in yellow letters on the front:

WHO'D HAVE THOUGHT IT,
PEAS AND PIES WOULD HAVE BOUGHT IT!

This outburst of lyric poetry was to inform the world that Joey had risen from humble beginnings to his present commercial eminence, and was not ashamed of the fact.

He called regularly about ten o'clock, and Jonah and Ada spent a delightful five minutes deciding which delicacy to choose for the night. When they tired of green peas they chose hot pies, full of rich gravy that ran out if you were not careful how you bit; or they preferred the plump saveloy, smoking hot from the can, giving out a savoury odour that made your mouth water. Then Ada fetched a jug of beer from the corner to wash it down. Soon Jonah stayed at the house on Saturday night as a matter of course.

But Jonah drew the line when the mother hinted that he might as well stay there altogether. He feared a trap; and when she pointed out the danger of two women living alone in the house, he looked at her brawny arms and smiled.

Haunted by her scheme for marriage, she set to work to undermine Jonah's obstinacy. She proceeded warily, and made no open attack; but Jonah began to notice with uneasiness that he could not talk for five minutes without stumbling on marriage. In the midst of a conversation on the weather, he would be amazed to find the theme turn to the praise of marriage, brought mysteriously to this hateful word as a man is led blindfold to a giddy cliff. When his startled look warned the mother, she changed the subject.

Still she persevered, sapping Jonah's prejudices with the terrible zeal of a priest making a convert. When he saw her drift, it set him thinking, and he watched Ada with curious attention as she moved about the house helping her mother.

It was Sunday morning, and Ada was shelling peas.

The pods split with a sharp crack under her fingers, and the peas rattled into a tin basin. She wore an old skirt, torn and shabby; her bodice was split under the arms, showing the white lining. Her hair lay flat on her forehead, screwed tightly in curling-pins, which brought into relief her flat face and high cheekbones, for she was no beauty. By a singular coquetry, she wore her best shoes, small and neat, with high French heels.

Jonah looked at the girl with satisfaction, but she stirred no sentiment, for all women were alike to him. His view of them was purely animal. The procession of Chook's loves crossed his mind, and he smiled. At regular intervals Chook "went barmy" over some girl or other, and, while the fit lasted, worshipped her as a savage worships an idol. And Jonah was stupefied by this passionate preference for one woman. He had never felt that way for Ada.

He returned to his own affairs. Marriage meant a wife, a family, and steady work, for Ada would leave the factory if he married her. The thought filled him with weariness. The vagabond in him recoiled from the set labours and common burdens of his kind. Ever since he could remember he had been more at home in the streets than in the four walls of a room. The Push, the corner, the noise and movement of the streets—that was life for him. And he decided the matter for ever; there was nothing in it.

But, as the months slipped by, and Jonah remained impregnable to her masked batteries, Mrs Yabsley attacked him openly. Jonah stood his ground, and pointed out, with cynical candour, his unfitness to keep a wife. But Mrs Yabsley seized the opportunity to sketch out a career for him, with voluminous instances, for she had foreseen and arranged all that.

"An' 'oo's ter blame fer that?" she cried, "a feller that oughter be gittin' 'is three pounds a week. W'y, look at Dave Brown. Don't I remember the time 'e used ter 'awk a basket o' fish on Fridays, an' doss in park? An' now 'e goes round in a white shirt, an' draws 'is rents. An' mark me, it was gittin' married did that fer 'im. W'en a man's married, 'e's got somethin' better to do than smokin' cigarettes an' playin' a mouth-orgin."

"Yes," said Jonah, grinning. "Git up an light the fire, an' graft 'is bloomin' 'ead off."

Mrs Yabsley feigned deafness.

"Anyhow, 'e didn't git 'is 'ouses 'awkin' fish," pursued Jonah; "'e got 'em while 'e kep' a pub."

Then, with feverish vivacity, Mrs Yabsley mapped out half a dozen careers for him, chiefly in connection with a shop, for to her, who lived by the sweat of her brow, shopkeepers were aristocrats, living in splendid ease.

"It's no go, missis," said Jonah. "Marriage is all right fer them as don't know better, but anyhow, it ain't wot it's cracked up ter be."

He avoided the house for some weeks after this conversation, patrolling the streets with the gang, with the zest of a drunkard returning to his cups. Mrs Yabsley, who saw that she had pushed her attack too far, waited in patience.

Jonah found the Push thirsting for blood. One of them had got three months for taking a fancy to a copper boiler that he had found in an empty house, and they discovered that a bricklayer, who lived next door, had put the police on his track. The Push resolved to stoush him, and had lain in wait for a week without success. Jonah took the matter in hand, and inquired secretly into the man's habits. He discovered that the bricklayer, sober as a judge through the week, was in the habit of fuddling himself on pay-day. Jonah arranged a plan, which involved a search of every hotel in the neighbourhood.

But one Saturday night, as they were stealthily scouting the streets for their man, Jonah suddenly thought of Ada. It was weeks since he had last seen her. He was surprised by a faint longing for her presence, and, with a word to Chook, he slipped away.

The cottage was in darkness and the door locked; but after a moment's hesitation, he took the key from under the flowerpot and went in. He struck a match and looked round. The irons were on the table. Mrs Yabsley had evidently gone out with the shirts. He lit the candle and sat down.

The room was thick with shadows, that fled and advanced as the candle flickered in the draught. He looked with quiet pleasure on the familiar objects—the deal table, propped against the wall on account of a broken leg, the ragged curtain stretched across the window, the new shelf that he had made out of a box. He studied, with fresh interest, the coloured almanacs on the wall, and spelt out, with amiable derision, the Scripture text over the door. He felt vaguely that he was at home.

Home!—the word had no meaning for him. He had been thrown on the streets when a child by his parents, who had rid themselves of his unwelcome presence with as little emotion as they would have tossed an empty can out of doors.

A street-arab, he had picked a living from the gutters, hardened to exposure, taking food and shelter with the craft of an old soldier in hostile country. Until he was twelve he had sold newspapers, sleeping in sheds and empty cases, feeding on the broken victuals thrown out from the kitchens of hotels and restaurants, and then, drifting by chance to Waterloo, had found a haven of rest with Paasch as an errand-boy at five shillings a week.

His cigarette was finished, and there was no sign of Ada. He swore at himself for coming, picked up his hat, and turned to go. But, at that moment, from the corner of the room, came a thin, wailing cry.

Jonah started violently, and then, as he recognized the sound, smiled grimly. It was the baby, awakened by the light. He remembered that Mrs Yabsley often left it alone in the house.

But the infant, thoroughly aroused, gave out a querulous note, thin and sustained. Jonah stooped to blow out the candle, and then, with a sudden curiosity, walked over to the cradle.

It was a box on rough rollers, made out of a packing-case, grimy with dirt from the hands that had rocked it. Jonah pulled it out of the corner into the light, and the child, pacified by the sight of a face, stopped crying.

Fearful of observation, he looked round, and then stared intently at the baby. It was a meeting of strangers, for Mrs Yabsley, aware of his aversion from the child, had kept it out of the way. It was the first baby that he had seen at close quarters, for he had never lived in a house with one. And he looked at this with the curiosity with

43

which one looks at a foreigner—surprised that he, too, is a man.

The child blinked feebly under the light of the candle, which Jonah was holding near. Its fingers moved with a mechanical, crab-like motion.

With an odd sensation Jonah remembered that this was his child—flesh of his flesh, bone of his bone—and, with a swift instinct, he searched its face for a sign of paternity.

The child's bulging forehead bore no likeness to Jonah's, which sloped sharply from the eyebrows, and the nose was a mere dab of flesh; but its eyes were grey, like his own. His interest increased. Gently he stroked the fine silky down that covered its head, and then, growing bolder, touched its cheek. The delicate skin was smooth as satin under his rough finger.

The child, pleased with his touch, smiled and clutched his finger, holding it with the tenacity of a monkey. Jonah looked in wonder at that tiny hand, no bigger than a doll's. His own fist, rough with toil, seemed enormous beside it.

Flesh of his flesh, he thought, half incredulous, as he compared his red, hairy skin with that delicate texture; amazed by this miracle of life—the renewal of the flesh that perishes.

Then he remembered his deformity, and, with a sudden catch in his breath, lifted the child from the cradle, and felt its back, a passionate fear in his heart: it was straight as a die. He drew a long breath, and was silent, embarrassed for words before this mite, searching his mind in vain for the sweet jargon used by women.

"Sool 'im!" he cried at last, and poked his son in

the ribs. The child crowed with delight. Jonah touched its mouth, and its teeth, like tiny pegs, closed tightly on his fingers. It lay contentedly on his knees, its eyes closed, already fatigued. And, as Jonah watched it, there suddenly vibrated in him a strange, new sensation—the sense of paternity, which Nature, crafty beyond man, has planted in him to fulfil her schemes, the imperious need to protect and rejoice in its young that preserves the race from extinction.

Jonah sat motionless, afraid to disturb the child, intoxicated by the first pure emotion of his life, his heart filled with an immense pity for this frail creature. Absorbed in his emotions, he was startled by a step on the veranda.

He rose swiftly to put the child in the cot, but it was too late, and he turned to the door with the child in his arms, ashamed and defiant, like a boy caught with the jam-pot. He expected Mrs Yabsley or Ada; it was Chook, breathless with haste.

He stood in the doorway, dumb with amazement as his eye took in this strange picture; then his face relaxed in a grin.

"Well, strike me pink," he cried, and shook with laughter.

Jonah stared at him with a deepening scowl, till chuckles died away.

"Garn!" he cried at last, and his voice was between a whine and a snarl; "yer needn't poke borak!"

5

THE PUSH DEALS IT OUT

It was near eleven, and the lights were dying out along the Road as the shopmen, fatigued by their weekly conflict with the people, fastened the shutters. At intervals trams and buses, choked with passengers from the city, laboured heavily past. Groups of men still loitered on the footpaths, careless of the late hour, for tomorrow was Sunday, the day of idleness, when they could lie a-bed and read the paper. And they gossiped tranquilly, no longer harassed by the thought of the relentless toil, the inexorable need for bread, that dragged them from their warm beds while the rest of the world lay asleep.

The Angel, standing at the corner, dazzled the eye with the glare from its powerful lamps, their rays reflected in immense mirrors fastened to the walls, advertising in frosted letters the popular brands of whisky. And it stood alone in the darkening street, piercing the night with an unwinking stare like an evil spirit, offering its warm, comfortable bars to the passer-by, drawing men into its deadly embrace like a courtesan, to reject them afterwards babbling, reeling, staggering, to rouse the street with quarrels, or to snore in the gutters like swine.

Cassidy the policeman, with the slow, leaden step of a man who is going nowhere, stopped for a moment in front of the hotel, and examined the street with a suspicious eye. He saw nothing but some groups of young men leaning against the veranda-posts at the opposite corner. They smoked and spat, tranquilly discussing the horses and betting for the next Cup meeting. Satisfied that the Road was quiet, he moved off, dragging his feet as if they weighed a ton. At once a sinister excitement passed through the groups.

"That was Cassidy; now we shan't be long."

"Wot price Jonah givin' us the slip?"

"'Ow'll Chook perform, if 'e ain't at Ada's?"

It was the Push, who had run their man to earth at the Angel, where he was drinking in the bar, alone. Chook had posted them with the instinct of a general, and then left in hurried search of Jonah. And they watched the swinging doors of the hotel with cruel eyes, their nerves already vibrating with the ancestral desire to kill, the wild beast within them licking his lips at the thought of the coming feast.

Meanwhile, in Cardigan Street, Chook was arguing with Jonah. When told that the Push was waiting for him, he had listened without interest; the matter seemed foreign and remote. The velvety touch of his son's frail body still thrilled his nerves; its sweet, delicate odour was still in his nostrils. And he flatly refused to go. Chook was beside himself with excitement; tears stood in his eyes.

"W'y, y'ain't goin' ter turn dawg on me, Jonah, are yer?"

"No bleedin' fear," said Jonah; "but I feel—I dunno 'ow I feel. The blasted kid knocked me endways," he explained, in confusion.

As he looked down the street, he caught sight of Mrs Yabsley on the other side. She walked slowly on account of the hill, gasping for air, the weekly load of meat and groceries clutched in her powerful arms. His eyes softened with tenderness. He felt a sudden kinship for this huge, ungainly woman. He wanted to run and meet her, and claim the sweet, straight-limbed child that he had just discovered. Chook, standing at his elbow, like the devil in the old prints, was watching him curiously.

"Well, I'm off," cried Chook at last. "Wot'll I tell the blokes?"

Jonah was silent for a moment, with a sombre look in his eyes. Then he pulled himself together.

"Let 'er go," he cried grimly; "the kid can wait."

On the stroke of eleven, as they reached the Angel, the huge lamps were extinguished, the doors swung open and vomited a stream of men on to the footpath, their loud voices bringing the noise and heat of the bar into the quiet street They dispersed slowly, talking immoderately, parting with the regret of lovers from the warm bar with its cheerful light and pleasant clink of glasses. The doors were closed, but the bar was still noisy, and the laggards slipped out cautiously by the side door, where a barman kept watch for the police. Presently the bricklayer came out, alone. He stood on the footpath, slightly fuddled, his giddiness increased by the fresh air. Immediately Chook lurched forward to meet him, with a drunken leer.

"'Ello, Bill, fancy meetin' yous!" he mumbled.

The man, swaying slightly, stared at him in a fog.

"I dunno you," he muttered.

"Wot, yer dunno me, as worked wid yer on that job in Kent Street? Dunno Joe Parsons, as danced wid yer missis at the bricklayers' picnic?"

The man stopped to think, trying to remember, but his brain refused the effort.

"Orl right," he muttered; "come an' 'ave a drink." And he turned to the bar.

"No fear," cried Chook, taking him affectionately by the arm, "no more fer me! I'm full up ter the chin, an' so are yous."

"Might's well 'ave another," said the man, obstinately.

Chook pulled him gently away from the hotel, along the street.

"It's gittin' late; 'ow'll yer ole woman rous w'en yer git 'ome?"

"Sez anythin' ter me, break 'er bleedin' jaw," muttered the bricklayer. And then his eyes flamed with foolish, drunken anger. "I earn the money, don' I, an' I spend it, don' I?" he inquired. And he refused to move till Chook answered his question.

The Push closed quietly in.

"'Oo are these blokes?" he asked uneasily.

"Pals o' mine, all good men an' true," said Chook, gaily.

They were near Eveleigh Station, and the street was clear. The red signal-lights, like angry, bloodshot eyes, followed the curve of the line as it swept into the terminus. An engine screamed hoarsely as it swept past with a rattle of jolting metal and the hum of swiftly revolving wheels. The time was come to strike, but the Push hesitated. The show of resistance, the spark to kindle their brutal fury, was wanting.

"Is this a prayer meetin'?" inquired Waxy Collins, with a sneer. "Biff him on the boko, an' we'll finish 'im in one act."

"Shut yer face," said Jonah, and he stepped up to the bricklayer.

"Ever 'ear tell of a copper boiler?" he inquired pleasantly. "Ever meet a bleedin' bastard as put the cops on a bloke, an' got 'im three months' 'ard?" he inquired again.

The bricklayer stared at him open-mouthed, surprised and alarmed by the appearance of this misshapen devil with the glittering eyes. Then a sudden suspicion ran through the fuddled brain.

"I niver lagged 'im. S'elp me Gawd, I niver put nobody away to the cops!" he cried.

"Yer rotten liar, take that!" cried Jonah, and struck him full on the mouth with his fist. The man clapped his hand to his cut lip, and looked at the blood in amazement. The shock cleared his brain, and he remembered with terror the tales of deadly revenge taken by the pushes. He looked wildly for help. He was in a ring of mocking, menacing faces.

"Let 'im out," cried Jonah, in a sharp, strident voice. "The swine lives about 'ere; give 'im a run for 'is money."

The Push opened out, and the man, sobered by his danger, stood for a moment with bewildered eyes. Then, with the instinct of the hunted, he turned for home and ran. The Push gave chase, with Chook in the lead. Again and again the quarry turned, blindly seeking refuge in the darkest lanes.

As his pursuers gained on him he gave a hoarse scream—the dolorous cry of a hunted animal.

But it was the cat playing with the mouse. The bricklayer ran like a cow, his joints stiffened by years of toil; the larrikins, light on their feet as hares, kept the pace with a nimble trot, silent and dangerous, conscious of nothing but the desire and power to kill.

As he turned into Abercrombie Street, Chook ran level with him, then stooped swiftly and caught his ankle. The bricklayer went sprawling, and in an instant the Push closed in on the fallen man as footballers form a scrum, kicking the struggling body with silent ferocity, drunk with the primeval instinct to destroy.

"Nit!" cried Jonah; and the Push scattered, disappearing by magic over fences and down lanes.

The bricklayer had ceased to struggle, and lay in a heap. Five minutes later some stragglers, noticing the huddled mass on the road, crossed the street cautiously and stared. Then a crowd gathered, each asking the other what had happened, each amazed at the other's ignorance.

The excitement seemed to penetrate the houses oppo-site. Heads were thrust out of windows, doors were opened, and a stream of men and women, wearing whatever they could find in the dark, shuffled across the footpath.

Some still fumbled at their braces; others, draped like Greek statues, held their garments on with both hands. A coarse jest passed round when a tall, bony woman came up, a man's overcoat, thrown over her shoulders, barely covering her nightdress. They stood shivering in the cold air, greedy to hear what sensation had come to their very doors.

"It's only a drunken man."

"They say 'e was knocked down in a fight."

"No; the Push stoushed 'im, an' then cleared."

Someone struck a match and looked at his face; it was smeared with blood. Then the crowd rendered "first aid" in the street fashion.

"Wot's yer name? W'ere d'yer live? 'Ow did it 'appen?"

And at each question they shook him vigorously, impatient at his silence. The buzz of voices increased.

"W'ere's the perlice?"

"Not w'ere they're wanted, you may be sure."

"It's my belief they go 'ome an' sleep it out these cold nights."

"Well, I s'pose a p'liceman 'as ter take care of 'imself, like everybody else," said one, and laughed.

"It's shameful the way these brutes are allowed to knock men about."

"An' the perlice know very well 'oo they are, but they're afraid of their own skins."

The woman in the nightdress had edged nearer, craning her neck over the shoulders of the men to see better. As another match was struck she saw the man's face.

"My Gawd, it's my 'usband!" she screamed. "Bill, Bill, wot 'ave they done ter yer?"

Her old affection, starved to death by years of neglect, sprang to life for an instant in this cry of agony. She dropped on her knees beside the bruised body, wiping the blood from his face with the sleeve of her nightdress. A dark red stain spread over the coarse, common calico. And she kissed passionately the bleeding lips, heedless of the sour smell of alcohol that tainted his breath. The bricklayer groaned feebly. With a sudden movement she stripped the coat from her shoulders, and covered him as if to protect him from further harm.

Her hair, fastened in an untidy knot, slipped from the hairpins, and fell, grey and scanty, over her neck; her bony shoulders, barely covered by the thin garment, moved convulsively.

"'Ere, missis, take this, or you'll ketch cold," said a man kindly, pulling off his coat.

Then, with the quick sympathy of the people, they began to make light of the matter, trying to persuade her that his injuries were not serious. A friendly rivalry sprang up among them as they related stories of wonderful recoveries made by men whose bodies had been beaten to a jelly. One, carried away by enthusiasm, declared that it did a man good to be shattered like glass, for the doctors, with satanic cunning, seized the opportunity to knead the broken limbs like putty into a more desirable shape. But their words fell on deaf ears. The woman crouched over the prostrate man, stroking the bruised limbs with a stupid, mechanical movement as an animal licks its wounded mate.

The crowd divided as a policeman came up with an important air. Brisk and cheerful, he made a few inquiries, enchanted with this incident that broke the monotony of the night's dreary round. The crowd breathed freely, feeling that the responsibility had shifted on to the official shoulders. He blew shrilly on his whistle, and demanded a cab.

"Cab this time o' night? No chance," was the common opinion.

But by great good luck a cab was heard rattling along the next street. Two men ran to intercept it.

The woman clung desperately to the crippled body as they lifted it into the cab, impeding the men in their efforts, imploring them to carry him to his own house, with the distrust of the ignorant for the hospitals, where the doctors amuse themselves by cutting and carving the bodies of their helpless patients. The policeman, a young man, embarrassed by the sight of this half-dressed woman, swore softly to himself.

"'Ere, missis, you'd better get 'ome; you can't do any good 'ere," he said, kindly. "Don't you worry; I've seen worse cases than this go 'ome to breakfast the next day."

As the cab drove off, some neighbours led her away, her thin, angular body shaken with sobs.

The street was quiet again, but some groups still lingered, discussing with relish the details of the outrage, searching their memories for stories of brutal stoushings that had ended in the death of the victim.

6

THE BABY DISCOVERS JONAH

An hour later Jonah and Chook, picking the most round-about way, reached home. The family was in bed, and the house in darkness. The two mates dropped silently over the fence, and, with the stealthy movements of cats, clambered through the window of the room which they shared, for Jonah believed that secrets were kept best by those who had none to tell.

"Gawd, I'm dry," said Chook, yawning. "I could do a beer."

"That comes of runnin' along the street so 'ard," said Jonah, grinning. "It must 'ave bin a fire by the way I see yer run. W'y was yer runnin' so 'ard?" Then his face darkened. "I wonder 'ow the poor bloke feels, that fell down an' 'urt 'imself?"

"D'ye think 'e knows enough ter give us away?" asked Chook, anxiously.

"No fear," said Jonah. "I make the Ivy Street Push a present of that little lot."

"Well, I s'pose a sleep's the next best thing," replied Chook, and in a minute was snoring.

Jonah finished undressing slowly. As he unlaced his boots, he noticed a dark patch on one toe. It looked as if he had kicked something wet. He examined the stain without repugnance, and thought of the bricklayer.

"Serve the cow right," he thought. "'Ope it stiffens 'im!"

Again he examined the patch of blood attentively, wondering if it would leave a mark on his tan boots, of which he was very proud. Dipping a piece of rag in water, he washed it off carefully. And, as he rubbed, the whole scenes passed through his brain in rapid succession—the Angel, bright and alluring with the sinister gleam of its powerful lamps, the swaying man in the midst of the Push, the wild-beast chase, and the fallen body that ceased to struggle as they kicked.

He lit a cigarette and stared at the candle, smiling with the pride of a good workman at the thought of his plan that had worked so neatly. The Push was secure, and the blame would fall on the Ivy Street gang, the terror of Darlington. For a moment he regretted the active part he had taken in the stoushing, as his hunchback made him conspicuous. He wondered carelessly what had happened after the Push bolted. These affairs were so uncertain. Sometimes the victim could limp home, mottled with bruises; just as often he was taken to the hospital in a cab, and a magistrate was called in to take down his dying words. In this case the chances were in favour of the victim recovering, as the

Push had been interrupted in dealing it out through Jonah's excessive caution. Still, they had no intention of killing the man; they merely wished to teach him a lesson.

True, the lesson sometimes went too far; and he thought with anxiety of the Surry Hills affair, in which, through an accident, a neighbouring push had disappeared like rats into a hole, branded with murder. The ugly word hung on his tongue and paralysed his thoughts. His mind recoiled with terror as he saw where his lawless ways had carried him, feeling already branded with the mark of Cain, which the instinct of the people has singled out as the unpardonable crime, destroying the life that cannot be renewed. And suddenly he began to persuade himself that the man's injuries were not serious, that he would soon recover; for it was wonderful the knocking about a man could stand.

He turned on himself with amazement. Why was he twittering like an old woman? Quarrels, fights, and bloodshed were as familiar to him as his daily bread. With a sudden cry of astonishment he remembered the baby. The affair of the bricklayer had driven it completely out of his mind. His thoughts returned to Cardigan Street. He remembered the quiet room dimly lit with a candle, the dolorous cry of the infant, and the intoxicating touch of its frail body in his arms.

His amazement increased. What had possessed him to take the brat in his arms and nurse it? His lips contracted in a cynical grin as he remembered the figure he cut when Chook appeared. He decided to look on the affair as a joke. But again his thoughts returned to the child, and he was surprised with a vibration of tenderness sweet as honey in his veins. A strange yearning came over him like a physical weakness for the touch of his son's body.

His eye caught his shadow on the wall, grotesque and forbidding; the large head, bunched beneath the square shoulders, thrust outwards in a hideous lump. Monster and outcast was he? Well, he would show them that only an accident separated the hunchback from his fellows. He thought with a fierce joy of his son's straight back and shapely limbs. This was his child, that he could claim and exhibit to the world. Then his delight changed to a vague terror—the fear of an animal that dreads a trap, and finds itself caught. He blew out the candle and fell asleep, to dream of enemies that fled and mocked at him, embarrassed with an infant that hung like a millstone round his neck.

Within a month the affair of the bricklayer had blown over. The police made inquiries, and arrested some of the Ivy Street Push, but released them for want of evidence. In the hospital the bricklayer professed a complete ignorance of his assailants and their motive. It was understood that he was too drunk to recognize anyone.

But it was his knowledge of Push methods that sealed his tongue. No one would risk his skin by giving evidence. If the police had brought the offenders to book, the magistrates, who seemed to regard these outrages as the playful excesses of wanton blood, would have let them off with a light punishment, and the streets would never have been safe for him again. So he held his tongue, thankful to have escaped so easily.

But burnt on his brain was the vision of a misshapen devil, who struck at him, with snarling lips, and a desperate flight through avenues of silent, impassive streets that heard with indifference his cry for help. In six weeks he was back at work, with no mark of his misadventure but a broken nose, caused by a clumsy boot.

So the Push took to the streets again, and Jonah resumed his visits to Cardigan Street on Saturday nights. He had concealed his adventure with the baby from Ada and her mother, feeling ashamed, as if he had discovered an unmanly taste for mud pies and dolls. But the imperious instinct was aroused, and he gratified it in secret, caressing the child by stealth as a miser runs to his hoard. In the women's presence he ignored its existence, but he soon discovered that Ada shared none of his novel sensations. And he grew indignant at her indifference, feeling that his child was neglected.

Mrs Yabsley, for ever on the alert, felt some change in his manner, and one Sunday morning received a shock. She was chopping wood in the yard. She swung the axe with a grunt, and the billet, split in two, left the axe wedged in the block. As she was wrenching it out, Jonah dropped his cigarette and cried:

"'Ere, missis, gimme that axe; I niver like ter see a woman chop wood."

She looked at him in amazement. Times without number he had watched her grunt and sweat without stirring a finger. Bitten with her one idea, she watched him curiously.

It was the baby that betrayed him at last. Ada was carrying it past him in furtive haste, when it caught sight of his familiar features. Jonah, off his guard, smiled. The child laughed joyously, and leaned out of Ada's arms towards him.

"W'y, wot's the matter, Joe?" cried Mrs Yabsley, all eyes.

Jonah hesitated. Denial was on his tongue, but he looked again at his child, and a lump rose in his throat.

"Oh, nuthin', missis," he replied, reddening. "Me an' the kid took a fancy ter one another long ago."

He smiled blandly, in exquisite relief, as if he had confessed a sin or had a tooth drawn. He took the child from Ada, and it lay in his arms, nestling close with animal content.

Ada looked in silence, astonished and slightly scornful at this development, jealous of the child's preference, already regretting her neglect.

Mrs Yabsley stood petrified with the face of one who has seen a miracle. For a moment she was too amazed to think; then, with a rapid change of front, she conquered her surprise and claimed the credit for this result.

"I knowed all along the kid 'ud fetch yer, Joe. I knowed yer'd got a soft 'eart," she cried. "An' 'e's the very image of yer, wi' the sweetest temper mortal child ever 'ad."

From that time Sunday became a marked day for Jonah, and he looked forward to it with impatience. It was spring. The temperate rays of the sun fell on budding tree and shrub; the mysterious renewal of life that stirred inanimate nature seemed to touch his pulse to a quicker and lighter beat. He sat for hours in the backyard, once a garden, screened from observation, with the child on his knees. The blood ran pleasantly in his veins; he felt in sympathy with the sunlight, the sky flecked with clouds, and the warm breath of the winds. It broke on him slowly that he was taking his place among his fellows, outcast and outlaw no longer.

Soon, he and the child were inseparable. He learned to attend to its little wants with deft fingers, listening with a smile to the kindly banter of the women. His manner changed to Ada and her mother; he was considerate, even kind. Then he began to drop in on Monday or Tuesday instead of loafing with the Push at the corner. Ada was at the factory; but Mrs Yabsley, sorting piles of dirty linen, with her arms bared to the elbow, welcomed him with a smile. He remarked with satisfaction that a change had come over the old woman. She never spoke of marriage; seemed to have given up the idea.

But one day, as he sat with the child on his knees, she stopped in front of the pair, with a bundle of shirts in her arms, and regarded them with a puzzling smile. The baby lay on its back, staring into space with solemn, unreflective eyes. From time to time Jonah turned his head to blow the smoke of his cigarette into the air.

"You'll be gittin' too fond of 'im, if y'ain't careful, Joe," she said at last.

"Git work; wot's troublin' yer?" said Jonah, with a grin.

"Nuthin'; only I was thinkin' wot a fine child 'e'd be in a few years. It's a pity 'e ain't got no real father."

"Wot d'yer mean?" said Jonah, looking up angrily. "W'ere do I come in? Ain't I the bloke?"

"Well, y'are an' y'ain't, yer know," said Mrs Yabsley. "There's two ways of lookin' at these things."

61

"'Strewth! I niver thought o' that," said Jonah, scratching his ear.

"No, but other people do, worse luck," said Mrs Yabsley.

Jonah stared at the child in silence. Mrs Yabsley turned and poked the fire under the copper boiler. Suddenly Jonah lifted his head and cried:

"I say, missis, I can see a hole in a ladder plain enough! Yer mean I've got ter marry Ada?"

The old woman left the fire and stood in front of him.

"Not a bit, Joe. I've give up that idea. Marriage wouldn't suit yous. Your dart is ter be King of the Push, an' knock about the streets with a lot of mudlarks as can't look a p'liceman straight in the face. You an' yer pals are seein' life now all right; but wait till yer bones begin ter stiffen, an' yer can't run faster than the cop. Then it'll be jail or worse, an' yous might 'ave bin a good workman, with a wife an' family, only yer knowed better—"

"'Ere, steady on the brake, missis," interrupted Jonah, with a frown.

"No, Joe, I don't mind sayin' that I 'ad some idea of marryin' yous an' Ada, but ye're not the man I took yer for, an' I give it up. I don't believe in a man marryin' because 'e wants a woman ter cook 'is meals. My idea is a man wants ter git married because 'e's found out a lot o' surprisin' things in the world 'e niver dreamt of before. An' it's only when 'e's found somethin' ter live for, an' work for, that 'e's wot yer rightly call a man. That's w'y I don't worry about you, Joe. I can see your time ain't come."

"Don't be too bleedin' sure," cried Jonah, angrily.

"Of course I'm only a fat old woman as likes 'er joke an' a glass o' beer. I'd be a fool ter lay down the law to a bloke as sharp as yous, that thinks 'e can see everything. But I wasn't always so fat I 'ad ter squeeze through the door, an' I tell yer the best things in life are them yer can't see at all, an' that's the feelin's. So take a fool's advice, an' don't think of marryin' till yer feel there's somethin' wrong wi' yer inside, fer that's w'ere it ketches yer."

"'Ere, 'old 'ard! Can't a bloke git a word in edgeways?"

Mrs Yabsley stopped, with an odd smile on her face.

Jonah stared at her with a perplexed frown, and then the words came in a rush.

"Look 'ere, missis, I wasn't goin' ter let on, but since yer on fer a straight talk, I tell yer there's more in me than yer think, an' if it's up ter me ter git married, I can do it without gittin' roused on by yous."

"Keep yer 'air on, Joe," said Mrs Yabsley, smiling. "I didn't mean ter nark yer, but yer know wot I say is true. An' don't say I ever put it inter yer 'ead ter git married. You've studied the matter, an' yer know it means 'ard graft an' plenty of worry. There's nuthin' in it, Joe, as yer said, an' besides, the Push is waitin' for yer.

"Of course, there's no 'arm in yer cumin' 'ere ter see the kid, but I 'ope yer won't stand in Ada's way w'en she gits a chance. There's Tom Mullins, that was after Ada before she ever took up wi' yous. Only last week 'e told Mrs Jones 'e'd take Ada, kid an' all, if he got the chance. I know yous don't want a wife, but yer shouldn't 'inder others as do."

"Yer talkin' through yer neck," cried Jonah, losing his

temper. "Suppose I tell yer that the kid's done the trick, an' I want ter git married, an' bring 'im up respectable?"

The old woman was silent, but a wonderful smile lit up her face.

"Yer've got a lot ter say about the feelin's. Suppose I tell yer there's somethin' in me trembles w'en I touch this kid? I felt like a damned fool at first, but I'm gittin' used to it."

"That's yer own flesh an' blood a-callin' yer, Joe," cried Mrs. Yabsley, in ecstasy—"the sweetest cry on Gawd's earth, for it goes to yer very marrer."

"That's true, said Jonah, sadly; "an' 'e's the only relation I've got in the wide world, as far as I know. More than that, 'e's the only livin' creature that looks at me without seein' my hump."

It was the first time in Mrs Yabsley's memory that Jonah had mentioned his deformity. A tremor in his voice made her look at him sharply. Tears stood in his eyes. With a sudden impulse she stopped and patted his head.

"That's all right, Joe," she said, gently. "I was only pullin' yer leg. I wanted yer to do the straight thing by Ada, but I wasn't sure yer'd got a 'eart, till the kid found it. But wot will the Push say w'en—"

"The Push be damned!" cried Jonah.

"Amen ter that," said Mrs Yabsley. "Gimme yer fist."

Jonah stayed to tea that night, contrary to his usual habit, for Mrs Yabsley was anxious to have the matter settled.

"Wot's wrong wi' you an' me gittin' married, Ada?" he said.

Ada nearly dropped her cup.

"Garn, ye're only kiddin'!" she cried with an uneasy grin.

"Fair dinkum!" said Jonah.

"Right-oh," said Ada, as calmly as if she were accepting an invitation to a dance.

But she thought with satisfaction that this was the beginning of a perpetual holiday. For she was incorrigibly lazy and hated work, going through the round of mechanical toil in a slovenly fashion, indifferent to the shower of complaints, threats and abuse that fell about her ears.

"Where was yer thinkin' of gittin' married, Joe?" inquired Mrs Yabsley after tea.

"I dunno," replied Jonah, suddenly remembering that he knew no more of weddings than a crow.

"At the Registry Office, of course," said Ada. "Yer walk in, an' yer walk out, an' it's all over."

"That's the idea," said Jonah, greatly relieved. He understood vaguely that weddings were expensive affairs, and he had thirty shillings in his pocket.

"Don't tell me that people are married that goes ter the Registry Office!" cried Mrs Yabsley. "They only git a licence to 'ave a family. I know all about them. Yer sign a piece of paper, an' then the bloke tells yer ye're married. 'Ow does 'e know ye're married? 'E ain't a parson. I was married in a church, an' my marriage is as good now as ever it was. Just yous leave it to me, an' I'll fix yez up."

Ever since Ada was a child, Mrs Yabsley had speculated on her marriage, when all the street would turn out to the wedding. And now, after years of planning and waiting,

65

she was to be married on the quiet, for there was nothing to boast about.

"Well, it's no use cryin' over skimmed milk," she reflected, adapting the proverb to her needs.

But she clung with obstinacy to a marriage in a church, convinced that none other was genuine. And casting about in her mind for a parson who would marry them without fuss or expense, she remembered Trinity Church, and the thing was done.

Canon Vaughan, the new rector of Trinity Church, had brought some strange ideas from London, where he had worked in the slums. He had founded a workman's club, and smoked his pipe with the members; formed a brigade of newsboys and riff-raff, and taught them elementary morality with the aid of boxing-gloves; and offended his congregation by treating the poor with the same consideration as themselves. And then, astonished by the number of mothers who were not wives, that he discovered on his rounds, he had announced that he would open the church on the first Saturday night in every month to marry any couples without needless questions. They could pay, if they chose, but nothing was expected.

Jonah and Ada jumped at the idea, but Mrs Yabsley thought with sorrow of her cherished dream—Ada married on a fine day of sunshine, Cardigan Street in an uproar, a feast where all could cut and come again, the clink of glasses, and a chorus that shook the windows. Well, such things were not to be, and she shut her mouth grimly. But she determined in secret to get in a dozen of beer, and invite a few friends after the ceremony to drink the health of the

66

newly married, and keep the secret till they got home. And as she was rather suspicious of a wedding that cost nothing, she decided to give the parson a dollar to seal the bargain and make the contract more binding.

7

A QUIET WEDDING

The following Saturday Mrs Yabsley astonished her customers by delivering the shirts and collars in the afternoon. There were cries of amazement.

"No, I'm quite sober," she explained; "but I'm changin' the 'abits of a lifetime just to show it can be done."

Then she hurried home to clean up the house. After much thought, she had decided to hold the reception after the wedding in the front room, as it was the largest. She spent an hour carrying the irons, boards, and other implements of the laundry into the back rooms. A neighbour, who poked her head in, asked if she were moving. But when she had finished the cleaning, she surveyed the result with surprise. The room was scrubbed as bare as a shaven chin. So she took some coloured almanacs from the bedroom and kitchen, and tacked them on the walls, studying the effect with the gravity of a decorative artist. The crude blotches of colour pleased her eye, and she considered the result with pride.

"Wonderful 'ow a few pitchers liven a place up," she thought.

She looked doubtfully at the chairs. There were only three, and, years ago, her immense weight had made them as uncertain on their legs as drunkards. She generally sat on a box for safety. Finally, she constructed two forms out of the ironing-boards and some boxes. Then she fastened two ropes of pink tissue paper, that opened out like a concertina, across the ceiling. This was the finishing touch, and lent an air of gaiety to the room.

For two hours past Ada and Pinkey had been decorating one another in the bedroom. When they emerged, Mrs Yabsley cried out in admiration, not recognizing her own daughter for the moment. Their white dresses, freshly starched and ironed by her, rustled stiffly at every movement of their bodies, and they walked daintily as if they were treading on eggs. Both had gone to bed with their hair screwed in curling-pins, losing half their sleep with pain and discomfort, but the result justified the sacrifice. Ada's hair, dark and lifeless in colour, decreased the sullen heaviness of her features; Pinkey's, worn up for the first time, was a barbaric crown, shot with rays of copper and gold as it caught the light.

"Yous put the kettle on, an' git the tea, an' I'll be ready in no time," said Mrs Yabsley. "W'en I was your age, I used ter take 'arf a day ter doll meself up, an' then git down the street with a brass band playin' inside me silly 'ead; but now, gimme somethin' new, if it's only a bit o' ribbon in me 'at, an' I feel dressed up ter the knocker."

At seven o'clock Jonah and Chook arrived. They were dressed in the height of larrikin fashion—tight-fitting suits of dark cloth, soft black felt hats, and soft white shirts with new black mufflers round their necks in place of collars—for the larrikin taste in dress runs to a surprising neatness. But their boots were remarkable, fitting like a glove, with high heels and a wonderful ornament of perforated toe-caps and brass eyelet-holes on the uppers.

Mrs Yabsley, moved by the solemn occasion, formally introduced Chook and Pinkey. They stared awkwardly, not knowing what to say. In a flash, Chook remembered her as the red-haired girl whom he had chiacked at the corner. As he stared at her in surprise, the impudence died out of his face, and he thought with regret of his ferocious jest and her stinging reply. Pinkey grew uneasy under his eyes. Again the curious pink flush coloured her cheeks, and she turned her head with a light, scornful toss. That settled Chook. In five minutes he was looking at her with the passionate adoration of a savage before an idol, for this Lothario of the gutter brought to each fresh experience a surprising virginity of emotion that his facile, ignoble conquests left untouched. Jonah broke the silence by complimenting the ladies on their appearance.

"My oath, yer a sight fer sore eyes, yous are!" he cried. "I'm glad yer don't know 'ow giddy yer look, else us blokes wouldn't 'ave a chance, would we, Chook?"

The girls bridled with pleasure at the rude compliments, pretending not to hear them, feeling very desirable and womanly in their finery.

70

"Dickon ter you," said Mrs Yabsley. "Yer needn't think they're got up ter kill ter please yous. Its only ter give their clobber an airin', an' keep out the moths."

When it was time to set out for the church, the five were quite at their ease, grinning and giggling at the familiar jokes on marriage, broad as a barn door, dating from the Flood. Mrs Yabsley toiled in the rear of the bridal procession, fighting for wind on account of the hill. She kept her fist shut on the two half-dollars for the parson; the wedding ring, jammed on the first joint of her little finger for safety, gave her an atrocious pain. At length they reached Cleveland Street, and halted opposite the church.

The square tower of Trinity Church threw its massive outline against the faint glow of the city lights, keeping watch and ward over the church, that had grown grey in the service of God, like a fortress of the Lord planted on hostile ground. And they stood together, the grim tower and the grey church, for a symbol of immemorial things—a stronghold and a refuge.

The wedding party walked into the churchyard on tiptoe as if they were trespassers. Then, unable to find the door in the dark, they walked softly round the building, trying to see what was going on inside through the stained-glass windows. Their suspicious movements attracted the attention of the verger, and he followed them with stealthy movements, convinced that they meditated a burglary. When he learned their errand, he took charge of the party. They entered the church like foreigners in a remote land. Another wedding was in progress, so they sat down in the narrow, uncomfortable pews, waiting their turn. When

Chook caught sight of the Canon in his surplice and bands, he uttered a cry of amazement.

"Look at the old bloke. 'E's wearin' 'is shirt outside!"

The two girls were convulsed, turning crimson with the effort to repress their giggles. Mrs Yabsley was annoyed, feeling that they were treating the matter as a farce.

"I'm ashamed o' yer, Chook," she remarked severely. "Yer the two ends an' middle of a 'eathen. That's wot they call 'is surplus, an' I wish I 'ad the job of ironin' it."

Order was restored, but at intervals the girls broke into ripples of hysterical laughter. Then Chook saw the organ, with its rows of painted pipes, and nudged Jonah.

"Wot price that fer a mouth-orgin, eh? Yer'd want a extra pair o' bellows ter play that."

Jonah examined the instrument with the interest of a musician, surprised by the enormous tubes, packed stiffly in rows, the plaything of a giant; but he still kept an eye on the pair that were being married, with the nervous interest of a criminal watching an execution. The women, to whom weddings were an afternoon's distraction, like the matinées of the richer, stared about the building. Mrs Yabsley, wedged with difficulty in the narrow pew, pretended that they were made uncomfortable on purpose to keep people awake during the sermon. Presently Ada and Pinkey, who had been examining the memorial tablets on the walls, began to argue whether the dead people were buried under the floor of the church. Pinkey decided they were, and shivered at the thought. Ada called her a fool; they nearly quarrelled.

When their turn came, the Canon advanced to meet

them, setting them at their ease with a few kindly words, less a priest than a courteous host welcoming his guests. He seemed not to notice Jonah's deformity. But, as he read the service, he was the priest again, solemn and austere, standing at the gates of Life and Death. He followed the ritual with scrupulous detail, scorning to give short measure to the poor. In the vestry they signed their names with tremendous effort, holding the pen as if it were a prop. Mrs Yabsley, being no scholar, made a mark. The Canon left them with an apology, as another party was waiting.

"Rum old card," commented Chook, when they got outside. "I reckon 'e's a man w'en 'e tucks 'is shirt in."

The party decided to go home by way of Regent Street, drawn by the sight of the jostling crowd and the glitter of the lamps. As they threaded their way through the crowd, Jonah stopped in front of a pawnshop and announced that he was going to buy a present for Ada and Pinkey to bring them luck. He ignored Ada's cries of admiration at the sight of a large brooch set with paste diamonds, and fixed on a thin silver bracelet for her, and a necklace of imitation pearls, the size of peas, for Pinkey. Ada thrust her fat fingers through the rigid band of metal; it slipped over the joints and hung loosely on her wrist. Then Pinkey clasped the string of shining beads round her thin neck, the metallic lustre of the false gems heightening the delicate pallor of her fine skin. The effect was superb. Ada, feeling that the bride was eclipsed, pretended that her wedding ring was hurting her, and drew all eyes to that badge of honour.

When they reached Cardigan Street, Mrs Yabsley went into the back room, and returned grunting under the weight of a dozen bottles of beer in a basket. Then, one by one, she set them in the middle of the table like a group of ninepins. It seemed a pity to break the set, but they were thirsty, and the pieman was not due for half an hour. A bottle was opened with infinite precaution, but the faint plop of the cork reached the sharp ears of Mrs Swadling, who was lounging at the end of the lane. The unusual movements of Mrs Yabsley had roused her suspicions, but the arrival of her husband, Sam, fighting drunk for his tea, had interrupted her observations. She was accustomed to act promptly, even if it were only to dodge a plate, and in an instant her sharp features were thrust past the door, left ajar for the sake of coolness.

"I thought I'd run across an' ask yer about that iron-mould on Sam's collar," she began.

Then, surprised by the appearance of the room, dressed for a festival, she looked around. Her eyes fell on the battalion of bottles, and she stood thunderstruck by this extravagance. But Ada, anxious to display her ring, was smoothing and patting her hair every few minutes. Already the movement had become a habit. Unconsciously she lifted her hand and flashed the ring in the eyes of Mrs Swadling.

"Well, I never!" she cried. "I might 'ave known wot yer were up to, an' me see a weddin' in me cup only this very mornin'."

Mrs Yabsley looked at Jonah and laughed.

"Might as well own up, Joe," she cried. "The cat's out of the bag."

"Right y'are," cried Jonah. "Let 'em all come. I can't be 'ung fer it."

Mrs Yabsley, delighted with her son-in-law's speech, invited Mrs Swadling to a seat, and then stepped out to ask a few of her neighbours in to drink a glass and wish them luck. In half an hour the room was full of women, who were greatly impressed by the bottles of beer, a luxury for aristocrats. When Joey the pieman arrived, some were sitting on the veranda, as the room was crowded. Mrs Yabsley anxiously reckoned the number of guests; she had reckoned on twelve, and there were twenty. She beckoned to Jonah, and they whispered together for a minute. He counted some money into her hand, and cried, "Let 'er go; it's only once in a lifetime."

Then Mrs Yabsley, as hostess, went to each in turn, asking what they preferred. The choice was limited to green peas, hot pies, and saveloys, and as each chose, she ticked it off on a piece of paper in hieroglyphics known only to herself, as she was used to number the shirts and collars. Joey, impressed by the magnitude of the order, got down from his perch in the cart and helped to serve the guests. And he passed in and out among the expectant crowd, helping them to make a choice, like a chef anxious to please even the most fastidious palates.

Cups, saucers, plates, and basins were pressed into service until Mrs Yabsley's stock ran out; the last served were forced to hold their delicacy wrapped in a scrap of paper in their hands, the hot grease sweating through the thin covering on to their fingers. The ladies hesitated, fearful of being thought vulgar if they ate in their usual manner; but Mrs Yabsley, seeing their embarrassment, cried out that fingers were made before forks, and bit a huge piece out of her pie.

Then the feast began in silence, except for the sound of chewing. Joey had surpassed himself. The peas melted in your mouth, the piecrusts were a marvel, and the saveloys were done to a turn. And they ate with solemn, serious faces, for it was not every day the chance came to fill their bellies with such dainties. Joey, with an eye to business, decided to stay in the street on the chance of selling out, for the crowd had now reached to the gutter. He rattled the shining lids of the hot cans from time to time to attract attention as his cracked voice chanted his familiar cry, "Peas an' pies, all 'ot, all 'ot!"

And he drove a brisk trade among the uninvited guests, who paid for their own. Inside, they drank the health of the married couple; but the dozen of beer barely wet their throats. Jonah and Chook went to the Woolpack with jugs, and the company settled down to the spree. At intervals the men offered to shout for a few friends, and, borrowing a dead marine from the heap of empty bottles, shuffled off to the hotel to get it filled. The noise grew to an uproar—a babel of tongues, sudden explosions of laughter, and the shuffling of feet.

Suddenly Mrs Yabsley looked at the clock.

"Good Gawd!" she cried. "Tomorrer's Sunday, an' there ain't a bite or sup in the blessed 'ouse!"

In the excitement of the wedding she had forgotten her weekly shopping. It was a catastrophe. But Chook had an idea.

"Cum on, blokes," he cried, "'oo'll cum down the road wi' Mother, an' 'elp carry the tucker? Blimey, I reckon it's 'er night out!"

76

A dozen volunteered, with a shout of applause. Jonah and Ada were left to entertain the guests, and the party set out. The grocer was going to bed, and the shop was in darkness, but they banged so fiercely on the door that he leaned over the balcony in his shirt, convinced that the Push had come to wreck his shop. Yet he came down, distressed in his shopkeeper's soul at the thought of losing his profit. He served her in haste, terrified by the boisterous noise of her escort.

Then they walked up the Road, shrieking with laughter, bumping against the passengers, who hurried past with scared looks. It was a triumphal procession to the butcher's and the greengrocer's. Mrs Yabsley, radiant with beer, gave her orders royally, her bodyguard, seizing on every purchase, fighting for the privilege of carrying it. The procession turned into Cardigan Street again, laden with provisions, yelling scraps of song, rousing the street with ungodly clamour.

Old Dad met them at the corner of Cooper Street. He stood for a moment, lurching with unpremeditated steps to the front and rear, astonished by the noise and the crowd. Then he recognized Mrs Yabsley, and became suddenly excited, under the impression that she was being taken to the lock-up by the police. He lurched gallantly into the throng, calling on his friends to rescue the old girl from her captors. When he learned that she was in no danger, he grew enthusiastic, and insisted on helping to carry the provisions.

"'Ere, Dad, yer've lost yer 'ead. Take this," said Chook, offering him a cabbage.

"Keep it sonny—keep it; you want it more than I do," cried Dad, scornfully.

So saying, he tore a shoulder of mutton out of Waxy's hands, and, carrying it in his arms as a woman carries a child, joined the procession with sudden, zigzag steps. When the party reached the cottage, it was met with a howl of welcome from the crowd, which now reached to the opposite footpath. Barney Ryan, seized with an inspiration, broke suddenly into "Mother Shipton". The chorus was taken up with a roar of discordant voices:

> *"Good old Mother has come again to prophesy*
> *Things that will surely occur as the days go rolling by,*
> *So listen to me if you wish to know,*
> *For I'll let you into the know, you know,*
> *And tell you some wonders before I go*
> > *To home, sweet home."*

Mrs Yabsley, delighted by the compliment, stood on her veranda, smiling and radiant, like Royalty receiving homage from its subjects. This set the ball rolling. Song followed song, the pick of the music-halls. Jonah gave a selection on the mouth-organ. Then Barney, who was growing hoarse, winked maliciously at Jonah and Ada, and struck into his masterpiece, "Trinity Church". It was the success of the evening.

> *"She told me her age was five-and-twenty,*
> *Cash in the bank of course she'd plenty,*
> *I like a lamb believed it all,*

78

I was an M.U.G.;
At Trinity Church I met my doom,
Now we live in a top back room,
Up to my eyes in debt for 'renty',
    That's what she's done for me."

The chorus rang out with a deafening roar. The guests, tickled by the words that fell so pat, twisted and squirmed with laughter, digging their fingers into their neighbours' ribs to emphasize the details. But Barney, in trying to imitate a stumpy man with an umbrella, as the song demanded, tripped and lay where he fell, too fatigued to rise.

Then, saddened by the beer they had drunk, they grew sentimental. Mrs Swadling, who never let herself be asked twice, for fear of being thought shy, led off with a pathetic ballad. She sang in a thin, quavering voice, staring into vacancy, with glassy eyes like the blind beggars at the corner, dragging the tune till it became a wail—a dirge for lost souls.

"Some are gone from us for ever,
    Longer here they might not stay;
They have reached a fairer region,
    Far away-ee, far away—
They have reached a fairer region,
    Far away-ee, far away."

The guests listened with a beery sadness in their eyes, suddenly reminded that you were here today and gone tomorrow, pierced with a sense of the tragic brevity of Life, their hearts oppressed with a pleasant anguish at the pity and wonder of this insubstantial world.

Mrs Yabsley had put the baby in her bed, where it had slept calmly through the night till awakened by the singing. Then it grew fretful, disturbed by the rude clamour. At length, in a sudden pause, a lusty yell from the bedroom fell on their ears. Everyone smiled. But, as Mrs Yabsley crossed the room to pacify it, the women called for the baby to be brought out. When Mrs Yabsley appeared with the infant in her arms, she was greeted with yells of admiration. Ada turned crimson with embarrassment. The women passed it from hand to hand, nursing it for a few minutes with little cries of emotion.

But suddenly Jonah walked up to Mrs Swadling and took his child in his arms. And he stood before the crowd, his eyes glittering with pride as he exhibited his own flesh and blood, the son whose shapely back and limbs proved that only an accident separated the hunchback from his fellows. The guests howled with delight, clapping their hands, stamping their feet, trying to add to the din. It was a triumph, the sensation of the evening. Then Old Dad, shutting one eye to see more distinctly, proposed the health of the baby. It was given with a roar.

The noise stimulated Dad to further effort and, swaying slightly, he searched his memory for a suitable quotation. A patent medicine advertisement zigzagged across his brain, and with a sigh of relief, he muttered,

"The 'and that slaps the baby rocks the world," beaming on the guests with the air of a man who has Shakespeare at his fingers' ends. There was a dead silence, and Dad looked round in wonder. Then a woman tittered, and a shout went up that rattled the windows.

It was nearly twelve when the party broke up, chiefly because the Woolpack was closed and the supply of beer was cut off. Some of the men had reached the disagreeable stage, maudlin drunk or pugnacious, anxious to quarrel, but forgetting the cause of dispute. The police, who had looked on with a tolerant eye, began to clear the footpaths, shaking the drowsy into wakefulness, threatening and coaxing the obstinate till they began to stagger homewards.

There was nearly a fight in the cottage. Pinkey's young man had called to take her home, and Chook had recognized him for an old enemy, a wool-washer, called "Stinky" Collins on account of the vile smell of decaying skins that hung about his clothes. Chook began to make love to Pinkey under his very eyes. And Stinky sat in sullen silence, refusing to open his mouth. Pinkey, amazed by Chook's impudence and annoyed that her lover should cut so poor a figure, encouraged him, with the feminine delight in playing with fire. Then Chook, with an insolent grin at Stinky, announced that he was going to see Pinkey home. Mrs Yabsley just parted them in time. Chook went swearing up to the corner on the chance of getting a final taste at the Woolpack.

Mrs Yabsley stood on the veranda and watched his departing figure, aching in every joint from the strain of the eventful day. Cardigan Street was silent and deserted. The air was still hot and breathless, but little gusts of wind began to rise, the first signs of a coming "buster". Then she turned to Jonah and Ada, who had followed her on to the veranda, and summed up the day's events.

"All's well that ends well, as the man said when he plaited the horse's tail, but this is a new way of gittin' married on the sly, with all the street to keep the secret. There's no mistake, secrets are dead funny. Spend yer last penny to 'elp yer friend out of a 'ole, an' it niver gits about; but pawn yer last shirt, an' nex' day all the bloomin street wants to know if yer don't feel the cold."

8

JONAH STARTS ON HIS OWN

It was Monday morning. Hans Paasch was at his bench cleaning up the dirt and litter of last week, setting the tools in order at one end of the bench, while he swept it clear of the scraps of leather that had gathered through the week. Then he set the heavy iron lasts on their shelves, where they looked like a row of amputated feet. The shining knives and irons lay in order, ready to hand. A light cloud of dust from the broom made him sneeze, and he strewed another handful of wet tea-leaves on the floor. These he saved carefully from day to day to lay the dust before sweeping. When the bench and the shop were swept clean, he looked round with mild satisfaction.

Once a week, in this manner, he gratified his passion for order and neatness; but when work began, everything fell into disorder, and he wasted hours peering over the bench with his short sight for tools that lay under his nose, buried in a heap of litter.

The peculiar musty odour of leather hung about the shop. A few pairs of boots that had been mended stood in a row, the shining black rim of the new soles contrasting with the worn, dingy uppers—the patched and mended shoes of the poor, who must wear them while upper and sole hang together. They betrayed the age and sex of the wearer as clearly as a photograph. The shoddy slipper, with the high, French heels, of the smart shop-girl; the heavy bluchers, studded with nails, of the labourer; the light tan boots, with elegant, pointed toes, of the clerk or counter-jumper; the shoes of a small child, with a thin rim of copper to protect the toes.

For the first time since he was on piecework, Jonah set out for the shop on Monday morning; but when he walked in, Paasch met him with a look of surprise, thinking he had mistaken the day of the week. He blinked uneasily when Jonah reached for his apron.

"It vas no use putting on your apron. Dere is not a stitch of work to be done," he cried in amazement.

Jonah looked round; it was true. He remembered that the repairs, which were the backbone of Paasch's trade, began to come in slowly on Monday. Paasch always began the week by making a pair of boots for the window, which he sold at half price when the leather had perished. In his eagerness for work, he had forgotten that Paasch's business was so small. He looked round with annoyance, realizing that he would never earn the wages here that he needed for his child. For he usually earned about fifteen shillings, except in the Christmas season, when trade was brisk. Then he drew more than a pound. This sum of money, which had formerly satisfied his wants, now seemed a mere flea-bite.

He looked round with a sudden scorn on the musty shop that had given him work and food since he was a boy. The sight of the old man, bending over the last, with his simple, placid face, annoyed him. And he felt a sudden enmity for this man whose old-fashioned ways had let him grow grey here like a rat in a hole.

He stared round, wondering if anything could be done to improve the business. The shop wanted livening up with a coat of paint. He would put new shelves up, run a partition across, and dress the windows like the shops down town. In his eager thoughts he saw the dingy shop transformed under his touch, spick and span, alive with customers, who jostled one another as they passed in and out, the coin clinking merrily in the till.

He awoke as from a dream, and looked with dismay on the small, grimy shop keeping pace with its master's old age. Suddenly an idea came into his head, and he stared at Paasch with a hard calculating look in his eyes. Then he got up, and walked abruptly out of the shop. The old German, who was used to his sudden humours and utter want of manners, peered after his retreating figure with a puzzled look.

Jonah had walked out of the door to look for work. He saw that it was useless to expect the constant work and wages that he needed from Paasch, for the old man's business had remained stationary during the twelve years that Jonah had worked for him. And he had decided to leave him, if a job could be found. He stood on the footpath and surveyed the Road with some anxiety. There were plenty of shops, but few of them in which he would be welcome, owing to his reputation as leader of the Push. For years he had been at daggers drawn with the owners of the three largest shops, and the small fry could barely make a living for themselves.

The street-arab in him, used to the freedom of a small shop, recoiled from the thought of Packard's, the huge factory where you became a machine, repeating one operation indefinitely till you were fit for nothing else. Paasch had taught him the trade thoroughly, from cutting out the insoles to running the bead-iron round the finished boot. As a forlorn hope, he resolved to call on Bob Watkins. Bob, who always passed the time of day with him, had been laid up with a bad cold for weeks. He might be glad of some help. Jonah found the shop empty, the bench and tools covered with dust. Mrs Watkins came in answer to his knock.

"Bob's done 'is last day's work 'ere," she said, using her handkerchief. "'E 'ad a terrible cold all the winter, an' at last 'e got so bad we 'ad to call the doctor in, an' 'e told 'im 'e was in a gallopin' consumption, an' sent 'im away to some 'ome on the mountains."

"It's no use askin' fer a job, then?" inquired Jonah.

"None at all," said the woman. "Bob neglected the work for a long time, as 'e was too weak to do it, an' the customers took their work away. In fact, I'm giving up the shop, an' going back to business. I was a dressmaker before I got married, and my sister's 'ad more work than

86

she could do ever since I left 'er. And Bob wrote down last week to say that I was to sell the lasts and tools for what they would fetch. And now I think of it, I wish you would run your eye over the lasts and bench, an' tell me what they ought to fetch. A man offered me three pounds for the lot, but I know that's too cheap."

"Yer'll niver get wot 'e gave fer 'em, but gimme a piece of paper, an' I'll work it out," said Jonah.

In half an hour he made a rough inventory based on the cost and present condition of the material.

"I make it ten pounds odd, but I don't think yer'll git it," he said at last. "Seven pounds would be a fair offer, money down."

"I'd be thankful to get that," said Mrs Watkins.

Jonah walked thoughtfully up Cardigan Street. Here was the chance of a lifetime, if a man had a few dollars. With Bob's outfit, he could open a shop on the Road, and run rings round Paasch and the others. But seven pounds! He had never handled so much money in his life, and there was no one to lend it to him. Mrs Yabsley was as poor as a crow. Well, he would fit up the back room as a workshop, and go on at Packard's as an outdoor finisher, carrying a huge bag of boots to and from the factory every week, like Tom Mullins.

When Jonah reached the cottage, he found Mrs Yabsley sorting the shirts and collars; Ada was reading a penny novelette. She had left Packard's without ceremony on her wedding-day, and was spending her honeymoon on the back veranda. Her tastes were very simple. Give her nothing to do, a novelette to read, and some lollies to suck, and she was satisfied. Ray, who was growing too big for the box-cradle, was lying on a sugar-bag in the shade.

"W'y, Joe, yer face is as long as a fiddle!" cried Mrs Yabsley, cheerfully. "Wot'ys up? 'Ave yer got the sack?"

"No, but Dutchy's got nuthin' fer me till We'n'sday. I might 'ave known that. An' anyhow, if I earned more than a quid, 'e'd break 'is 'eart."

"Well, a quid's no good to a man wi' a wife an' family," replied the old woman. "Wot do yer reckon on doin'?"

She knew that her judgment of Jonah was being put to the test, and she remarked his gloomy face with satisfaction.

"I'm goin' ter chuck Dutchy, if I can git a job," said Jonah. "I went round ter Bob Watkins, but 'e's in the 'orspital, an' 'is wife's sellin' 'is tools."

"Wot does she want for 'em?" asked Mrs Yabsley, with a curious look.

"Seven quid, an' they'd set a man up fer life," said Jonah.

"Ah! that's a lot o' money," said Mrs Yabsley, raking the ashes from under the copper. "Wait till this water boils, an' we'll talk things over."

Ada returned to her novelette. Ray, sitting upright with an effort, gurgled with pleasure to see his father. Jonah tilted him on his back, and tickled his fat legs, pretending to worry him like a dog. The pair made a tremendous noise.

"Oh, gi' the kid a bit o' peace!" cried Ada, angry at being disturbed.

"Yous git round, an' 'elp Mum wi' the clothes," snapped Jonah.

"Me? No fear!" cried Ada, with a malicious grin. "I didn't knock off work to carry bricks. Yous married me, an' yer got ter keep me."

Jonah looked at her with a scowl. She knew quite well that he had married her for the child's sake alone. A savage retort was on his tongue, but Mrs Yabsley stepped in.

"Well, Joe, now I see yer dead set on earnin' a livin', I don't mind tellin' yer I've got somethin' up me sleeve. No, I don't mean a guinea-pig an' a dozen eggs, like the conjurer bloke I see once," she explained in reply to his surprised look; "but if yer the man I take yer for, we'll soon 'ave the pot a-boiling. Many's the weary night I've spent in bed thinkin' about you w'en I might 'ave bin snorin'. That reminds me. Did y'ever notice yer can niver tell exactly w'en yer drop off? I've tried all I know, but ye're awake one minit, an' chasin' a butterfly wi' a cow's 'ead the next. But that ain't wot I'm a-talkin' about. Paasch 'e's blue mouldy, an' couldn't catch a snail unless yer give 'im a start; an' if yer went ter Packard's, yer'd tell the manager ter go to 'ell, an' git fired out the first week. Yous must be yer own boss, Joe. I've studied yer like a book, an yer nose wasn't made that shape for nuthin'."

"W'y, wot's wrong wi' it?" laughed Jonah, feeling his nose with its powerful, predatory curve.

"Nuthin', if yer listen to me...'Ave yer got pluck enough 'ter start on yer own?" she inquired, suddenly.

"Wot's the use, w'en I've got no beans?" replied Jonah.

"I'll find the beans, an' yer can go an' buy Bob Watkins's shop out as it stands," said Mrs Yabsley, proudly.

"Fair dinkum!" cried Jonah, in amazement.

89

Ada put down her novelette and stared, astonished at the turn of the conversation. It flashed through her mind that her mother had some mysterious habits. Suppose she were like the misers she had read of in books, who lived in the gutter, and owned terraces of houses? For a moment Ada saw herself riding in a carriage, with rings on every finger, and feathers in her hat, with the childlike faith of the ignorant in the marvellous.

But Mrs Yabsley was studying some strange hieroglyphics like Chinese, pencilled on the cupboard. She knitted her brows in the agony of calculation.

"I can lay me 'ands on thirty pounds in solid cash," she announced. She spoke as if it were a million. Jonah cried out in amazement; Ada felt disappointed.

"W'ere is it, Mum? In the bank?" asked Jonah.

"No fear," said Mrs Yabsley, with a crafty smile. "It's as safe as a church. I was niver fool enough ter put my money in the bank. I know all about them. Yer put yer money in fer years, an' then, w'en they've got enough, they shut the door, an' the old bloke wi' the white weskit an' gold winkers cops the lot. No banks fer me, thank yer!"

Then she explained that ever since she opened the laundry, she had squeezed something out of her earnings as one squeezes blood out of a stone. She had saved threepence this week, sixpence that, sometimes even a shilling went into the child's money-box that she had chosen as a safe deposit. When the coins mounted to a sovereign, she had changed them into a gold piece. Then, her mind disturbed by visions of thieves bent on plunder, she had hit on a plan. A floorboard was loose in the kitchen. She had levered this up, and probed with a stick till she touched solid earth. Then the yellow coin, rolled carefully in a ball of paper, was dropped into the hole. And for years she had added to her unseen treasure, dropping her precious coins into that dark hole with more security than a man deposits thousands in the bank. But the time was come to unearth the golden pile.

She trembled with excitement when Jonah ripped up the narrow plank with the poker. Then he thrust his arm down till he touched the soft earth. He seemed a long time groping, and Mrs Yabsley wondered at the delay. At last he sat up, with a perplexed look.

"I can't feel nuthin'," he said. "Are yez sure this is the place?"

"Of course it is," said Mrs Yabsley, sharply. "I dropped them down right opposite the 'ead of that nail."

Jonah groped again without success.

"'Ere, let me try," said Mum, impatiently.

She knelt over the hole to get her bearings, and then plunged her arm into the gap. Jonah and Ada, on their knees, watched in silence.

At last, with a cry of despair, Mrs Yabsley sat up on the floor. There was no doubt, the treasure was gone! In this extremity, her wit, her philosophy, her temper, her very breath deserted her, and she wept. She looked the picture of misery as the tears rolled down her face. Jonah and Ada stared at one another in dismay, each wondering if this story of a hidden treasure was a delusion of the old woman's mind. Like her neighbours, who lived from hand to mouth, she was given to dreaming of imaginary riches falling on her from the clouds. But her grief was too real for doubt.

"Well, if it ain't there, w'ere is it?" cried Jonah, angrily, feeling that he, too, had been robbed. "If it's gone, somebody took it. Are yer sure yer niver got a few beers in, an' started skitin' about it?" He looked hard at Ada.

"Niver a word about it 'ave I breathed to a livin' soul till this day," wailed Mrs Yabsley, mopping her eyes with her apron.

"Rye buck!" said Jonah. "'Ere goes! I'll find it, if the blimey house falls down. Gimme that axe."

The floor-boards cracked and split as he ripped them up. Small beetles and insects, surprised by the light, scrambled with desperate haste into safety. A faint, earthy smell rose from the foundations. Suddenly, with a yell of triumph, Jonah stooped, and picked up a dirty ball of paper. As he lifted it, a glittering coin fell out.

"W'y, wot's this?" he cried, looking curiously at the wad of discoloured paper. One side had been chewed to a pulp by something small and sharp. "Rats an' mice!" cried Jonah. "They've boned the paper ter make their nests. Every dollar's 'ere, if we only look."

"Thank Gawd!" said Mrs Yabsley, heaving a tremendous sigh. "Ada, go an' git a jug o' beer."

In an hour Jonah had recovered twenty-eight of the missing coins; the remaining two had evidently been dragged down to their nests by the industrious vermin. Late in the afternoon Jonah, who looked like a sweep, gave up the search. The kitchen was a wreck. Mrs Yabsley sat with the coins in her lap, feasting her eyes on this heap of glittering gold, for she had rubbed each coin till it shone like new. Her peace of mind was restored, but it was a long time before she could think of rats and mice without anger.

9

PADDY'S MARKET

Chook was standing near the entrance to the market where his mates had promised to meet him, but he found that he had still half an hour to spare, as he had come down early to mark a pak-ah-pu ticket at the Chinaman's in Hay Street. So he lit a cigarette and sauntered idly through the markets to kill time.

The three long, dingy arcades were flooded with the glare from clusters of naked gas-jets, and the people, wedged in a dense mass, moved slowly like water in motion between the banks of stalls. From the stone flags underneath rose a sustained, continuous noise—the leisurely tread and shuffle of a multitude blending with the deep hum of many voices, and over it all, like the upper notes in a symphony, the shrill, discordant cries of the dealers.

Overhead, the light spent its brightness in a gloomy vault, like the roof of a vast cathedral fallen into decay, its ancient timbers blackened with the smoke and grime of half a century.

On Saturdays the great market, silent and deserted for six nights in the week, was a debauch of sound and colour and smell. Strange, pungent odours assailed the nostrils; the ear was surprised with the sharp, broken cries of dealers, the cackle of poultry, and the murmur of innumerable voices; the stalls, splashed with colour, astonished the eye like a picture, immensely powerful, immensely crude.

The long rows of stalls were packed with the drift and refuse of a great city. For here the smug respectability of the shops were cast aside, and you were deep in the romance of traffic in merchandise fallen from its high estate—a huge welter and jumble of things arrested in their ignoble descent from the shops to the gutter.

At times a stall was loaded with the spoils of a sunken ship or the loot from a city fire, and you could buy for a song the rare fabrics and costly dainties of the rich, a stain on the cloth, a discoloured label on the tin, alone giving a hint of their adventures. Then the people hovered round like wreckers on a hostile shore, carrying off spoil and treasure at a fraction of its value, exulting over their booty like soldiers after pillage.

There was no caprice of the belly that could not be gratified, no want of the naked body that could not be supplied in this huge bazaar of the poor; but its cost had to be counted in pence, for those who bought in the cheapest market came here.

A crowd of women and children clustered like flies round the lolly stall brought Chook to a standstill; the trays heaped with sweets coloured like the rainbow, pleased his eye, and, remembering Ada's childish taste for lollies, he thought suddenly of her friend, Pinkey the red-haired, and smiled.

Near at hand stood a collection of ferns and pot-plants, fresh and cool, smelling of green gardens and moist earth. Over the way, men lingered with serious faces, trying the edge of a chisel with their thumb, examining saws, planes, knives, and shears with a workman's interest in the tools that earn his bread.

Chook stopped to admire the art gallery, gay with coloured pictures from the Christmas numbers of English magazines. On the walls were framed pictures of Christ crucified, the red blood dropping from His wounds, or the old rustic bridge of an English village, crude as almanacs, printed to satisfy the artistic longings of the people.

Opposite, a cock crowed in defiance; the hens cackled loudly in the coops; the ducks lay on planks, their legs fastened with string, their eyes dazed with terror or fatigue.

A cargo of scented soap and perfume, the damaged rout of a chemist's shop, fascinated the younger women, stirring their instinctive delight in luxury; and for a few pence they gratified the longing of their hearts.

The children pricked their ears at the sudden blare of a tin trumpet, the squeaking of a mechanical doll. And they stared in amazement at the painted toys, surprised that the world contained such beautiful things. The mothers, harassed with petty cares, anxiously considered the prices; then the pennies were counted, and the child clasped in its small hands a Noah's ark, a wax doll, or a wooden sword.

Chook stared at the vegetable stalls with murder in his eyes, for here stood slant-eyed Mongolians behind heaps of potatoes, onions, cabbages, beans, and cauliflowers, crying the prices in broken English, or chattering with their neighbour's in barbaric, guttural sounds. To Chook they were the scum of the earth, less than human, taking the bread out of his mouth, selling cheaply because they lived like vermin in their gardens.

But he forgot them in watching the Jews driving bargains in second-hand clothes, renovated with secret processes handed down from the Ark. Coats and trousers, equipped for their last adventure with mysterious darns and patches, cheated the eye like a painted beauty at a ball. Women's finery lay in disordered heaps—silk blouses covered with tawdry lace, skirts heavy with gaudy trimming—the draggled plumage of fine birds that had come to grief. But here buyer and seller met on level terms, for each knew to a hair the value of the sorry garments; and they chaffered with crafty eyes, each searching for the silent thought behind the spoken lie.

Chook stared at the bookstall with contempt, wondering how people found the time and patience to read. One side was packed with the forgotten lumber of bookshelves—an odd volume of sermons, a collection of scientific essays, a technical work out of date. And the men, anxious to improve their minds, stared at the titles with the curious reverence of the illiterate for a printed book. At their elbows boys gloated over the pages of a penny dreadful, and the women fingered penny novelettes with rapid movements, trying to judge the contents from the gaudy cover.

The crowd at the provision stall brought Chook to a standstill again. Enormous flitches hung from the posts, and the shelves were loaded with pieces of bacon tempting the eye with a streak of lean in a wilderness of fat. The buyers watched hungrily as the keen knife slipped into the rich meat, and the rasher, thin as paper, fell on the board like the shaving from a carpenter's plane. The dealer, wearing a clean shirt and white apron, served his customers with smooth, comfortable movements, as if contact with so much grease had nourished his body and oiled his joints.

When Chook elbowed his way to the corner where Joe Crutch and Waxy Collins had promised to meet him, there was no sign of them, and he took another turn up the middle arcade. It was now high tide in the markets, and the stream of people filled the space between the stalls like a river in flood. And they moved at a snail's pace, clutching in their arms fowls, pot-plants, parcels of groceries, toys for the children, and a thousand odd, nameless trifles, bought for the sake of buying, because they were cheap. A babel of broken conversation, questions and replies, jests and laughter, drowned the cries of the dealers, and a strong, penetrating odour of human sweat rose on the hot air. From time to time a block occurred, and the crowd stood motionless, waiting patiently until they could move ahead.

In one of these sudden blocks Chook, who was craning his neck to watch the vegetable stalls, felt someone pushing, and turning his head, found himself staring into the eyes of Pinkey, the red-haired.

"'Ello, fancy meetin' yous," cried Chook, his eyes dancing with pleasure.

The curious pink flush spread over the girl's face, and then she found her tongue.

"Look w'ere ye're goin'. Are yer walkin' in yer sleep?"

"I am," said Chook, "an' don't wake me; I like it."

But the twinkle died out of his eyes when he saw Stinky Collins, separated from Pinkey by the crowd, scowling at him over her shoulder. He ignored Chook's friendly nod, and they stood motionless, wedged in that sea of human bodies until it chose to move.

Chook felt the girl's frail body pressed against him. His nostrils caught the odour of her hair and flesh, and the perfume mounted to his brain like wine. The wonderful red hair, glittering like bronze, fell in short curls round the nape of her neck, where it had escaped from the comb. A tremor ran through his limbs and his pulse quickened. And he was seized with an insane desire to kiss the white flesh, pale as ivory against her red hair. The crowd moved, and Pinkey wriggled to the other side.

"I'll cum wid yer, if yer feel lonely," said Chook as she passed.

"Yous git a move on, or yer'll miss the bus," cried Pinkey, as she passed out of sight.

When Chook worked his way back to the corner, little Joe Crutch and Waxy Collins stepped forward.

"W'ere the 'ell 'ave yer bin? We've bin waitin' 'ere this 'arf 'our," they cried indignantly.

"Wot liars yer do meet,' said Chook, grinning.

The three entered the new market, an immense red-brick square with a smooth, cemented floor, and a lofty roof on steel girders. It is here the people amuse themselves with the primitive delights of an English fair after the fatigue of shopping.

The larrikins turned to the chipped-potato stall as a hungry dog jumps at a bone, eagerly sniffing the smell of burning fat as the potatoes crisped in the spitting grease.

"It's up ter yous ter shout," cried Joe and Waxy.

"Well, a tray bit won't break me," said Chook, producing threepence from his pocket.

The dealer, wearing the flat white cap of a French cook, and a clean apron, ladled the potatoes out of the cans into a strainer on the counter. His wife, with a rapid movement, twisted a slip of paper into a spill, and, filling it with chips, shook a castor of salt over the top. Customers crowded about, impatient to be served, and she went through the movements of twisting the paper, filling it with chips, and shaking the castor with the automatic swiftness of a machine.

When they were served, the larrikins stood on one side, crunching the crisp slices of potato between their teeth with immense relish as they watched the cook stirring the potatoes in the cauldron of boiling fat. Then they licked the grease off their fingers, lit cigarettes, and sauntered on. But the chips had whetted their appetites, and the sight of green peas and saveloys made their mouths water.

Men, women, and children sat on the forms round the stall with the stolid air of animals waiting to be fed. When each received a plate containing a squashy mess of peas and a luscious saveloy, they began to eat with slow, animal satisfaction, heedless of the noisy crowd. The larrikins sat down and gave their order, each paying for his own.

"Nothin' like a feed ter set a man up," said Chook, wiping his mouth with the back of his hand.

As he turned, he was surprised to see Stinky Collins and Pinkey in front of the electric battery. These machines had a singular attraction for the people. The mysterious fluid that ran silently and invisibly through the copper wires put them in touch with the mysteries of Nature. And they gripped the brass handles, holding on till the tension became too great, with the conscientious air of people taking medicine.

Stinky, full of jealous fear, had dragged Pinkey to the new market, where he meant to treat her to green peas and ice-cream. But as they passed the battery, a sudden desire swept through him to give an exhibition of his strength and endurance to this girl, to force her admiration with the vanity of a cock strutting before his hens.

He took hold of the brass handles, and watched the dial, like a clock-face, that marked the intensity of the current. The muscles of his face contracted into a rigid stare as the electric current ran through his limbs. He had the face of one visiting the dentist, but he held on until the pointer marked half-way. Then he nodded, and dropped the handles with a sigh of relief as the current was turned off.

But as he looked to Pinkey for the applause that he had earned, Chook stepped up to the machine and, with an impudent grin at Pinkey, grasped the handles. The pointer moved slowly round, and passed Stinky's mark, but Chook held on, determined to eclipse his rival. His muscles seemed to be cracking with pain, the seconds lengthened into intolerable hours. Suddenly, as the dial marked three-quarters, he dropped the handles with a grin of triumph at Pinkey.

Stinky, smarting with defeat, instantly took up the challenge.

"That's no test of strength," he cried angrily. "Women can stand a lot more than men."

"Orl right; choose yer own game, an' I'm after yer," said Chook.

Behind them a hammer fell with a tremendous thud, and a voice cried, "Try yer strength—only a penny, only a penny."

"'Ow'll that suit yer?" inquired Stinky, with a malicious grin, for he counted on his superior weight and muscle to overcome his rival.

"Let 'er go!" cried Chook.

Stinky spat on his hands, and seized the wooden mallet. Cripes, he would show Pinkey which was the better man of the two! He tightened his muscles with tremendous effort as he swung the hammer, turning red in the face with the exertion. The mallet fell, and a little manikin flew up the pillar, marking the weight of the blow. It was a good stroke, and he threw down the hammer with the air of a Sandow.

Then Chook seized the mallet, still with his provoking grin at Pinkey, and swung it with the ease of a man using an axe. The manikin flew level with Stinky's mark. And they disputed angrily which was the heavier blow. But Stinky, whose blood was up, seized the mallet again, and forced every ounce of his strength into the blow. The manikin flew a foot higher than the previous mark. The contest went on, each striving to beat the other's mark, with blows that threatened to shatter the machine, till both were tired. But Stinky's second blow held the record. Chook was beaten.

"Is there any other game yer know?" sneered Stinky.

Near them were the shooting-galleries, looking like enormous chimneys that had blown down. A sharp, spitting crack came from each rifle as it was fired.

"A dollar even money yer can't ring the bell in six shots," cried Chook.

"Done!" shouted Stinky.

The stakes, in half-crowns, were handed to the proprietor of the gallery, and they took turns with the pea-rifle, resting their elbows on the ledge as they stared down the black tube at a white disc that seemed miles away. Each held the gun awkwardly like a broom-handle, holding their breath to prevent the barrel from wobbling. At the fifth shot, by a lucky fluke, Chook rang the bell. When he put down the rifle, Stinky was already dragging Pinkey away, his face black with anger. But Chook cried out, "'Ere, 'arf a mo'—this is my shout!"

They were near the ice-cream stall, where trade was brisk, for the people's appetite for this delicacy is independent of the season. Pinkey, who adored ice-cream, looked with longing eyes, but Stinky turned angrily on his heel.

"'Ave a bit o' common, an' don't make a 'oly show of yerself 'cause yer lost a dollar," she whispered in disgust.

She pulled him to a seat, and the party sat down to wait their turn. Then the dealer scooped the frozen delicacy out of the can, and plastered it into the glasses as if it were mortar. And they swallowed the icy mixture in silence, allowing it to melt on the tongue to extract the flavour before swallowing. All but Stinky, who held his glass as if it belonged to someone else, disdaining to touch it. Chook's gorge rose at the sight.

"Don't eat it, if it chokes yer," he cried.

With an oath Stinky threw the glass on the ground, where it broke with a noisy crash that jerked every head in their direction as if pulled by strings.

"I can pay fer wot I eat," he cried. "Come on, Liz."

The others had sprung to their feet, astonished at this prodigal waste of a delicacy fit for kings. Chook stood for a moment, glowering with rage, and then ran at his enemy; but Pinkey jumped between them.

"You do!—you do!" she cried, pushing him away with the desperate valour of a hen defending her chickens.

"Orl right, not till next time," said Chook, smiling grimly.

She pulled Stinky by the arm, and they disappeared in the crowd.

"It's all right, missis; I'll pay fer the glass," said Chook to the dealer, who began to jabber excitedly in Italian. The woman began to scrape the pieces of broken glass together, and the sight reminded Chook of the insult. His face darkened.

"Cum on, blokes, an' see a bit o' fun," he cried with a mirthless grin that showed he was dangerously excited.

The three larrikins caught up with Stinky and the girl as they were crossing into Belmore Park. Stinky was explaining to some sympathizers the events that had led up to the quarrel.

"Wot would yous do if a bloke tried to sneak yer moll?" he inquired in an injured tone.

"Break 'is bleedin' neck," said Chook as he stepped up.

"When I want yer advice, I'll ask fer it," cried Stinky.

"Yer'll git it now without askin'," said Chook. "Don't open yer mouth so wide, or yer'll ketch cold."

"I don't want ter talk ter anybody as 'awks rotten cabbages through the streets," cried Stinky.

"The cabbages don't stink worse than some people I've met," Chook replied.

Stinky, who was very touchy on the score of the vile smell of his trade, boiled over.

"Never mind my trade," he shouted, "I'm as good a man as yous."

"Garn, that's only a rumour! I wouldn't let it git about," sneered Chook.

The smouldering hate of months burst suddenly into flame, and the two men rushed at each other. The others tried to separate them.

"Don't be a fool."

"Yer'll only git lumbered."

"'Ere's the traps."

But the two enemies, with a sudden twist, broke away from their advisers, and threw off their hats and coats. And as suddenly, the others formed a ring round the two antagonists, who faced each other with the savage intensity of gamecocks, with no thought but to maim and kill the enemy in front of them. A crowd gathered, and Pinkey was pushed to the outside of the ring, where she could only judge the progress of the fight by the cries of the onlookers.

"Use yer left, Chook."

"Wot price that?"

"Time!"

"Wait fer 'is rush, an' use yer right."

"Foller 'im up, Chook."

"Oh, dry up! I tell yer 'e slipped."

"Not in the same class, I tell yer."

"Mix it, Chook—mix it. Yer've got 'im beat."

The last remark was true, for Stinky, in spite of his superior weight and height, was no match for Chook, the cock of Cardigan Street. It was the fifth round, and Chook was waiting for an opening to finish his man before the police came up, when a surprising thing happened. As Stinky retreated in exhaustion before the fists that rattled on his face like drumsticks, his hand struck his enemy's lower jaw by chance, and the next minute he was amazed to see Chook drop to the ground as if shot. And he stared with open mouth at his opponent, wondering why he didn't move.

"Gawd, 'e's stiffened 'im!"

"I 'eard 'is neck crack!"

Stinky stood motionless, his wits scattered by this sudden change—the stillness of his enemy, who a moment ago was beating him down with murderous fists.

"'Ere's the johns," cried someone.

"Come on, Liz," cried Stinky, and turned to run.

"Cum with yous, yer great 'ulkin', stinkin' coward," cried Pinkey, her face crimson with passion, "yer'll be lucky if y'ain't hung fer murder."

Stinky listened in amazement. Here was another change that he was too dazed to understand, and, hastily grabbing his coat, he ran.

Pinkey ran to Chook's prostrate body, and listened.

"I can 'ear 'im breathin'," she cried.

105

The others listened, and the breathing grew louder, a curious, snoring sound.

"Gorblimey! A knock-out!"

"'E'll be right in a few minutes."

It was true. Stinky, with a haphazard blow, had given Chook the dreaded knock-out, a jolt beside the chin that, in the expressive phrase, "sent him to sleep".

But now the police came up, glad of this chance to show their authority and order the people about. The crowd melted.

Chook's mates had pulled him into a sitting position, when, to Pinkey's delight, he opened his eyes and spat out a mouthful of blood.

"W'ere the 'ell am I?" he muttered, like a man awaking from a dream.

"What's this? You've been fighting," said the policeman.

"Me? No fear," growled Chook. "I was walkin' along, quiet as a lamb, when a bloke come up an' landed me on the jaw."

"Well, who was he?" asked the policeman.

"I dunno. I never set eyes on 'im before," said Chook, lying without hesitation to their common enemy, the police.

The policeman looked hard at him, and then cried roughly, "Get out of this, or I'll lock you up."

Chook's mates helped him to his feet, and he staggered away like a drunken man. Suddenly he became aware that someone was crying softly near him, and, turning his head, found that it was Pinkey, who was holding his arm and guiding his steps. He wrenched his arm free with an oath, remembering that she was the cause of his fight and defeat.

"Wot the 'ell are yous doin' 'ere? Go an' tell yer bloke I nearly got lumbered.'

"I ain't got no bloke," sobbed Pinkey.

"Wotcher mean?" cried Chook.

"I don't run after people I don't want," said Pinkey, smiling through her tears.

"Fair dinkum?" cried Chook.

Pinkey nodded her head, with its crown of hair that glittered like bronze.

Chook stopped to think.

"I'm orl right," he said to Waxy and Joe; "I'll ketch up with yer in a minit." They understood and walked on.

He stood and stared at Pinkey with a scowl that softened imperceptibly into a smile, and then a passionate flame leapt into his eyes.

"Cum 'ere," he said; and Pinkey obeyed him like a child.

He looked at her with a gloating fondness in his eyes, and then caught her in his arms and kissed her with his bleeding lips.

"Ugh, I'm all over blood!" cried the girl with a shuddering laugh, as she wiped her lips with her handkerchief.

10

JONAH DECLARES WAR

As it promised to be a slack week, Paasch had decided to dress the window himself, as he felt that the goods were not displayed to their proper advantage. This was a perquisite of Jonah's, for which he was paid eighteenpence extra once a fortnight; but Jonah had deserted him—a fact which he discovered by finding that Jonah's tools, his only property, were missing.

So he had spent a busy morning in renovating his entire stock with double coats of Peerless Gloss, the stock that the whole neighbourhood knew by sight—the watertight bluchers with soles an inch thick that a woolwasher from Botany had ordered and left on his hands; the pair of kangaroo tops that Pat Riley had ordered the week he was pinched for manslaughter; the pair of flash kid lace-ups, high in the leg, that Katey Brown had thrown at his head because they wouldn't meet round her thick calves; and half a dozen pairs of misfits into which half the neighbourhood had tried to coax their feet because they were dirt cheap.

But the pride of the collection was a monstrous abortion of a boot, made for a clubfoot, with a sole and heel six inches deep, that had cost Paasch weeks of endless contrivance, and had only one fault—it was as heavy as lead and unwearable. But Paasch clung to it with the affection of a mother for her deformed offspring, and gave it the pride of place in the window. And daily the urchins flattened their noses against the panes, fascinated by this monster of a boot, to see it again in dreams on the feet of horrid giants. This melancholy collection was flanked by odd bottles of polish and blacking, and cards of bootlaces of such unusual strength that elephants were shown vainly trying to break them.

The old man paused in his labours to admire the effect of his new arrangement, and suddenly noticed a group of children gathered about a man painting a sign on the window opposite. Paasch stared; but the words were a blur to his short sight, and he went inside to look for his spectacles, which he had pushed up on his forehead in order to dress the window. By the time he had looked everywhere without finding them, the painter had finished the lettering, and was outlining the figure of something on the window with rapid strokes.

Paasch itched with impatience. He would have crossed the street to look, but he made it a rule never to leave the shop, even for a minute, lest someone should steal the contents in his absence. As he fidgeted with impatience, it occurred to him to ask a small boy, who was passing, what was being painted on the window.

"Why, a boot of course," replied the child.

Paasch's amazement was so great that, forgetting the caution of a lifetime, he walked across until the words came into range. What he saw brought him to a standstill in the middle of Botany Road, heedless of the traffic, for the blur of words had resolved themselves into:

JOSEPH JONES,

BOOTMAKER.

Repairs neatly executed.

And, underneath, the pattern of a shoe, which the painter was finishing with rapid strokes.

So, thought Paasch, another had come to share the trade and take the bread out of his mouth, and he choked with the egotistical dread of the shopkeeper at another rival in the struggle for existence. Who could this be? he thought, with the uneasy fear of a man threatened with danger. For the moment he had forgotten Jonah's real name, and he looked into the shop to size up his adversary with the angry curiosity of a soldier facing the enemy. Then, through the open door, he spied the familiar figure of the hunchback moving about the shop and placing things in order. He swallowed hastily, with the choking sensation of a parent whose child has at last revolted, for his rival was the misshapen boy that he had taken off the streets, and clothed and fed for years. Jonah came to the door for a moment, and, catching sight of the old man, stared at him fixedly without a sign of recognition.

And suddenly, with a contraction at his heart, a fear and dread of Jonah swept through Paasch, the vague, primeval distrust and suspicion of the deformed that lurks in the normal man, a survival of the ancient hostility that in olden times consigned them to the stake as servants of the Evil One.

He forgot where he was till the warning snort of a steam tram made him jump aside and miss the wheels of a bus from the opposite direction by the skin of his teeth.

And the whole street smiled at the sight of the bewildered old man, with his silvery hair and leather apron, standing in the middle of the Road to stare at a dingy shop opposite.

Paasch crossed the street and entered his door again with the air of a man who has been to a funeral. He had never made any friends, but, in his gruff, reserved way, he liked Jonah. He had taught him his trade, and here, with a sudden sinking in his heart, he remembered that the pupil had easily surpassed the master in dexterity. Then another fear assailed him. How would he get through his work? for most of it had passed through Jonah's nimble fingers. Ah well, it was no matter! He was a lonely old man with nothing but his fiddle to bring back the memories of the Fatherland.

The week ran to an end, and found Jonah out of pocket. He had planted himself like a footpad at the door of his old master to rob him of his trade and living; and day by day he counted the customers passing in and out of the old shop, but none came his way. As he stared across the street at his rival's shop, his face changed; it was like a hawk's, threatening and predatory, indifferent to the agony of the downy breast and fluttering wings that it is about to strike.

It maddened him to see the stream of people pass his shop with indifference, as if it were none of their business whether he lived or starved. The memory of his boyish days returned to him, when every man's hand was against him, and he took food and shelter with the craft of an old soldier in hostile country. Even the shop which he had furnished and laid out with such loving care, seemed a cunning trap to devour his precious sovereigns week by week.

True, he had drawn some custom, but it was of the worst sort—that of the unprincipled rogues who fatten upon tradesmen till the back of their credit is broken, and then transfer their sinister custom to another. Jonah recognized them with a grim smile, but he had taken their work, glad of something to do, although he would never see the colour of their money.

Meanwhile the weeks ran into a month, and Jonah had not paid expenses. He could hold out for three months according to his calculation, but he saw the end rapidly approaching, when he must retire covered with ignominious defeat. He would have thrown up the sponge there and then, but for the thought of the straight-limbed child in Cardigan Street, for whom he wanted money—money to feed and clothe him for the world to admire.

One Saturday night, weary of waiting for the custom that never came, he closed the shop, and joined Ada, who was waiting on the footpath. They sauntered along, Ada stopping every minute to look into the shop windows, while Jonah, gloomy and taciturn, turned his back on the

112

lighted windows with impatience. Presently Ada gave a cry of delight before the draper's.

"I say, Joe, that bonnet would suit the kid all to pieces. An' look at the price! Only last week they was seven an' a kick."

Jonah turned and looked at the window. The bonnet, fluffy and absurd, was marked with a ticket bearing an enormous figure 4 in red ink, and beside it, faintly marked in pencil, the number 11.

"W'y don't yer say five bob, an' be done with it?" said Jonah.

"But it ain't five bob; it's only four an' eleven," insisted Ada, annoyed at his stupidity.

"An' I suppose it 'ud be dear at five bob?" sneered Jonah.

"Any fool could tell yer that," snapped Ada.

Jonah included the whole feminine world in a shrug of the shoulders, and turned impatiently on his heel. But Ada was not to be torn away. She ran her eye over the stock, marvelling at the cheapness of everything. Jonah, finding nothing better to do, lit a cigarette, and turned a contemptuous eye on the bales of calico, cheap prints, and flimsy lace displayed. Presently he began to study the tickets with extraordinary interest. They were all alike. The shillings in gigantic figures of red or black, and across the dividing line elevenpence three-farthings pencilled in strokes as modest as the shy violet. When Jonah reached Cardigan Street, he was preoccupied and silent, and sat on the veranda, smoking in the dark, long after Ada and her mother had gone to bed.

About one o'clock Mrs Yabsley, who was peacefully ironing shirts in her sleep, was awakened by a loud hammering on the door. She woke up, and instantly recognized what had happened. Ada had left the candle burning and had set the house on fire, as her mother had daily predicted for the last ten years. Then the hammering ceased.

"Are yez awake, Mum?" cried Jonah's voice.

"No," said Mrs Yabsley firmly. "'Ow did it 'appen?"

"'Appen wot?" cried Jonah roughly.

"'Ow did the 'ouse ketch fire?" said Mrs Yabsley, listening for the crackling.

"The 'ouse ain't a-fire, an' ye're talkin' in yer sleep."

"Wot!" cried Mrs Yabsley, furiously, "yer wake me up out o' me sleep to tell me the 'ouse ain't a-fire. I'll land yer on the 'ead wi' me slipper, if yer don't go to bed."

"I say, Mum," entreated Jonah, "will yer gimme five quid on Monday, an' ask no questions?"

Mrs Yabsley's only answer was a snore.

But a week later the morning procession that trudged along Botany Road towards the city was astonished at the sight of a small shop, covered with huge calico signs displaying in staring red letters on a white ground the legend:

WHILE U WAIT.
Boots and Shoes Soled and Heeled.
Gents, 2/11; Ladies, 1/11; Childs, 1/6.

The huge red letters, thrown out like a defiance and a challenge, caused a sensation in the Road. The pedestrians stopped to read the signs, looked curiously at the shop, and went on their way. The passengers in the trams and buses craned their necks, anxious to read the gigantic advertisement before they were carried out of sight. A group of urchins, stationed at the door, distributed handbills to the curious, containing the same announcement in bold type.

Across the street hung Paasch's dingy sign from which the paint was peeling:

Repairs neatly executed
GENTS, 3/6; LADIES, 2/6; CHILDS, 1/9

—the old prices sanctioned by usage, unchangeable and immovable as the laws of nature to Paasch and the trade on Botany Road.

The shop itself was transformed. On one side were half a dozen new chairs standing in a row on a strip of bright red carpet. Gay festoons of coloured tissue paper, the work of Mrs Yabsley's hands, stretched in ropes across the ceiling. The window had been cleared and at a bench facing the street Jonah and an assistant pegged and hammered as if for dear life. Another, who bore a curious likeness to Chook, with his back to the street and a last on his knees, hammered with enthusiasm. A tremendous heap of old boots, waiting to be repaired, was thrown carelessly in front of the workers, who seemed too busy to notice the sensation they were creating.

The excitement increased when a customer, Waxy Collins by name, entered the shop, and, taking off his boots, sat down while they were repaired, reading the morning paper as coolly as if he were taking his turn at the barber's. The thing spread like the news of a murder, and through the day a group of idlers gathered, watching with intense relish the rapid movements of the workmen. Jonah had declared war.

Six weeks after he had opened the shop, Jonah found twelve of Mrs Yabsley's sovereigns between him and ignominious defeat. Then the tickets in the draper's window had given him an idea, and, like a general who throws his last battalion at the enemy, he had resolved to stake the remaining coins on the hazard. The calico signs, then a novelty, the fittings of the shop, and the wages for a skilful assistant, had swallowed six of his precious twelve pounds. With the remaining six he hoped to hold out for a fortnight. Then, unless the tide turned, he would throw up the sponge. Chook, amazed and delighted with the idea, had volunteered to disguise himself as a snob, and help to give the shop a busy look; and Waxy Collins jumped at the chance of getting his boots mended for the bare trouble of walking in and pretending to read the newspaper.

The other shopkeepers were staggered. They stared in helpless anger at the small shop, which had suddenly become the most important in their ken. Already they saw their families brought to the gutter by this hunchback ruffian, who hit them below the belt in the most ungentlemanly fashion in preference to starving. But the simple manoeuvre of cutting down the prices of his rivals was only a taste of the unerring instinct for business that was later to make him as much feared as respected in the trade. By a single stroke he had shown his ability to play on the weakness

116

as well as the needs of the public, coupled with a pitiless disregard for other interests than his own, which constitutes business talent.

The public looked on, surprised and curious, drawn by the novelty of the idea and the amazing prices, but hesitating like an animal that fears a tempting bait. The ceaseless activity of the shop reassured them. One by one the customers arrived. Numbers bred numbers, and in a week a rush had set in. It became the fashion on the Road to loll in the shop, carelessly reading the papers for all the world to see, while your boots were being mended. On Saturday for the first time Jonah turned a profit, and the battle was won.

Among the later arrivals Jonah noticed with satisfaction some of Paasch's best customers, and every week, with an apologetic smile, another handed in his boots for repair. Soon there was little for Paasch to do but stand at his door, staring with frightened, short-sighted eyes across the Road at the octopus that was slowly squeezing the life out of his shop. But he obstinately refused to lower his prices, though his customers carried the work from his counter across the street. It seemed to him that the prices were something fixed by natural laws, like the return of the seasons or the multiplication table.

"I haf always charge tree an' six for men's, an' it cannot be done cheaper without taking de bread out of mine mouth," he repeated obstinately.

In three months Jonah hired another workman, and the landlord came down to see if the shop could be enlarged to meet Jonah's requirements. Then a traveller called with

117

an armful of samples. He was travelling for his brother, he explained, who had a small factory. Jonah looked longingly, and confessed that he wanted to stock his shop, but had no money to buy. Then the traveller smiled, and explained to Jonah, alert and attentive, the credit system by which his firm would deliver fifty pounds' worth of boots at three months. Jonah was quick to learn, but cautious.

"D'ye mean yer'd gimme the boots, an' not want the money for three months?"

The traveller explained that was the usual practice.

"An' can I sell 'em at any price I like?"

The man said he could give them away if he chose.

Jonah spent a pound on brass rods and glass stands, and sold the lot in a month at sixpence a pair profit. His next order ran into a hundred pounds, and Jonah had established a cash retail trade. Meanwhile, he worked in a way to stagger the busy bee. Morning and night the sound of his hammer never ceased, except the three nights a week he spent at a night school, where he discovered a remarkable talent for mental arithmetic and figures. Jonah the hunchback had found his vocation.

And in the still night, when he stopped to light a cigarette, Jonah could hear the mournful wail of a violin in Paasch's bedroom across the street. In his distress the old man had turned to his beloved instrument as one turns to an old friend. But now the tunes were never merry, only scraps and fragments of songs of love and despair, the melancholy folk-songs of his native land, long since forgotten, and now returning to his memory as its hold on the present grew feebler.

11

THE COURTING OF PINKEY

It was Monday morning, and, according to their habit, the Partridges were moving. Every stick of their furniture was piled on the van, and Pinkey, who was carrying the kerosene lamp for fear of breakage, watched the load anxiously as the cart lurched over a rut. A cracked mirror, swinging loosely in its frame, followed every movement of the cart, one minute reflecting Pinkey's red hair and dingy skirt, the next swinging vacantly to the sky.

The cart stopped outside a small weatherboard cottage, and the vanman backed the wheels against the kerbstone, cracking his whip and swearing at the horse, which remained calm and obstinate, refusing to move except of its own accord. The noise brought the neighbours to their doors. And they stood with prying eyes, ready to judge the social standing of the newcomers from their furniture.

It was the old battered furniture of a poor family, dragged from the friendly shelter of dark corners into the naked light of day, the back, white and rough as a packing-case, betraying the front, varnished and stained to imitate walnut and cedar. Every scratch and stain showed plainly on the tables and chairs fastened to their companions in misery—odd, nameless contrivances made of boxes and cretonne, that took the place of the sofas, wardrobes, and toilet-tables of the rich. Every mark and every dint was noted with satisfaction by the furtive eyes. The new arrivals had nothing to boast about.

Mrs Partridge, who collected gossip and scandal as some people collect stamps, generally tired of a neighbourhood in three months, after she had learned the principal facts—how much of the Browns' money went in drink, how much the Joneses owed at the corner shop, and who was really the father of the child that the Smiths treated as a poor relation. When she had sucked the neighbourhood dry like an orange, she took a house in another street, and Pinkey lost a day at the factory to move the furniture.

Pinkey's father was a silent, characterless man, taking the lead from his wife with admirable docility, and asking nothing from fortune but regular work and time to read the newspaper. He had worked for the same firm since he was a boy, disliking change; but since his second marriage he had been dragged from one house to another. Sometimes he went home to the wrong place, forgetting that they had moved. Every week he planned another short cut to Grimshaw's works, which landed him there half an hour late.

Her mother had died of consumption when Pinkey was eleven, and two years later her father had married his housekeeper. She proved to be a shiftless slattern, never dressed, never tidy, and selfish to the core under the cloak of a good-natured smile. She was always resting from the fatigue of imaginary labours, and her house was a pigsty. Nothing was in its place, and nothing could be found when it was wanted. This, she always explained with a placid smile, was owing to the fact that they were busy looking for a house where they could settle down.

The burden of moving fell on Pinkey, for her father had never lost a day at Grimshaw's in his life; and after Mrs Partridge had hindered for half an hour by getting in the way and mislaying everything, Pinkey usually begged her in desperation to go and wait for the furniture in the new house.

Meanwhile, lower down the street, Chook was slowly working his way from house to house, hawking a load of vegetables. In the distance he remarked the load of furniture, and resolved to call before a rival could step in and get their custom. As he praised the quality of the peas to a customer, he found time to observe that the unloading went on very slowly. The vanman stood on the cart and slid the articles on to the shoulders of a girl, who staggered across the pavement under a load twice her size. It looked like an ant carrying a beetle. Five minutes later Chook stood at the door and rapped with his knuckles.

"Any vegetables today, lydy?" he inquired, in his nasal, professional sing-song.

121

The answer to his question was Pinkey, dishevelled, sweating in beads, covered with dust, her sleeves tucked up to the elbows, showing two arms as thin as broomsticks. She flushed pink under the sweat and grime, feeling for her apron to wipe her face. They had not seen each other since the fight, for in a sudden revulsion of feeling Pinkey had decided that Chook was too handy with his fists to make a desirable bloke, and a change of address on the following Monday had enabled her to give him the slip easily. And after waiting at street corners till he was tired, Chook had returned to his old love, the two-up school. Pinkey broke the silence with a question that was furthest from her thoughts.

"'Ow are yer sellin' yer peas?"

Chook dropped his basket and roared with laughter.

"If yer only come ter poke borak, yer better go," cried Pinkey, with an angry flush.

Chook sobered instantly.

"No 'arm meant," he said, quite humbly, "but yer gimme the knock-out every time I see yer. But wot are yer doin'?" he asked.

"We're movin'," said Pinkey, with an important air.

"Oh, are yer?" said Chook, looking round with interest. "Yous an' old Jimmy there?" He nodded familiarly to the vanman, who was filling his pipe. "Well, yer must excuse me, but I'm on in this act."

"Wotcher mean?" said Pinkey, looking innocent, but she flushed with pleasure.

"Nuthin'," said Chook, seizing the leg of a table; "but wait till I put the nosebag on the moke."

122

"Whose cart is it?" inquired Pinkey.

"Jack Ryan's," answered Chook; "'e's bin shickered since last We'n'sday, an' I'm takin' it round fer 'is missis an' the kids."

Mrs Partridge received Chook very graciously when she learned that he was a friend of Pinkey's and had offered to help in passing. She had been reading a penny novelette under great difficulties, and furtively eating some slices of bread-and-butter which she had thoughtfully put in her pocket. But now she perked up under the eyes of this vigorous young man, and even attempted to help by carrying small objects round the room and then putting them back where she found them. In an hour the van was empty, and Jimmy was told to call next week for his money. It was well into the afternoon when Chook resumed his hawking with the cart and then only because Pinkey resolutely pushed him out of the door.

Chook's previous love-affairs had all been conducted in the open air. Following the law of Cardigan Street, he met the girl at the street corner and spent the night in the park or the dance-room. Rarely, if she forgot the appointment, he would saunter past the house, and whistle till she came out. What passed within the house was no concern of his. Parents were his natural enemies, who regarded him with the eyes of a butcher watching a hungry dog. But his affair with Pinkey had been full of surprises; and this was not the least, that chance had given him an informal introduction to Pinkey's stepmother and the furniture.

He had called again with vegetables, and when he adroitly remarked that no one would have taken Mrs

123

Partridge to be old enough to be the mother of Pinkey, she had spent a delightful hour leaning against the door-post telling him how she came to marry Partridge, and the incredible number of offers she had refused in her time. Charmed with his wit and sympathy, she forgot what she was saying, and invited him to tea on the following Sunday. Chook was staggered. He knew this was the custom of the law-abiding, who nodded to the police and went to church on Sunday. But here was the fox receiving a pressing invitation from the lamb. He decided to talk the matter over with Pinkey. But when he told her of the invitation, she flushed crimson.

"She asked yous to tea, did she? The old devil!"

"W'y," said Chook mortified.

"W'y? 'Cause she knows father 'ud kill yer, if yer put yer nose inside the door."

"Oh! would 'e?" cried Chook, bristling.

"My word, yes! A bloke once came after Lil, an' 'e run 'im out so quick 'e forgot 'is 'at, an' waited at the corner till I brought it."

"Well, 'e won't bustle me," cried Chook.

"But y'ain't goin'?" said Pinkey, anxiously.

"My oath, I am!" cried Chook. "I'm doin' the square thing this time, don't yous fergit, an' no old finger's goin' ter bustle me, even if 'e's your father."

"Yous stop at 'ome while yer lucky," said Pinkey. "Ever since Lil cleared out wi' Marsden, 'e swears 'e'll knife the first bloke that comes after me."

"Ye're only kiddin'," said Chook, cheerfully; "an' wot'll 'e do ter yous?"

"Me! 'E niver rouses on me. W'en 'e gits shirty, I just laugh, an' 'e can't keep it up."

"Right-oh!" said Chook. "Look out fer a song an' dance nex' Sunday."

About five o'clock on the following Sunday afternoon, Chook, beautifully attired in the larrikin fashion, sauntered up to the door and tried the knocker. It was too stiff to move, and he used his knuckles. Then he heard footsteps and a rapid whispering, and Pinkey, white with anxiety, opened the door. Mrs Partridge, half dressed, slipped into the bedroom and called out in a loud voice, "Good afternoon, Mr Fowles! 'Ave yer come to take Elizabeth for a walk?"

Ignoring Pinkey's whispered advice, he pushed in and looked round. He was in the parlour, and a large china dog welcomed him with a fixed grin.

"W'ere's the old bloke?" muttered Chook.

Pinkey pointed to the dining-room, and Chook walked briskly in. He found Partridge in his arm-chair, scowling at him over the newspaper.

"Might I ask 'oo you are?" he growled.

"Me name's Fowles—Arthur Fowles," replied Chook, picking a seat near the door and smoothing a crease in his hat.

"Ah! that's all I wanted to know," growled Partridge. "Now yer can go."

"Me? No fear!" cried Chook, affecting surprise. "Yer missis gave me an invite ter tea, an' 'ere I am. Besides, I ain't such a stranger as I look; I 'elped move yer furniture in."

"An' yer shove yer way into my 'ouse on the strength of wot a pack o' silly women said ter yer?"

"I did," admitted Chook.

"Now you take my advice, an git out before I break every bone in yer body."

Chook stared at him with an unnatural stolidity for fear he should spoil everything by grinning.

"Well, wot are yer starin at?" inquired Partridge, with irritation.

"I was wonderin' 'ow yer'd look on the end of a rope," replied Chook, quietly.

"Me on the end of a rope?" cried Partridge in amazement.

"Yes. They said yous 'ud stiffen me if I cum in, an' 'ere I am."

"An' yet you 'ad the cheek?"

"Yes," said Chook; "I niver take no notice o' wot women say."

Partridge glared at him as if meditating a spring, and then, with a rapid jerk, turned his back on Chook and buried his nose in the newspaper. Pinkey and her stepmother, who were listening to this dialogue at the door, ready for flight at the first sound of breaking glass or splintered wood, now ventured to step into the room. Chook, secure of victory, criticized the weather, but Partridge remained silent as a graven image. Mrs Partridge set the table for tea with nervous haste.

"Tea's ready, William," she cried at last.

William took his place, and, without lifting his eyes, began to serve the meat. Mrs Partridge had made a special effort. She had bought a pig's cheek, some German sausage, and a dozen scones at seven for threepence. This was flanked by bread-and-butter, and a newly opened tin of jam with the jagged lid of the tin standing upright. She thought, with pride, that the young man would see he was in a house where no expense was spared. She requested Chook to sit next to Pinkey, and talked with feverish haste.

"Which do yer like, Mr Fowles? Lean or fat? The fat sometimes melts in yer mouth. Give 'im that bit yer cut for me, William."

"If 'e don't like it, 'e can leave it," growled Partridge.

"Now, that'll do, William. I always said yer bark was worse than yer bite. You'll be all right w'en yer've 'ad yer beer. 'E's got the temper of an angel w'en 'e's 'ad 'is beer," she explained to Chook, as if her husband were out of hearing.

Partridge sat with his eyes fixed on his plate with the face of a sulky schoolboy. His long features reminded Chook of a horse he had once driven. When he had finished eating, he pulled his chair back and buried his silly, obstinate face in the newspaper. He had evidently determined to ignore Chook's existence. Mrs Partridge broke the silence by describing his character to the visitor as if he were a naughty child.

"William always sulks w'en 'e can't get 'is own way. Not another word will we 'ear from 'im tonight. 'E knows 'e ought to be civil to people as eat at 'is own table, an' that only makes 'im worse. But for all 'is sulks, 'e's got the temper of an angel w'en 'e's 'ad 'is beer. I've met all sorts—them as smashes the furniture for spite, an' them as bashes their wives 'cause it's cheaper, but gimme William every time."

Partridge took no notice, except to bury his nose deeper in the paper. He had reached the advertisements, and a careful study of these would carry him safely to bed. After tea, Pinkey set to work and washed up the dishes, while Mrs Partridge entertained the guest. Chook took out his cigarettes, and asked if Mr Partridge objected to smoke. There was no answer.

"You must speak louder, Mr Fowles," said Mrs Partridge. "William's 'earing ain't wot it used to be."

William resented this remark by twisting his chair farther away and emitting a grunt.

Pinkey, conscious of Chook's eyes, was bustling in and out with the airs of a busy housewife, her arms, thin as a broomstick, bared to the elbow. His other love-affairs had belonged to the open-air, with the street for a stage and the park for scenery, and this domestic setting struck Chook as a novelty. Pinkey, then, was not merely a plaything for an hour, but a woman of serious uses, like the old mother who suckled him and would hear no ill word of him. And as he watched with greedy eyes the animal died within him, and a sweeter emotion than he had ever known filled his ignorant, passionate heart. For the first time in his life he understood why men gave up their pals and the freedom of the streets for a woman. Mrs Partridge saw the look in his eyes, and wished she were twenty years younger. When Pinkey got her hat and proposed a walk, Chook, softened by his novel emotions, called out "Good night, boss!"

For a wonder, Partridge looked up from his paper and grunted "Night!"

"There now," cried Mrs Partridge, delighted, "William wouldn't say that to everybody, would you, William? Call again any time you like, an' 'e'll be in a better temper."

When they reached the park, they sat on a seat facing the asphalt path. Near them was another pair, the donah, with a hat like a tea-tray, nursing her bloke's head in her lap as he lay full length along the seat. And they exchanged caresses with a royal indifference to the people who were sauntering along the paths. But, without knowing why, Chook and Pinkey sat as far apart as if they had freshly studied a book on etiquette. For to Chook this frail girl with the bronze hair and shabby clothes was no longer a mere donah, but a laborious housewife and a potential mother of children; and to Pinkey this was a new Chook, who kept his hands to himself, and looked at her with eyes that made her forget she was a poor factory girl.

Chook looked idly at the stars, remote and lofty, strewn like sand across the sky, and wondered at one that gleamed and glowed as he watched. A song of the music-hall about eyes and stars came into his head. He looked steadily into Pinkey's eyes, darkened by the broad brim of her hat, and could see no resemblance, for he was no poet. And as he looked, he forgot the stars in an intense desire to know the intimate details of her life—the mechanical, monotonous habits that fill the day from morning till night, and yet are too trivial to tell. He asked some questions about Packard's factory where she worked, and Pinkey's tongue ran on wheels when she found a sympathetic listener. Apart from the boot factory, the great events of her life had been the death of her mother, her father's second marriage, and the flight of her elder sister, Lil, who had gone to the bad. She blamed her stepmother for that. Lil had acted like a fool, and Mrs Partridge, with her insatiable greed for gossip, had gathered hints and rumours from the four corners of Sydney, and Lil had bolted rather than argue it out with her father. That and the death of Pinkey's mother had soured his temper, and his wits, never very powerful, had grown childish under the blow.

"So don't yous go pokin' borak at 'im," she cried, flushing pink. "'E's a good father to me, if she lets 'im alone. But she's got 'im under 'er thumb with 'er nasty tongue."

Chook thought Mrs Partridge was an agreeable woman. Instantly Pinkey's eyes blazed with anger.

"Is she? You ought ter 'ear 'er talk. She's got a tongue like a dog's tail; it's always waggin'. An' niver a good word for anybody. I wish she'd mind 'er own business, an' clean up the 'ouse. W'en my mother was alive, you could eat yer dinner off the floor, but Sarah's too delicate for 'ousework. She'd 'ave married the greengrocer, but she was too delicate to wait in the shop. We niver see a bit o' fresh meat in the 'ouse, an' if yer say anythin' she bursts into tears, an' sez somethin' nasty about Lil. She makes believe she's got no more appetite than a canary, but she lives on the pick of the 'am shop w'en nobody's lookin'. Look 'ow fat she is. W'en she married Dad, you could 'ear 'er bones rattle. I wouldn't mind if she did the washin'. But she puts the things in soak on Monday, an' then on Saturday I 'ave ter turn to an' do the lot, 'cause she's delicate. I ain't delicate. I'm only skin an' bone."

Her face was flushed and eager; her eyes sparkled. Chook remembered the song about eyes and stars, and agreed with the words. And as suddenly the sparkle died out of her eyes, her mouth drooped, and the colour left her face, pale as ivory in the faint gleam of the stars.

"Yous don't think any worse o' me 'cause Lil's crook, do yer?" she asked piteously.

Chook swore a denial.

"P'raps yer think it runs in the family; but Lil 'ud 'a' gone straight if she 'adn't been driven out o' the 'ouse by Sarah's nasty tongue."

Chook declared that Lil was spotless.

"No, she ain't," said Pinkey; "she's as bad as they make 'em now; but...wot makes yer tail up after me?" she inquired suddenly.

Chook answered that she had sent him fair off his dot.

"Oh yes, that's wot yer said to Poll Corcoran, an' then went skitin' that she'd do anythin' yer liked, if yer lifted yer finger. I've 'eard all about yous."

Chook swore that he would never harm a hair of her head.

"The worst 'arm is done without meanin' it," said Pinkey, wisely, "an' that's w'y I'm frightened of yer."

"Wotcher got ter be frightened o' me?" asked Chook, softly.

"I'm frightened o' yer...'cause I like yer," said Pinkey, bursting into tears.

Mrs Partridge was disappointed in Chook. He was too much taken up with that red-headed cat, and he ate nothing when he came to tea on Sunday, although she ransacked the ham-and-beef shop for dainties—black pudding, ham-and-chicken sausage, and brawn set in a mould of appetizing jelly. She flattered herself she knew her position as hostess, and made up for William's sulks by loading the table with her favourite delicacies. And Chook's healthy stomach recoiled in dismay before these doubtful triumphs of the cookshop. His mother had been a cook before she married, and, as a shoemaker believes in nothing but leather, she pinned her faith to good cooking. The family might go without clothes or boots, but they always had enough to eat. Chook's powerful frame, she asserted, was due entirely to careful nourishment in his youth. "Good meals keep people out of jail," was her favourite remark. Chook had learned this instead of the catechism, and the sight of Pinkey's starved body stirred his anger. What she wanted was proper nourishment to cover her bones.

The next Sunday, while Pinkey was frying some odds and ends in the pan to freshen them up for breakfast, Mrs Partridge, who was finishing a novelette in bed, heard a determined knock on the door. It was only eight o'clock. She called Pinkey, and ran to the window in surprise. It was Chook, blushing as nearly as his face would permit, and carrying two plates wrapped in a towel. He pushed through to the kitchen with the remark "I'll just 'ot this up agin on the stove."

"But wot is it?" cried Pinkey, in astonishment.

Chook removed the upper plate, and showed a dish of sheep's brains, fried with eggs and breadcrumbs—a thing to make the mouth water.

"Mother sent these; she thought yer might like somethin' tasty fer yer breakfast," he muttered gruffly, in fear of ridicule. Pinkey tried to laugh, but the tears welled into her eyes.

"Oh, Sarah will be pleased!" she cried.

"No, she won't," said Chook, grimly. "Wot yer can't eat goes back fer the fowls."

While Mrs Partridge was dressing, they quarrelled fiercely, because Chook swore she must eat the lot. Sarah ended the dispute by eating half, but Chook watched jealously till Pinkey declared she could eat no more.

The next Sunday it was a plate of fish fried in the Jewish fashion—a revelation to Pinkey after the rancid fat of the fish shop—then a prime cut off the roast for dinner, or the breast and wing of a fowl; and he made Pinkey eat it in his presence, so that he could take the plates home to wash. One Sunday he was so late that Mrs Partridge fell back on pig's cheek; but he arrived, with a suspicious swelling under his eye. He explained briefly that there had been an accident. They learned afterwards that an ill-advised wag in the street had asked him if he were feeding Pinkey up for the show. During the two rounds that followed, Chook had accidentally stepped on the plates.

Whenever Ada met Pinkey, she wanted to know how things were progressing; but Pinkey could turn like a hare from undesirable questions.

"Are you an' 'im goin' to git spliced?" she inquired, for the hundredth time.

"I dunno," said Pinkey, turning scarlet; "'e sez we are."

PART TWO

THE SIGN OF THE SILVER SHOE

12

THE SIGN OF THE SILVER SHOE

The suburban trains slid into the darkness of the tunnel at Cleveland Street, and, as they emerged into daylight on the other side, paused for a moment like intelligent animals before the spider's web of shining rails that curved into the terminus, as if to choose the pair that would carry them in safety to the platform. It was in this pause that the passengers on the left looked out with an upward jerk of the head, and saw that the sun had found a new plaything in Regent Street.

It was the model of a shoe, fifteen feet long, the hugest thing within sight, covered with silver leaf that glittered like metal in the morning sun. A gang of men had hoisted it into position last night by the flare of naphtha lamps, and now it trod securely on air above the new bootshop whose advertisement sprawled across half a page of the morning paper.

In Regent Street a week of painting and hammering had prepared them for surprises; two shops had been knocked into one, with two plate-glass windows framed in brass, and now the shop with its triumphant sign caught the eye like a check suit or a red umbrella. Every inch of the walls was covered with lettering in silver leaf, and across the front in huge characters ran the sign:

JONAH'S SILVER SHOE EMPORIUM

Meanwhile, the shop was closed, the windows obscured by blinds; but the children, attracted by the noise of hammering, flattened their noses against the plate glass, trying to spy out the busy privacy within. Evening fell, and the hammering ceased. Then, precisely on the stroke of seven, the electric lights flashed out, the curtains were withdrawn, and the shop stood smiling like a coquette at her first ball.

Everything was new. The fittings glistened with varnish, mirrors and brass rods reflected the light at every angle, and the building was packed from roof to floor with boots. The shelves were loaded with white cardboard boxes containing the better sort of boot. But there was not room enough on the shelves, and boots and shoes hung from the ceiling like bunches of fruit; they clung to brass rods like swarming bees. The strong, peculiar odour of leather clogged the air. The shopmen stood about, whispering to one another or changing the position of a pair of boots as they waited for the customers.

A crowd had gathered round the window on the left, which was fitted out like a workshop. On one side a clicker was cutting uppers from the skin; beside him a girl sat at a machine stitching the uppers together at racing speed. On the other side a man stood at a bench lasting the uppers to the insoles, and then pegging for dear life; near him sat a finisher, who shaved and blackened the rough edges, handing the finished article to a boy, who gave it a coat of gloss and placed it in the front of the window for inspection. A placard invited the public to watch the process of making Jonah's Famous Silver Shoes. The people crowded about as if it were a play, delighted with the novelty, following the stages in the growth of a boot with the pleasure of a boy examining the inside of a watch.

At eight o'clock another surprise was ready. A brass band began to play popular airs on the balcony, hung about with Chinese lanterns, and a row of electric bulbs flashed out, marking the outline of the wonderful silver shoe, glittering and gigantic in the white light.

The crowd looked up, and made bets on the length of the shoe, and recalled the time, barely five years ago, when the same man—Jonah the hunchback—had astonished Botany Road with his flaring signs in red and white. True, his shop was still on the Road, for Regent Street is but the fag end of a long, dusty road where it saunters into town, snobbishly conscious of larger buildings and higher rents. Since then his progress had been marked by removals, and each step had carried him nearer to the great city. He had outgrown his shops as a boy outgrows his trousers.

It was reported that everything turned to gold that he touched. It was certain that he had captured the trade of the Road, and this move meant that he had fastened his teeth in the trade of the roaring city. And not so long ago people could remember when he was a common larrikin, reputed leader of the Cardigan Street Push, and working for old Paasch, whose shop was now empty, his business absorbed by Jonah with the ease one swallows a lozenge. And they say he began life as a street-arab, selling papers and sleeping in the gutter. Well, some people's luck was marvellous!

The crowd became so dense that the police cleared a passage through it, and the carts and buses slackened to a walk as they passed the shop, where the electric lights glittered, the Chinese lanterns swung gaily in the breeze, and the band struck noisily into the airs from a comic opera.

Meanwhile the shop was crowded with customers, impatient to be served, each carrying a coupon cut from the morning paper, which entitled the holder to a pair of Jonah's Famous Silver Shoes at cost price. And near the door, in an interval of business, stood the proprietor, a hunchback, his grey eyes glittering with excitement at seeing his dream realized, the huge shop, spick and span as paint could make it, the customers jostling one another as they passed in and out, and the coin clinking merrily in the till.

Yes, they were quite right. Everything that he touched turned to gold. Outsiders confused his fortune with the luck of the man who draws the first prize in a sweep, enriched without effort by a chance turn of Fortune's wrist. They were blind to the unresting labour, the ruthless devices that left his rivals gaping, and the fixed idea that shaped everything to its needs. In five years he had fought his way down the Road, his line of march dotted with disabled rivals.

140

Old Paasch, the German, had been his first victim. Bewildered and protesting, he had succumbed to Jonah's novel methods of attack as a savage goes down under the fire of machine-guns. His shop was closed years ago, and he lived in a stuffy room, smelling vilely of tobacco-smoke, where he taught the violin to hazardous pupils for little more than a crust. He always spoke of Jonah with a vague terror in his blue eyes, convinced that he had once employed Satan as an errand-boy.

People were surprised to find that Jonah meant to live in the rooms over the new shop, when he could well afford to take a private house in the suburbs. It was said he treated his wife like dirt; that they lived like cat and dog; that he grudged her bare living and clothing. Jonah set his lips grimly on a hint of these rumours.

Three years ago he had planted Ada in a house of her own, and had gone home daily to rooms choked with dirt, for with years of ease she had grown more slovenly. Servants were a failure, for she made a friend of them, and their families lived in luxury at her expense. And when Ada was left alone, the meals were never ready, the house was like a pigsty, and she sat complacently amidst the dirt, reading penny novelettes in a gaudy dressing-jacket, or entertaining her old pals from the factory.

These would sit through an afternoon with envy in their hearts, and cries of wonder on their lips at the sight of some useless and costly article, which Ada, with the instinct of the parvenu, had bought to dazzle their eyes. For she remained on the level where she was born, and the gaping admiration of her poorer friends was the only profit

141

she drew from Jonah's success. If Jonah arrived without warning, they tumbled over one another to get out unseen by the back door, but never forgot to carry away some memento of their visit—a tin of salmon, a canister of tea, a piece of bacon, a bottle whose label puzzled them—for Ada bestowed gifts like Royalty, with the invariable formula "Oh! take it; there's plenty more where that comes from."

But the worst was her neglect of Ray, now seven years old, and the apple of Jonah's eye. She certainly spent part of the morning in dressing him up in his clothes, which were always new, for they were discarded by Jonah when the creases wore off; but when this duty, which she was afraid to neglect, was ended, she sent him out into the street to play in the gutter. His meals were the result of hazard, starving one day, and over-eating the next. And then, one day, some stains which Ada had been unable to sponge out elicited a stammering tale of a cart-wheel that had stopped three inches from the prostrate child.

This had finished Jonah, and with an oath he had told Ada to pack up, and move into the rooms over the shop, when they could be got ready. Ada made a scene, grumbled and sulked, but Jonah would take no more risks. His son and his shop, he had fathered both, and they should be brought together under his watchful eye, and Ada's parasites could sponge elsewhere.

It had happened in time for him to have the living-rooms fitted up over the shop, for the part which was required as a store-room left ample space for a family of three. Ada gave in with a sullen anger, refusing to notice the splendours of the new establishment. But she had a real terror, besides her objection to being for ever under Jonah's sharp eyes.

Born and bred in a cottage, she had a natural horror of staircases, looking on them as dangerous contrivances on which people daily risked their lives. She climbed them slowly, feeling for safety with her feet, and descended with her heart in her mouth. The sight of others tripping lightly up and down impressed her like a dangerous performance on the tight-rope in a circus. And the new rooms could only be reached by two staircases, one at the far end of the shop, winding like a corkscrew to the upper floor, and another, sickening to the eye, dropping from the rear balcony in the open air to the kitchen and the yard.

Mrs Yabsley continued to live in the old cottage in Cardigan Street. Jonah made her an allowance, but she still worked at the laundry, not for a living, as she carefully explained to every new customer, but for the sake of exercise. And she had obstinately refused to be pensioned off.

"I've seen too many of them pensioners, creepin' an' coughin' along the street, because they thought they was too old fer work, an' one fine mornin' they fergit ter come down ter breakfast, an' the neighbours are invited to the funeral. An' but for that they might 'ave lived fer years, drawin' their money an standin' in the way of younger men. No pensions fer me, thank yer!"

When Jonah had pointed out that she could not live alone in the cottage, she had listened with a mysterious smile. With Jonah's allowance and her earnings, she was the rich woman, the lady chatelaine of the street, and she chose a companion from the swarm of houseless women

143

that found a precarious footing in the houses of their relations—women with raucous voices, whose husbands had grown tired of life and fled; ladies who were vaguely supposed to be widows; comely young women cast on a cold world with a pitiful tale and a handbag. And she fed them till they were plump and vicious again, when they invariably disappeared, taking everything of value they could lay hands on. When Jonah, exasperated by these petty thefts, begged her to come and live with them, she shook her head, with a humorous twinkle in her eyes.

"No, yer'd 'ave ter pull me up by the roots like that old tree if yer took me out of this street. I remember w'en 'arf this street was open paddicks, an' now yer can't stick a pin between the 'ouses. I was a young gell then, an' a lot better lookin' than yer'd think. Ada's father thought a lot o' me, I tell yer. That was afore 'e took ter drink. I was 'is first love, as the sayin' is, but beer was 'is second. 'E was a good 'usbind ter me wot time 'e could spare from the drink, an' I buried 'im out of this very 'ouse, w'en Ada could just walk. I often think life's a bloomin' fraud, Joe, w'ichever way yer look at it. W'en ye're young, it promises yer everythin' yer want, if yer only wait. An' w'en ye're done waitin', yer've lost yer teeth an' yer appetite, or forgot wot yer were waitin' for. Yes, Joe, the street an' me's old pals. We've seen one another in sickness an' sorrer an' joy an' jollification, an' it 'ud be a poor job ter part us now. Funny, ain't it? This street is more like a 'uman bein' ter me than plenty I know. Yer see, I can't read the paper, an' see 'oo's bin married and murdered through the week, bein' no scholar, but I can read Cardigan Street like a book. An' I've found that wot 'appens in this street 'appens everywhere else, if yer change the names an' addresses."

About a week after the triumphant opening of the Silver Shoe, Jonah was running his eye down some price-lists, when he was disturbed by a loud noise. He looked round, and was surprised to see Miss Giltinan, head of the ladies' department, her lips tight with anger, replacing a heap of cardboard boxes with jerks of suppressed fury.

She was his best saleswoman, gathered in from the pavement a week after she had been ejected from Packard's factory for cheeking the boss. She had spent a few weeks dusting shoes and tying up parcels, and then, brushing the old hands aside, had taken her place as a born saleswoman. Sharp as a needle, the customers were like clay in her hands. She recognized two classes of buyers—those who didn't know what they wanted, and always, under her guidance, spent more than they intended; and those who knew quite well what they wanted, the best quality at an impossible price. Both went away satisfied, for she took them into her confidence, and, with covert glances for fear she should be overheard, gave them her private opinion of the articles in a whisper. And they went away satisfied that they had saved money, and, made a friend who would always look after their interests. But this morning she was blazing.

"Save the pieces, Mary," said Jonah, "wot's the matter?"

"A woman in there's got me beat," replied the girl savagely—"says she must 'ave Kling & Wessel's, an' we 'aven't got a pair in the place. Not likely either, when the firm's gone bung; but I wasn't goin' to tell 'er that. Better come an' try 'er yourself, or she'll get away with 'er money."

145

As Jonah entered, the troublesome customer looked up with an air of great composure. She was a young woman of five-and-twenty, tall, dark, and slight, with features more uncommon than beautiful. Her face seemed quite familiar to Jonah.

"Good mornin', Miss. Can I 'elp you in any way?" he said, trying to remember where he had seen her before.

"So sorry to trouble you, but my feet are rather a nuisance," she said, in a voice that broke like the sound of harps and flutes on Jonah's ear.

Jonah noted mechanically that her eyes were brown, peculiar, and luminous as if they glowed from within. They were marked by dark eyebrows that formed two curves of remarkable beauty. She showed her teeth in a smile; they were small, and white and even, so perfect that they passed for false with strangers. She explained that she had an abnormally high instep, and could only be fitted by one brand of shoe. She showed her foot, cased in a black stocking, and the sight of it carried Jonah back to Cardigan Street and the push, for the high instep was a distinguished mark of beauty among the larrikins, adored by them with a Chinese reverence.

"I can only wear Kling & Wessel's, and your assistant tells me you are out of them at present," she continued, "so I am afraid I must give it up as a bad job." She picked up her shoe, and Jonah was seized with an imperious desire to keep her in the shop at any cost.

"I'm afraid yer've worn yer last pair of that make," said Jonah. "The Americans 'ave driven them off the market, and the agency's closed."

"How annoying! I must wear shoes. Whatever shall I do?" she replied, staring at the shelves as if lost in thought.

Jonah marked with an extraordinary pleasure every detail of her face and dress. The stuff was a cheap material, but it was cut and worn with a daintiness that marked her off from the shopgirls and others that Jonah was most familiar with. And as he looked, a soft glow swept through him like the first stage of intoxication. Sometimes at the barber's a similar hypnotic feeling had come over him, some electric current stirred by the brushing of his hair, when common sounds and movements struck on his nerves like music. Again his nerves vibrated tunefully, and he became aware that she was speaking.

"So sorry to have troubled you," she said, and prepared to go.

He felt he must keep her at any cost. "A foot like yours needs a special last shaped to the foot. I don't make to order now, as a rule, but I'll try wot I can do fer yer, if yer care to leave an order," he said. He spoke like one in a dream.

She looked at him with a peculiar, intense gaze. "I should prefer that, but I'm afraid they would be too expensive," she said.

"No, I can do them at the same price as Kling & Wessel's," said Jonah.

Miss Giltinan started and looked sharply from Jonah to his customer. She knew that was impossible. And she looked with a frown at this woman who could make Jonah forget his business instincts for a minute. For she worshipped him in secret, grateful to him for lifting her out of the gutter, and regarded him as the arbiter of her destiny.

He went to the desk and found the sliding rule and tape. As he passed the tape round the stranger's foot, he found that his hands were trembling. And as he knelt before her on one knee, the young woman studied, with a slight repugnance, the large head, wedged beneath the shoulders as if a giant's hand had pressed it down, and the hump projecting behind, monstrous and inhuman. Suddenly Jonah looked up and met her eyes. She coloured faintly.

"Wot sort of fit do yer like?" he asked. His voice, usually sharp and nasal, was rather hoarse.

All her life she remembered that moment. The huge shop, glittering with varnish, mirrors, and brass rods, the penetrating odour of leather, the saleswoman silently copying the figures into the book, and the misshapen hunchback kneeling before her and looking up into her face with his restless grey eyes, grown suddenly steady, that asked one question and sought another. She frowned slightly, conscious of some strange and disagreeable sensation.

"I prefer them as tight as possible without hurting me," she replied nervously; "but I'm afraid I'm giving you too much trouble."

"Not a bit," replied Jonah, clearing his throat.

As he finished measuring, a small boy, dressed in a Fauntleroy velvet suit, with an enormous collar and a flap cap, ran noisily into the shop, dragging a toy train at his heels.

"Get upstairs at once, Ray," said Jonah, without looking round.

The child, puffing and snorting like an engine, took no notice of the command.

"Did yer 'ear me speak?" cried Jonah, angrily.

148

The child laughed, and stopped with his train in front of the customer, staring at her with unabashed eyes.

"What a pretty boy!" said the young woman. "Won't you tell me your name?"

"My name's Ray Jones, and I'll make old bones," he cried, with the glibness of a parrot.

The young woman laughed, and Jonah's face changed instantly. It wore the adoring gaze of the fond parent, who thinks his child is a marvel and a prodigy.

"Tell the lady 'ow old yer are," he said.

"I'm seven and a bit old-fashioned," cried the child, looking into the customer's face for the amused look that always followed the words. The young woman smiled pleasantly as she laced her shoe.

"'E's as sharp as a needle," said Jonah, with a proud look, "but I 'aven't put 'im to school yet, 'cause 'e'll get enough schooling later on. But I'll 'ave ter do somethin' with 'im soon; 'e's up ter 'is neck in mischief. I wish 'e was old enough ter learn the piano. 'E's got a wonderful ear fer music."

"But he is old enough," said the young woman with a sudden interest. "I have two pupils the same age as he."

"Ah?" said Jonah, inquiringly.

"I am a teacher of music," continued the young woman, "and in my opinion, they can't start too early, if they have any gift."

"An' 'ow would yer judge that?" said Jonah, delighted at the turn of the conversation.

"I generally go by the width of the forehead at the temples. Phrenologists always look for that, and I have

149

never found it fail. Come here," she said to the child, in a sharp, businesslike tone. She passed her hand over his forehead, and pointed out to Jonah a fullness over the corner of the eye. "That is the bump of music. You have it yourself," she said, suddenly looking at Jonah's face. "I'm sure you're fond of music. Do you sing or play?"

"I can do a bit with the mouth-organ," said Jonah, off his guard. He turned red with shame at this vulgar admission, but the young woman only smiled.

"Well, about the boy," said Jonah, anxious to change the subject, "I'd like yer to take 'im in 'and, if yer could make anythin' of 'im."

"I should be very pleased," said the young woman.

"Very well, we'll talk it over on Thursday, when yer come fer yer shoes," said Jonah, feeling that he was making an appointment with this fascinating stranger.

As she left the shop she handed Jonah a card, on which was printed:

MISS CLARA GRIMES,
Teacher of Music.
Terms: £1. 1s. per quarter.

"Well, I'm damned!" said Jonah. "Old Grimes's daughter, of course." And as he watched her crossing the street with a quick, alert step, an intense yearning and loneliness came over him. Something within him contracted till it hurt. And suddenly there flashed across his mind some half-forgotten words of Mrs Yabsley's:

"Don't think of marryin' till yer feel there's somethin' wrong wi' yer inside, for that's w'ere it ketches yer."

He sighed heavily, and went into the shop, preoccupied and silent for that day.

13

A FAMILY IN EXILE

Dad Grimes had just finished the story of his nose and the cabman, and the group in the bar of the Angel exploded like a shell. Dicky Freeman's mouth seemed to slip both ways at once till it reached his ears. The barman put down the glass he was wiping and twisted the cloth in his fingers till the tears stood in his eyes. The noise was deafening.

"An' 'e sez, 'Cum on, you an' yer nose, an' I'll fight the pair o' yez,'" spluttered Dicky, with hysterical gasps, and went off again. His chuckles ended in a dead silence. There was no sound but the rapid breathing of the men. The barman flattened a mosquito on his cheek; the smack sounded like a kiss. Dicky Freeman emptied his glass, and then stared through the bottom as if he wondered where the liquor had gone.

"I assure you for the moment I was staggered," said Dad, rounding off his story. "I am aware that my nose has added to the gaiety of nations, but it was the first time that it had been reckoned as a creature distinct from myself with an individuality of its own."

Dad Grimes was a man of fifty, wearing a frock coat that showed a faint green where the light fell on the shoulders, and a tall silk hat that had grown old with the wearer. But for his nose he might have been an undertaker. It was an impossible nose, the shape and size of a potato, and the colour of pickled cabbage—the nose for a clown in the Carnival of Venice. Its marvellous shape was none of Dad's choosing, but the colour was his own, laid on by years of patient drinking as a man colours a favourite pipe. Years ago, when he was a bank manager, his heart had bled at the sight of this ungainly protuberance; but since his downfall, he had led the chorus of laughter that his nose excited, with a degraded pride in his physical defect.

It was Dicky Freeman's turn to shout, and he began another story as Dad sucked the dregs of beer off his moustache. Dad recognized the opening sentence. It was one of the interminable stories out of the Decameron of the bar-room, realistic and obscene, that circulate among drinkers. Dad knew it by heart. He looked at his glass, and remembered that it was his fourth drink. Instantly he thought of the Duchess. With his usual formula "'Scuse me; I'm a married man, y'know," he hurried out of the bar in search of his little present.

It was nine o'clock, and the Duchess would be waiting for him with his tea since six. And always when he stopped at the Angel on his way home, he tried to soften her icy looks with a little present. Sometimes it was a bunch of grapes

153

that he crushed to a pulp by rolling on them; sometimes a dozen apples that he spilt out of the bag, and recovered from the gutter with lurching steps. But tonight he happened to stop in front of the fish shop, and a lobster caught his eye. The beer had quickened the poetry in his soul, and the sight of this fortified inhabitant of the deep pleased him like a gorgeous sunset. He shuffled back to the Angel with the lobster under his arm, wrapped in a piece of paper.

One more drink and he would go home. He put the lobster carefully at his elbow and called for drinks. But Dicky was busy with a new trick with a box of matches, and Dad, who was a recognized expert in the idle devices of bar-room loafers—picking up glasses and bottles with a finger and thumb, opening a footrule with successive jerks from the wrist, drinking beer out of a spoon—forgot the lapse of time with the new toy.

Punctually on the stroke of eleven the swinging doors of the Angel were closed and the huge street lamps were extinguished. Dad's eye was glassy, but he remembered the lobster.

"Whersh my lil' present?" he wailed. "Mush 'ave lil' present for the Duchess, y'know. 'Ow could I g'ome, d'ye think?"

He made so much noise that the landlord came to see what was the matter, and then the barman pointed to where he had left the lobster on the counter. He tucked it under his arm and lurched into the street. Now, Dad could run when he couldn't walk. He swayed a little, then suddenly broke into a run whose speed kept him from falling and preserved his balance like a spinning top.

The Duchess, seen through a haze, seemed unusually stern tonight; but with beery pride he produced his little present, the mail-clad delicacy, the armoured crustacean. But Dicky Freeman, offended by Dad's sudden departure in the middle of the story, had taken a mean revenge with the aid of the barman, and, as Dad unfastened the wrapping, there appeared, not the shellfish in its vermilion armour, but something smooth and black—an empty beer-bottle! Dad stared and blinked. A look at the Duchess revealed a face like the Ten Commandments. The situation was too abject for words; he grinned vacantly and licked his lips.

The Grimes family lived in the third house in the terrace, counting from the lamp-post at the corner of Buckland Street, where, running parallel to Cardigan Street, it tumbles over the hill and is lost to sight on its way to Botany Road. It was a long, ugly row of two-storey houses, the model lodging-houses of the crowded suburbs, so much alike that Dad had forced his way, in a state of intoxication, into every house in the terrace at one time or another, under the impression that he lived there.

Ten years ago the Grimes family had come to live in Waterloo, when the Bank of New Guinea had finally dispensed with Dad's services as manager at Billabong. His wife had picked on this obscure suburb of working men to hide her shame, and Dad, who could make himself at home on an ant-hill, had cheerfully acquiesced. He had started in business as a house-agent, and the family of three lived from hand to mouth on the profits that escaped the publican. Not that Dad was idle. He was for ever busy; but it was the busyness of a fly. He would call for the rent, and spend half the morning fixing a tap for Mrs Brown, instead of calling in the plumber; he would make a special journey to the other end of Sydney for Mrs Smith, to prove that he had a nose for bargains.

Mrs Grimes forgot with the greatest ease that her neighbours were made of the same clay as herself, but she never forgot that she had married a bank manager, and she never forgave Dad for lowering her pride to the dust. True, she was only the governess at Nullah Nullah station when Dad married her, but her cold aristocratic features had given her the pick of the neighbouring stations, and Dad was reckoned a lucky man when he carried her off. It was her fine, aquiline features and a royal condescension in manner that had won her the title of "Duchess" in this suburb of workmen. She tried to be affable, and her visitors smarted under a sense of patronage. The language of Buckland Street, coloured with oaths, the crude fashions of the slop-shop, and the drunken brawls, jarred on her nerves like the sharpening of a saw. So she lived, secluded as a nun, mocked and derided by her inferiors.

She was born with the love of the finer things that makes poverty tragic. She kept a box full of the tokens of the past—a scarf of Maltese lace, yellow with age, that her grandmother had sent from England; a long chain of fine gold, too frail to be worn; a brooch set with diamonds in a bygone fashion; a ring with her father's seal carved in onyx.

Her daughter Clara was the image of herself in face and manner, and her grudge against her husband hardened every time she thought of her only child's future. Clara was fifteen when they descended to Buckland Street, a

156

pampered child, nursed in luxury. The Duchess belonged to the Church of England, and it had been one of the sights of Billabong to see her move down the aisle on Sunday like a frigate of Nelson's time in full sail; but she had overcome her scruples, and sent Clara to the convent school for finishing lessons in music, dancing, and painting.

We each live and act our parts on a stage built to our proportions, and set in a corner of the larger theatre of the world, and the revolution that displaces princes was not more surprising to them than the catastrophe that dropped the Grimes family in Buckland Street was to Clara and her mother.

Clara had been taught to look on her equals with scorn, and she stared at her inferiors with a mute contempt that roused the devil in their hearts. She had lived in the street ten years, and was a stranger in it. Buckland Street was never empty, but she learned to pick her time for going in and out when the neighbours were at their meals or asleep. She attended a church at an incredible distance from Waterloo, for fear people should learn her unfashionable address. Her few friends lived in other suburbs whose streets she knew by heart, so that they took her for a neighbour.

When she was twenty-two she had become engaged to a clerk in a Government office, who sang in the same choir. A year passed, and the match was suddenly broken off. This was her only serious love-affair, for, though she was handsome in a singular way, her flirtations never came to anything. She belonged to the type of woman who can take her pick of the men, and remains unmarried while her plainer friends are rearing families.

The natural destiny of the Waterloo girls was the factory, or the workshops of anaemic dressmakers, stitching slops at racing speed, for the warehouses. A few of the better sort, marked out by their face and figure, found their way to the tea-rooms and restaurants. But the Duchess had encouraged her daughter's belief that she was too fine a lady to soil her hands with work, and she strummed idly on the dilapidated piano while her mother roughened her fine hands with washing and scrubbing. This was in the early days, when Dad, threatened with starvation, had passed the hotels at a run to avoid temptation, for which he made amends by drinking himself blind for a week at a time. Then, after years of genteel poverty, the Duchess had consented to Clara giving lessons on the piano—that last refuge of the shabby-genteel. But pupils were scarce in Waterloo, and Clara's manner chilled the enthusiasm of parents who only paid for lessons on the understanding that their child was to become the wonder of the world for a guinea a quarter.

This morning Clara was busy practising scales, while her mother dusted and swept with feverish haste, for Mr Jones, the owner of the great boot-shop, was bringing his son in the afternoon to arrange for lessons on the piano. The Duchess knew the singular history of Jonah, the boot king, and awaited his arrival with intense curiosity. She had married a failure, and adored success. She decided to treat Jonah as an equal, forgiving his lowly origin with a confused idea that it was the proper thing for millionaires to spring from the gutter, the better to show their contempt for the ordinary advantages of education and family. She had decided to wear her black silk, faded and darned, but by drawing the curtains she hoped it would pass. From some receptacle unknown to Dad she had fished out a few relics of her former grandeur—an old-fashioned card-tray of solid silver, and the quaint silver tea-set with the tiny silver spoons that her grandmother had sent as a wedding present from England.

Clara had just finished a variation with three tremendous fortissimo chords when she heard the wheels of a cab. This was an event in itself, for cabs in Buckland Street generally meant doctors, hospitals, or sudden death. She ran to the window and saw the hunchback and the boy stepping out. Clara opened the door with an air of surprise, and led them to the parlour where the Duchess was waiting. Years and misfortune had added to her dignity, and Jonah felt his shop and success and money slip away from him, leaving him the street-arab sprung from the gutter before this aristocrat. Ray took to her at once, and climbed into her lap, bringing her heart into her mouth as he rubbed his feet on the famous black silk.

"I have never had the pleasure of meeting you, but I have heard of your romantic career," she said.

"Well, I've got on, there's no denying that," said Jonah. "Some people think it's luck, but I tell 'em it's 'ard graft."

"Exactly," said the Duchess, wondering what he meant by graft.

Jonah looked round the stuffy room. It had an indescribable air of antiquity. Every piece of furniture was of a pattern unknown to him, and there was a musty flavour in the air, for the Duchess, valuing privacy more than fresh air, never opened the windows. On the wall opposite was a large picture in oils, an English scene, with the old rustic bridge and the mill in the distance, painted at Billabong by Clara at an early age. The Duchess caught Jonah's eye.

"That was painted by my daughter ten years ago. Her teachers considered she had a wonderful talent, but misfortune came, and she was unable to follow it up," she said.

Jonah's amazement increased. It was a mere daub, but to his untrained eye it was like the pictures in the Art Gallery, where he had spent a couple of dull afternoons. Over the piano a framed certificate announced that Clara Grimes had passed the junior grade of Trinity College in 1890. And Jonah, who had an eye for business like a Jew, who moved in an atmosphere of profit and loss, suddenly felt ill at ease. His shop, his money, and his success must seem small things to these women who lived in the world of art. His thoughts were brought back to earth by a sudden crash. Ray was sitting on a chair, impatient for the music to begin, and, as he never sat on a chair in the ordinary fashion, he had paralysed the Duchess with a series of gymnastic feats, twining his legs round the chair, sitting on his feet, kneeling on the seat with his feet on the back of the chair, until at last an unlucky move had tilted the chair backwards into a pot-stand. The jar fell with a crash, and Ray laughed. The Duchess uttered a cry of terror.

"Yer young devil, keep still," cried Jonah, angrily. "Yer can pay fer that out of yer pocket-money," he added.

"It was of no value," said the Duchess, with frigid dignity.

160

"Perhaps Miss Grimes will play something," said Jonah. "Ray's talked of nothing else since daylight this morning."

Clara sat down at the piano and ran her fingers over the keys. She had selected her masterpiece, "The Wind Among the Pines", a tone-picture from a shilling album. Her fingers ran over the keys with amazing rapidity as she beat out the melody with the left hand on the groaning bass, while with the right she executed a series of scales to the top of the keyboard and back. Jonah listened spellbound to the clap-trap arrangement. He had the native ear for music, and he recognized that he was in the presence of a born musician. Ray crept near, and listened with open mouth to this display of musical fireworks. When she had finished, Clara turned to Jonah with a languid smile, the look of the artist conscious of divine gifts.

"My daughter was considered the best player at the convent where she was educated," said the Duchess—"a great talent wasted in this dreadful place."

"I niver 'eard anythin' like that in my natural," said Jonah with enthusiasm. "If yer can teach Ray ter play like that, I'm satisfied."

"You may depend upon her doing her best with your son, but it is not everyone who has Clara's talent," said the Duchess.

"Play some more," said Ray.

This time she selected a grand march, striking the dilapidated piano a series of stunning blows with both hands, filling the air with the noise of battle.

"That must be terrible 'ard," said Jonah.

"It takes it out of one," replied Clara, with the simplicity of an artist.

Then she gave Ray his first lesson, showing him how to sit and place his hands, anxious to impress the parent that she was a good teacher. She declared that Ray was very apt, and would learn rapidly. An hour later, Jonah paid for Ray's first quarter. Clara's terms were a guinea, but Jonah insisted on two guineas on the understanding that Ray would receive special attention.

But in spite of her promises, Ray's progress was slow. As Jonah had no piano, the boy came half an hour early to his lesson to practise, but the twenty minutes' journey from the Silver Shoe occupied the best part of an hour, for Ray, who took to the streets as a duck takes to water, could spend a morning idling before shop windows, following fiddlers on their rounds, watching navvies dig a drain, with a frank, sensuous delight in the sights and sounds of the streets, an inheritance from Jonah's years of vagabondage. Then the street-arabs fell on him, annoyed by his new clothes and immense white collar, and at the end of the third week he reached home after dark with a cut on his forehead and spattered with mud.

The next day Jonah called on Clara to make some other arrangements. His tone was brusque, and Clara noticed with surprise that he was inclined to blame her for Ray's mishap. He seemed to forget everything when it was a question of his son. But all of the Duchess in Clara came to the surface in her annoyance, and she suggested that the lessons had better come to an end. Absorbed in his egotistic feelings, Jonah looked up in surprise, and his anger vanished. He saw that he had offended her, and apologized. Then he remembered what had brought him. His overpowering desire to see this woman had surprised him like the first symptoms of an illness. He had not seen her for three weeks, and in the increased flow of business at the Silver Shoe had half forgotten his amazing emotions as one forgets a powerful dream. Women, he repeated, were worse than drink for taking a man's mind off his work.

In his experience he had observed with some curiosity that drink and women were alike in throwing men off their balance. Drink, fortunately, had no power over him. Beer only fuddled his brain, and he looked on its effect with the curious dislike women look on smoking, blind to its fascinations. As for women, Ada was the only one he had ever been on intimate terms with, and, judging by his sensations, people who talked about love were either fools or liars. True, he had heard Chook talking like a fool about Pinkey, swearing that he couldn't live without her, but thought naturally that he lied. And they had quarrelled so fiercely over the colour of her hair, that for years each looked the other way when they met in the street. But as he looked at Clara again, something vibrated within him, and he was conscious of nothing but a desire to look at her and hear her speak.

"My idea was to buy a piano, an' then yer could give Ray 'is lessons at 'ome," he said.

"That is the only way out of the difficulty," said Clara.

Jonah thought awhile, and made up his mind with a snap.

"Could yer come with me now, an' pick me a piano? I can tell a boot by the smell of the leather, but pianos are out of my line."

Clara's manner changed instantly as she thought of the commission she would get from Kramer's, where she had a running account for music.

"I shall be only too pleased," she said.

As they left the house she remembered, with a slight repugnance, Jonah's deformity. She hoped people wouldn't notice them as they went down the street. But to her surprise and relief, Jonah hailed a passing cab.

"Time's money to me," he said, with an apologetic look.

Cabs were a luxury in Buckland Street, and Clara was delighted. She felt suddenly on the level of the rich people who could afford to ride where others trudged afoot. She leaned forward, hoping that the people would notice her.

At Kramer's she took charge of Jonah as a guide takes charge of tourists in a foreign land, anxious to show him that she was at home among this display of expensive luxuries. The floor was packed with pianos, glittering with varnish which reflected the strong light of the street. From another room came a monotonous sound repeated indefinitely, a tuner at work on a piano.

The salesman stepped up, glancing at the hunchback with the quick look of surprise which Clara had noticed in others. They stopped in front of an open piano, and Clara, taking off her gloves, ran her fingers over the keys. The rich, singing notes surprised Jonah; they were quite unlike those he had heard on Clara's piano. Clara played as much

as she could remember of "The Wind Among the Pines",
and Jonah decided to buy that one.

"'Ow much is that?" he inquired.

"A hundred guineas," replied the shopman, indifferently.

"Garn! Yer kiddin'?" cried Jonah, astounded.

The salesman looked in surprise from Jonah to Clara.
She coloured slightly. Jonah saw that she was annoyed.
The salesman led them to another instrument, and, with
less deference in his tone, remarked that this was the firm's
special cheap line at fifty guineas. But Jonah had noticed the
change in Clara's manner, and decided against the cheaper
instrument instantly. They thought he wasn't good for a
hundred quid, did they? Well, he would show them. But,
to his surprise, Clara opposed the idea. The Steinbech,
she explained, was an instrument for artists. It would be
a sacrilege for a beginner to touch it. Jonah persisted, but
the shopman agreed with Clara that the celebrated Ropp
at eighty guineas would meet his wants. A long discussion
followed, and Jonah listened while Clara tried to beat the
salesman down below catalogue price for cash. Here was a
woman after his own heart, who could drive a bargain with
the best of them. At the end of half an hour Jonah filled in
a cheque for eighty guineas, and the salesman, reading the
signature, bowed them deferentially out of the shop.

Clara walked out of the shop with the air of a million-
aire. To be brought in contact even for a moment with this
golden stream of sovereigns excited her like wine. All her
life she had desired things whose price put them beyond her
reach, and she felt suddenly friendly to this man who took

what he wanted regardless of cost. She thought pleasantly of the ride home in the cab, but she was pulled up with a jerk when Jonah led the way to the tram. He wore an anxious look, as if he had spent more than he could afford, and yet the money was a mere flea-bite to him. But whenever he spent money, a panic terror seized him—a survival of the street-arab's instinct, who counted his money in pennies instead of pounds.

14

ADA MAKES A FRIEND

Ada moved uneasily, opened her eyes and stared at the patch of light on the opposite wall. As she lay half awake, she tried to remember the day of the week, and, deceived by the morning silence, decided that it was Sunday. She thought, with lazy pleasure, that a day of idleness lay before her, and felt under the pillow for the tin of lollies that she hid there every night. This movement awakened her completely, and stretching her limbs luxuriously between the warm sheets, she began to suck the lollies, at first slowly revolving the sticky globules on her tongue, and then scrunching them between her firm teeth with the tranquil pleasure of a quadruped.

This was her only pleasure and the only pleasant hour of the day. She looked at Jonah, who lay on his side with his nose buried in the pillow, without repugnance and without liking. That had gone long ago. And as she looked, she remembered that he was to be awakened early and that it was Friday the hardest day of the week, when she must make up her arrears of scrubbing and dusting. Her luxurious mood changed to one of dull irritation, and she looked sullenly at the enormous wardrobe and dressing-table with their speckled mirrors. These had delighted her at first, but in her heart she preferred the battered, makeshift furniture of Cardigan Street. A few licks with the duster and her work was done; but here the least speck of dust showed on the polished surface. Jonah, too, had got into a nasty habit of writing insulting words on the dusty surface with his finger.

Well, let him! There had been endless trouble since he bought the piano. As sure as Miss Grimes came to give Ray his lesson, he declared the place was a pigsty and tried to shame her by taking off his coat and dusting the room himself. Not that she blamed Miss Grimes. She was quite a lady in her way, and had won Ada's heart by telling her that she hated housework. She thought Ada must be a born housekeeper to do without a servant, and Ada didn't trouble to put her right. Anyhow, Jonah should keep a servant. He pretended that their servants in Wyndham Street had made game of her behind her back, and robbed her right and left. What did that matter? she thought—Jonah could afford it.

The real reason was that he wanted no one in the house to see how he treated his wife. She cared little herself whether she had a girl or not, for she had always been accustomed to make work easy by neglecting it. If Jonah wanted a floor that you could eat your dinner off, let him get a servant. He was as mean as dirt. A fat lot she got out of his money. Here she was, shut up in these rooms, little better than a prisoner, for her old pals never dared show their noses in this house, and she could never go out without all the shop-hands knowing it. She never bought a new dress, but Jonah stormed like a madman, declaring that she looked like a servant dressed up. Well, her clothes knocked Cardigan Street endways when she paid her mother a visit, and that was all she wanted.

There was her mother, too. She had never been a real mother to her; you could never tell what she was thinking about. Other people took their troubles to her, but she treated her own daughter like a stranger. And, of course, she sided with Jonah and talked till her jaw ached about her duty to her child and her husband. She would have married Tom Mullins if it hadn't been for the kid, and lived in Cardigan Street like her pals. Her thoughts travelled back to Packard's and the Road. She remembered with intense longing the group at the corner, the drunken rows, and the nightly gossip on the doorstep. That was life for her. She had been like a fish out of water ever since she left it. She thought with singular bitterness of Jonah's attempts to introduce her to the wives of the men he met in business, women who knew not Cardigan Street, and annoyed her by staring at her hands, and talking of their troubles with servants till they made her sick.

Her thoughts were suddenly interrupted by Jonah. He turned in his sleep and pushed the sheet from his face, but a loud scrunch from Ada's jaw woke him completely. He tugged at the pillow and his hand fell on the tin of sticky lollies.

"Bah!" he cried in disgust, and rubbed his fingers on the sheet. "Only kids eat that muck."

"Kid yerself!" cried Ada furiously. "Anybody 'ud think I was eatin' di'monds. Yer'd grudge me the air I breathe, if yer thought it cost money."

"Yah, git up an' light the fire!" replied Jonah.

"Yes, that's me all over. Anybody else 'ud keep a servant; but as long as I'm fool enough ter slave an' drudge, yer save the expense."

"You slave an' drudge?" cried Jonah in scorn—"that was in yer dream. Are yer sure ye're awake?"

"Yes, I am awake, an' let me tell yer that it's the talk of the neighbourhood that yer've got thousands in the bank, an' too mean ter keep a servant."

"That's a lie, an' yer know it!" cried Jonah. "Didn't yez 'ave a girl in Wyndham Street, an' didn't she pinch enough things to set up 'er sister's 'ouse w'en she got married?"

"Yous couldn't prove it," said Ada, sullenly.

"No, I couldn't prove it without showing everybody wot sort of wife I'd got."

"She's a jolly sight too good fer yous, an' well yer know it."

"Yes, that's wot I complain of," said Jonah. "I'd prefer a wife like other men 'ave that can mind their 'ouse, an' not make a 'oly show of themselves w'en they take 'em out."

"A fat lot yer take me out!"

"Take yous out! Yah! Look at yer neck!"

Ada flushed a sullen red. So far the quarrel had been familiar and commonplace, like a conversation about the weather, but her neck, hidden under grubby lace, was Ada's weak point.

"Look at the hump on yer back before yer talk about my neck," she shouted. It was the first time she had ever dared to taunt Jonah with his deformity, and the sound of her words frightened her. He would strike her for certain.

Jonah's face turned white. He raised himself on his elbow and clenched his fist, the hard, knotty fist of the shoemaker swinging at the end of the unnaturally long arms, another mark of his deformity. Jonah had never struck her—contrary to the habit of Cardigan Street—finding that he could hit harder with his tongue; but it was coming now, and she nerved herself for the blow. But Jonah's hand dropped helplessly.

"You low, dirty bitch," he said. "If a man said that to me, I'd strangle him. I took yer out of the factory, I married yer, an' worked day an' night ter git on in the world, an' that's yer thanks. Pity I didn't leave yer in the gutter w'ere yer belonged. I wonder who yer take after? Not after yer mother. She is clean an' wholesome. Any other woman would take an interest in my business, an' be a help to a man; but you're like a millstone round my neck. I thought I'd done with Cardigan Street, an' the silly loafers I grew up with, but s'elp me Gawd, when I married you I married Cardigan Street. I could put up with yer want of brains— you don't want much brains ter git through this world—but it's yer nasty, sulky temper, an' yer bone idleness. I suppose yer git them from yer lovely father. The 'ardest work 'e ever did was to drink beer. It's a wonder yer don't take after 'im in that. I suppose I've got something to be thankful for."

"Yes, I suppose yer'd like me ter drink meself ter death, so as yer could marry again. But yer needn't fear I'll last yous out," cried Ada, recovering her tongue now that she was no longer in fear of a blow.

"Ah well, yer can't make a silk purse out of a sow's ear, they say," said Jonah. There was an intense weariness in his voice as he turned his back on Ada.

"No more than yer can make a man out of a monkey on a stick," muttered Ada to herself as she got out of bed.

Ada got the breakfast and went about the house in sullen silence. Jonah was used to this. For days together after a quarrel she would sulk without speaking, proud of her stubborn temper that forced others to give in first. And they would sit down to meals and pass one another in the rooms, watching each other's movements to avoid the necessity for speaking. The day had begun badly for Ada, and her anger increased as she brooded over her wrongs. Heavy and sullen by nature, her wrath came to a head hours after the provocation, burning with a steady heat when others were cooling down.

But as she was pegging out some towels in the yard she heard a discreet cough on the other side of the fence. Ada recognized the signal. It was her neighbour, the woman with the hairy lip, housekeeper to Aaron the Jew. It had taken Ada weeks to discover Mrs Herring's physical defect, which she humoured by shaving. Now Ada could tell in an instant whether she was shaven or hairy, for when her lip bristled with hairs for lack of the razor, she peered over the fence so as to hide the lower part of her face. Ada, being used to such things, thought at first she was hiding a black eye. But who was there to give her one? Aaron the pawnbroker, not being her husband, could not take such a liberty.

She had introduced herself over the fence the week of Ada's arrival, giving her the history of the neighbourhood in an unceasing flow of perfect English, her voice never rising above a whisper. For days she would disappear altogether, and then renew the conversation by coughing gently on her side of the fence. This morning her lip was shaven, and she leaned over the fence, full of gossip. But Ada's sullen face caught her eye, and instantly she was full of sympathy, a peculiar look of falsity shining in her light blue eyes.

"Why, what's the matter, dearie?" she inquired.

"Oh, nuthin'," said Ada roughly.

"Ah, you mustn't tell me that! When my poor husband was alive, I've often looked in my glass and seen a face like that. He was my husband, and I suppose I should say no more, but men never brought any happiness to me or any other woman that I know of. The first day I set eyes on you, I said, 'That's an unhappy woman.'"

"Well, yer needn't tell the bloomin' street," growled Ada.

"What you want is love and sympathy, but I suppose your husband is too busy making money to spare the time for that. Ah, many's the time, when my poor dear husband was alive, did I pine for a kind word, and get a black look instead! And a woman can turn to no one in a trouble like that. She feels as if her own door had been slammed in her face. What you want is a cheerful outing with a sympathetic friend, but I hear you're little more than a prisoner in your own house."

"Who told yer that?" cried Ada, flushing angrily.

"A little bird told me," said the woman, with a false grin.

173

"Well, I'd wring its neck, if I 'eard it," cried Ada. "And as fer bein' a prisoner, I'm goin' out this very afternoon."

"Why, how curious!" cried Mrs Herring. "This is my afternoon out. We could have a pleasant chat, if you have nothing better to do."

Ada hesitated. Jonah always wanted to know where she was going, and had forbidden her to make friends with the neighbours, for in Cardigan Street friendship with neighbours generally ended in a fight or the police court. She had never defied Jonah before, but her anger was burning with a steady flame. She'd show him!

"I'll meet yer at three o'clock opposite the church," she cried, and walked away.

She gave Jonah his meal in silence, and sent Ray off on a message before two o'clock. But Jonah seemed to have nothing to do this afternoon, and sat, contrary to custom, reading the newspaper. Ada watched the clock anxiously, fearing she would be baulked. But, as luck would have it, Jonah was suddenly called into the shop, and the coast was clear. It never took Ada long to dress; her clothes always looked as if they had been thrown on with a pitchfork, and she slipped down the outside stairs into the lane at the back. It was the first time she had gone out without telling Jonah where she was going and when she would be back. And afterwards she could never understand why she crept out in this furtive manner. Mrs Herring was waiting, dressed in dingy black, a striking contrast to Ada's flaring colours. They walked up Regent Street, as Mrs Herring said she wanted to buy a thimble. But when they reached Redfern Street, Mrs Herring put her hand suddenly to her breast and cried "Oh, dearie, if you could feel how my heart is beating! I really feel as if I am going to faint. I've suffered for years with my heart, and the doctor told me always to take a drop of something soothing, when I had an attack."

They were opposite the Angel, no longer sinister and forbidding in the broad daylight. The enormous lamps hung white and opaque; the huge mirrors reflected the cheerful light of the afternoon sun. The establishment seemed harmless and respectable, like the grocer's or baker's. But from the swinging doors came a strong odour of alcohol, enveloping the two women in a vinous caress that stirred hidden desires like a strong perfume.

"Do you think we could slip in here without being seen?" said the housekeeper.

"If ye're so bad as all that, we can," replied Ada.

Mrs Herring turned and slipped in at the side door with the dexterity of customers entering a pawnshop, and Ada followed, slightly bewildered. The housekeeper, seeming quite familiar with the turnings, led the way to a small room at the back. Ada looked round with great curiosity. She had never entered a hotel before in this furtive fashion. In Cardigan Street she had always fetched her mother's beer in a jug from the bar. On the walls were two sporting prints of dogs chasing a hare, and a whisky calendar. On the table was a small gong, which Mrs Herring rang. Cassidy himself, the landlord, answered the ring.

"Good day, good day to you, Mrs Herring," he said briskly. "The same as usual, I suppose? And what'll your friend take?" he added, grinning at Ada.

"My friend, Mrs Jones," said the housekeeper.

175

"Glad to meet you," cried Cassidy. "A terrible hill this," he continued, winking at Ada. "We should never see Mrs Herring, if it wasn't for the hill."

"Nothing for me," said Ada, shaking her head.

"Now just a drop to keep me company," begged Mrs Herring.

As Ada continued to shake her head, Cassidy went out, and returned with a bottle of brandy and three glasses on a tray.

"Sure, I forgot to tell you I'm a father again; father number nine, unless I've lost count. Sure your friend will join us in a glass to wet the head of the baby?"

He filled three glasses as he spoke, and winked at Mrs Herring. Ada's brain was in a whirl. She saw that she had been trapped, and that Mrs Herring was a liar and a comedian. She might as well drink now she was here. But Jonah would kill her, if he smelt drink on her. Well, let him! It was little enough fun she got out of life anyhow. She nodded to Cassidy. They clinked the three glasses and drank, the landlord and Mrs Herring at a gulp, Ada with tiny sips as if it were poison.

"Well, I'll leave you to your bit of gossip; I think I hear the child crying," said the landlord, backing out of the door with a grin.

Mrs Herring, who had forgotten her palpitations, filled her glass again, and sipped slowly to keep Ada company. In half an hour Ada finished her second glass. A pleasant glow had spread through her body. The weight was lifted off her mind, and she felt calm and happy. She thought of Jonah with indifference. What did he matter? She listened cheerfully to Mrs Herring's ceaseless whisper, only catching the meaning of one word in ten.

"And many's the time, when my poor dear husband was alive, have I gone out meaning to throw myself into the harbour, and a drop of cordial has changed my mind."

Ada nodded to show that she understood that the late Mr Herring was a brute and a tyrant.

"And then he went with the contingent to South Africa, and the next I heard was that he was dead. And the thought of my poor dear lying with his face turned to the skies would have driven me mad, if the doctor hadn't insisted on my taking a drop of cordial to bear my grief. And when I recovered, I vowed I would never marry again. The men, dearie, are all alike. They marry one woman, and want twenty. And if you as much as look at another man, they smash the furniture and threaten to get a divorce. I can see you've found that out."

"Ye're barkin' up the wrong tree," said Ada. "My old man's as 'ard as nails, but 'e don't run after women. 'E's the wrong shape, see."

Ada had never spent such a pleasant time in her life. She had never tasted brandy till that afternoon. Cardigan Street drank beer, and the glasses Ada had drunk at odd times had only made her sleepy without excitement. But this seductive liquid leapt through her veins, bringing a delicious languor and a sense of comfort. Her mind, dull and heavy by habit, ran on wheels. She wanted to interrupt Mrs Herring to make some observations of her own which seemed too good to lose. She felt a silly impulse to ask her whether she was born with a moustache, who taught her to shave, whether she could grow a moustache if she left it alone. She wanted to ask why her palpitations had gone off so quickly, and why she seemed perfectly at home in the Angel, but her thoughts crowded heel on heel so fast that she had forgotten them before she could speak.

She remembered that a few weeks ago the housekeeper's husband had died of typhoid in the Never Never country, and Mrs Herring had nursed him bravely to the end. She tried to reconcile this with his death this afternoon in the Boer War, and decided that it didn't matter. He must have died somewhere, for no one had ever seen him. She was discovering slowly that this woman was a consummate liar, who lied as the birds sing, but forgot her many inventions, a born liar without a memory. Suddenly Mrs Herring said she must be going, and Ada got up to leave. She lurched as she stood, and pushed her chair over with a clumsy movement.

"I b'lieve I'm drunk," she muttered, with a foolish titter.

MRS PARTRIDGE LENDS A HAND

Since ten o'clock in the morning the large house, standing in its own grounds, had been invaded by a swarm of dealers, hook-nosed and ferret-eyed, prying into every corner, searching each lot for hidden faults, judging at a glance the actual value of every piece of furniture, their blood stirred with the hereditary joy in chaffering, for an auction is as full of surprises as a battle, the prices rising and falling according to the temper of the crowd. And they watched one another with crafty eyes that had long lost the power to see anything but the faults and defects in the property of others. Those who had commissions from buyers marked the chosen lots in their catalogue with a stumpy pencil.

Mother Jenkins was one of these. She was the auction-eer's scavenger, snapping up the dishonoured, broken remnants disdained by the others, buying for a song the job lots on the way to the rubbish-heap. All was fish that came to her net, for her second-hand shop in Bathurst Street had taught her to despise nothing that had an ounce of wear left in it. Her bids never ran beyond a few shillings, but today she had an important commission, twenty pounds to lay out on the furnishing of three rooms for a married couple. These were her windfalls. Sometimes she got a wedding order, and furnished the house out of her amazing collection, supplemented by her bargains at the next auction sale. This had brought her to the sale early, for the young couple, deciding to furnish in style, had exhausted her resources by demanding wardrobes, dressing-tables, and washstands with marble tops.

The young woman with the mop of red hair followed on her heels, amazed by the luxury of the interior harmonized in a scheme of colour. Her day-dreams, coloured by the descriptions of ducal mansions in penny novelettes, came suddenly true. And she lingered before carved cabinets, strange vases like frozen rainbows, and Oriental tapestry with the instinctive delight in luxury planted in women.

But Mother Jenkins had no time to spare. She had found the very thing for Pinkey, and led the way to the servants' quarters, hidden at the back of the house. Pinkey's visions of grandeur fled at the sight. The rooms were small, and a sour smell hung on the air, the peculiar odour of servants' rooms where ventilation is unknown. Pinkey recognized the curtains and drapes at a glance, the pick of a suburban rag-shop. One room was as bare as a prison cell, merely a place to sleep in, but the next was royally furnished with a wardrobe, toilet-table, and washstand, solid and old-fashioned like the generation it had outlived. By its look it had descended in regular stages from the bedrooms of the family to the casual guests' room and then to the servants. But Pinkey had seen nothing so beautiful at home, and her heart swelled at the thought of possessing such genteel furniture. Mother Jenkins explained that with a lick of furniture polish they would look as good as new, but Pinkey's only fear was that they would be too expensive. Then the dealer reckoned that she could get the lot for seven pounds. The only rivals she feared were women, who, if they set their heart on anything, sometimes forced the price up till you could buy it for less in the shop.

Meanwhile the sale had begun, and in the distance Pinkey could hear the monotonous voice of the auctioneer forcing the bids up till he reached the limit. From time to time there was a roar of laughter as he cracked a joke over the heads of his customers. The buyers stood wedged like sardines in the room, craning their necks to see each lot as it was put up. As the crowd moved from room to room, Pinkey's excitement increased. Mother Jenkins had gone to the kitchen, where she always found a few pickings. She came back and found Pinkey's husband, the young man with the ugly face and dancing eyes, who was waiting outside with the cart, watching while Pinkey polished a corner of the wardrobe to show him its quality. She hurried them down to the kitchen to examine the linoleum on the floor, as it would fit their dining-room, if the worn parts were cut out.

The crowd moved like a mob of sheep into the servants' rooms, standing in each other's way, tired of the strain on their attention. Mother Jenkins whispered that things would go cheap because the auctioneer was in a hurry to get to his lunch. Pinkey stood behind her, ready to poke her in the ribs if she wished her to keep on bidding.

"Now, gentlemen," said the auctioneer, "lot one hundred and seventy-five. Duchesse wardrobe, dressing-table with bevelled mirrors, and marble-top washstand, specially imported from England by Mrs Harper. What am I offered?"

"Specially imported from England?" cried a dealer. "Yes, came out in the first fleet."

"What's that?" cried the auctioneer. "Thank you for telling me, Mr Isaacs." And he began again: "What offer for this solid ash bedroom suite, imported in the first fleet, guaranteed by Mr Isaacs, who was in leg-irons and saw it."

There was a roar of laughter at the dealer's discomfiture.

"Now, Mr Isaacs, how much are you going to bid, for old times' sake?" cried the auctioneer, pushing his advantage. But Isaacs had turned sulky.

"A pound," said Mother Jenkins.

"No, mother, you don't mean it," cried the auctioneer, grinning. "That'll leave you nothing to pay your tram fare home." But he went on: "I'm offered a pound for this solid ash bedroom suite that cost thirty guineas in London."

The bids crawled slowly up to six pounds.

"It's against you, mother," cried the auctioneer; "don't let a few shillings stand in the way of your getting married. I knew the men couldn't leave you alone with that face. Thank you, six-five."

The old hag showed her toothless gums in a hideous smile, the woman that was left in the dried shell still tickled at the reference to marriage. But her look changed to one of intense pain as Pinkey, trembling with excitement, nudged her violently in the ribs as a signal to keep on bidding. However, there was no real opposition, and the bidding stopped suddenly at seven pounds, forced up to that price by a friend of Mother Jenkins's to increase her commission.

In the kitchen the auctioneer lost his temper, and knocked down to Mother Jenkins enough pots and pans to last Pinkey a lifetime for ten shillings before the others could get in a bid. Chook, who had borrowed Jack Ryan's cart for the day, drove off with his load in triumph, while Pinkey went with Mother Jenkins to her shop in Bathurst Street to sort out her curtains, bed-linen, and crockery from that extraordinary collection. Twenty pounds would pay for the lot, and leave a few shillings over.

One Saturday morning, two years ago, Pinkey had set out for the factory as usual, and had come home to dinner with her wages in her handkerchief and a wedding ring on her finger. Mrs Partridge gave up novelettes for a week when she learned that her stepdaughter had married Chook that morning at the registry office. Partridge had taken the news with a look that had frightened the women; the only sign of emotion that he had given was to turn his back without a word on his favourite daughter. Since then they had lived with Chook's mother, as he had no money to furnish; but last month Chook had joined a syndicate of three to buy a five-shilling sweep ticket, which, to their amazement, drew a hundred-pound prize. With Chook's share they had decided to take Jack Ryan's shop in Pitt Street just round the corner from Cardigan Street. It was a cottage that had been turned into a shop by adding a false front to it. The rent, fifteen shillings a week, frightened Chook, but he reserved ten pounds to stock it with vegetables, and buy the fittings from Jack Ryan, who had tried to conduct his business from the bar of the nearest hotel, and failed. If the money had run to Jack's horse and cart, their fortunes would have been made.

Mrs Partridge's wanderings had ended with the marriage of Pinkey. Only once had she contrived to move, and the result had frightened her, for William had mumbled about his lost time in his sleep. And she had lived in Botany Street for two years, a stone's throw from the new shop in Pitt Street. She remembered that Chook had helped to move her furniture in at their first meeting, and, not liking to be outdone in generosity, resolved to slip round after tea and lend a hand. She knew, if any woman did, the trouble of moving furniture and setting it straight. She prepared for her labours by putting on her black silk blouse and her best skirt, and as William was anchored by the fireside with the newspaper, she decided to wear her new hat with the ostrich feathers, twenty years too young for her face, which she had worn for three months on the quiet out of regard for William's feelings, for it had cost the best part of his week's wages, squeezed out in shillings and sixpences, the price of imaginary pounds of tea, butter, and groceries.

She found Chook with his mouth full of nails, hanging pictures at five shillings the pair; Pinkey, dishevelled, sweating in beads, covered with dust, her sleeves tucked up

to the elbows, ordering Chook to raise or lower the picture
half an inch to increase the effect. It was some time before
Mrs Partridge could find a comfortable chair where she
ran no risk of soiling her best clothes, but when she did
she smiled graciously on them, noting with intense satisfaction Pinkey's stare of amazement at the black hat, twenty
years too young for her face.

"I thought I'd come round and give you a hand," she
explained.

"Thanks, Missis," said Chook, thankful for even a
little assistance.

Pinkey stared again at the hat, and Mrs Partridge felt
a momentary dissatisfaction with life in possessing such a
hat without the right to wear it in public. In half an hour
Chook and Pinkey had altered the position of everything
in the room under the direction of Mrs Partridge, who
sat in her chair like a spectator at the play. At last they sat
down exhausted, and Mrs Partridge, who felt as fresh as
paint, gave them her opinion on matrimony and the cares
of housekeeping. But Pinkey, unable to sit in idleness among
this beautiful furniture, got to work with her duster.

"Ah," said Mrs Partridge, "it's natural to take a pride
in the bit of furniture you start with, but when you've been
through the mill like I 'ave, you'll think more of your own
comfort. There was yer Aunt Maria wore 'er fingers to the
bone polishing 'er furniture on the time-payment plan, an'
then lost it all through the death of 'er 'usband, an' the
furniture man thanked 'er kindly fer keepin' it in such beautiful order when 'e took it away. An' Mrs Ross starved 'erself
to buy chairs an' sofas, which she needed, in my opinion,

185

being too weak to walk about; an' then 'er 'usband dropped a match, an' they 'ad the best fire ever seen in the street, an' 'ave lived in lodgings ever since."

"That's all right," said Chook uneasily, "but this ain't time-payment furniture, an' I ain't goin' ter sling matches about like some people sling advice."

"That's very true," said Mrs Partridge, warming up to her subject, "but there's no knowin' 'ow careless yer may git when yer stomach's undermined with bad cookin'."

"Wot rot ye're talkin'!" cried Chook. "Mother taught her to cook a fair treat these two years. She niver got anythin' to practise on in your 'ouse."

"That's true,' said Mrs Partridge, placidly. "I was never one to poison meself with me own cooking. When I was a girl I used ter buy a penn'orth of everythin', peas-pudden, saveloys, pies, brawn, trotters, Fritz, an' German sausage. Give me the 'am shop, an' then I know who ter blame, if anythin' goes wrong with me stomach."

Chook gave his opinion of cookshops.

"Ah well," said Mrs Partridge, "what the eye doesn't see the 'eart doesn't grieve over, as the sayin' is! An' that reminds me. Elizabeth suffers from 'er 'eart, an' that means a doctor's bill which I could never understand the prices they charge, knowin' plenty as got better before the doctor could cure 'em, an' so takin' the bread out of 'is mouth, as the sayin' is. Though I make it my business to be very smooth with them as might put somethin' nasty in the medsin an' so carry you off, an' none the wiser, as the sayin' is."

"'Ere, this ain't a funeral," cried Chook, in disgust.

"An' thankful you ought ter be that it ain't," cried Mrs Partridge, "after what I read in the paper only last week about people bein' buried alive oftener than dead, an' fair gave me the creeps thinkin' I could see the people scratchin' their way out of the coffin, an' sittin' on a tombstone with nuthin' but a sheet round 'em. It would cure anybody of wantin' ter die. I've told William to stick pins in me when my time comes."

"Anybody could tell w'en you're dead," said Chook.

"Why, 'ow?" cried Mrs Partridge, eagerly.

"Yer'll stop gassin' about yerself," cried Chook, roughly.

Mrs Partridge started to smile, and then stopped. It dawned slowly on her mind that she was insulted, and she rose to her feet.

"Thanks fer yer nasty remark," she cried. "That's all the thanks I get fer comin' to give a 'elpin' 'and. But I know when I'm not wanted."

"Yer don't," said Pinkey, "or yer'd 'ave gone 'ours ago."

Mrs Partridge turned to go, the picture of offended dignity, when her eyes fell on an apparition in the doorway, and she quailed. It was William, left safely by the fireside for the night, and now glowering, not at her as she swiftly divined, but at the hat with the drooping feathers, twenty years too young for her face. For the first time in her life she lost her nerve, but with wonderful presence of mind, she smiled in her agony.

"Why, there you are, William," she cried. "Yer gave me quite a start. I was just tryin' on Elizabeth's new 'at, to see if it suited me."

As she spoke, she tore out the hatpins with feverish dexterity, and thrust the hat into Pinkey's astonished hand.

"Take it, yer little fool," she whispered, savagely.

Her face looked suddenly old and withered under the scanty grey hair.

"Good evenin', Mr Partridge—glad ter see yer," cried Chook, advancing with outstretched hand; but the old man ignored him. His eyes travelled slowly round the room, taking in every detail of the humble furniture. The others stood silent with a little fear in their hearts at the sight of this old man with the face of a sleep-walker; but suddenly Pinkey walked up to him, and, reaching on tiptoe, kissed him, her face pink with emotion. It was the first time since her unforgiven marriage. And she hung on him like a child, her wonderful hair, the colour of a new penny, heightening the bloodless pallor of the old man's face. The stolid grey eyes turned misty, and, in silence, he slowly patted his daughter's cheek.

Chook kept his distance, feeling that he was not wanted. Mrs Partridge, who had recovered her nerve, came as near cursing as her placid, selfish nature would permit. She could have bitten her tongue for spite. She thought of a thousand ways of explaining away the hat. She should have said that a friend had lent it to her; that she had bought it for half price at a sale. She had meant to show it to William some night after his beer with a plausible story, but his sudden appearance had upset her apple-cart, and the lie had slipped out unawares. She wasn't afraid of William; she scorned him in her heart. And now that little devil must keep it, for if she went back on her word it would put William on the track of other little luxuries that she squeezed out of his wages unknown to him—luxuries whose chief charm lay in their secrecy. She felt ready to weep with vexation. Instead she cried gaily, "I've been tellin' them what a nice little 'ome they've got together. I've seen plenty would be glad to start on less."

Partridge seemed not to hear his wife's remark. His mind, dulled by shock and misfortune, was slowly revolving forgotten scenes. He saw with incredible sharpness of view his first home, with its few sticks of second-hand furniture like Pinkey's, and Pinkey's mother, the dead image of her daughter. That was where he belonged—to the old time, when he was young and proud of himself, able to drink his glass and sing a song with the best of them. Someone pulled him gently. He looked round, wondering what he was doing there. But Pinkey pulled him across the room to Chook, who was standing like a fool. He looked Chook up and down as if he were a piece of furniture, and then, without a word, held out his hand. The reconciliation was complete.

"Well, we must be goin', William," said Mrs Partridge, wondering how she was to get home without a hat; but Partridge followed Chook into the kitchen, where a candle was burning. Chook held the candle in his hand to show the little dresser with the cups and saucers and plates arranged in mathematical precision. The pots and pans were already hung on hooks. They had all seen service, and in Chook's eyes seemed more at home than the brand-new things that hung in the shops. As Chook looked round with pride, he became aware that Partridge was pushing something into his hand. It seemed like a wad of dirty paper, and Chook

189

held it to the candle in surprise. He unrolled it with his fingers, and recognized banknotes.

"'Ere, I don't want yer money," cried Chook, offering the wad of paper to the old man; but he pushed it back into Chook's hand with an imploring look.

"D'ye mean it fer Liz?" asked Chook.

Partridge nodded; his eyes were full of tears.

"Yous are a white man, an' I always knew it. Yer niver 'ad no cause ter go crook on me, but I ain't complainin'," cried Chook hoarsely.

The tears were running a zigzag course over the grey stubble of Partridge's cheeks.

"Yer'll be satisfied if I think as much of 'er as yous did of her mother?" asked Chook, feeling a lump in his throat.

Partridge nodded, swallowing as if he were choking.

"She's my wife, an' the best pal I ever 'ad, an' a man can't say more than that," cried Chook proudly, but his eyes were full of tears.

Without a word the grey-haired old man shook his head and hurried to the front door, where Mrs Partridge was waiting impatiently. She had forced the hat on Pinkey in a speech full of bitterness, and had refused the loan of a hat to see her home. To explain her bare head, she had prepared a little speech about running down without a hat because of the fine night, but Partridge was too agitated to notice what she wore.

When they stepped inside, the first thing that met Chook's eyes was the hat with the wonderful feathers lying on a chair where Pinkey had disdainfully thrown it. He stood and laughed till his ribs ached as he thought of the

190

figure cut by Mrs Partridge. He looked round for Pinkey to join in, and was amazed to find her in tears.

"W'y, wot's the matter, Liz?" he cried, serious in a moment.

"Nuthin'," said Pinkey, drying her eyes. "I was cryin' because I'm glad father made it up with yous. 'E's bin a good father to me. W'en Lil an' me was kids, 'e used ter take us out every Saturday afternoon, and buy us lollies," and the tears flowed again.

Chook wisely decided to say nothing about the banknotes till her nerves were steadier.

"'Ere, cum an' try on yer new 'at," he cried, to divert her thoughts.

"Me?" cried Pinkey, blazing. "Do yer think I'd put anythin' on my 'ead belongin' to 'er?"

"All right," said Chook, with regret, "I'll give it to mother fer one of the kids."

"Yer can burn it, if yer like," cried Pinkey.

Chook held up the hat, and examined it with interest. It was quite unlike any he had seen before.

"See 'ow it looks on yer," he coaxed.

"Not me," said Pinkey, glaring at the hat as if it were Mrs Partridge.

But Chook had made up his mind, and after a short scuffle, he dragged Pinkey before the glass with the hat on her head.

"That's back ter front, yer silly," she said, suddenly quiet.

A minute later she was staring into the glass, silent and absorbed, forgetful of Mrs Partridge, Chook, and her father.

The hat was a dream. The black trimmings and drooping feathers set off the ivory pallor of her face and made the wonderful hair gleam like threads of precious metal. She turned her head to judge it at every angle, surprised at her own beauty. Presently she lifted it off her head as tenderly as if it were a crown, with the reverence of women for the things that increase their beauty. She put it down as if it were made of glass.

"I'll git Miss Jones to alter the bow, an' put the feathers farther back," she said, like one in a dream.

"I thought yer wouldn't wear it at any price," said Chook, delighted, but puzzled.

"Sometimes you talk like a man that's bin drinkin'," said Pinkey, with the faintest possible smile.

16

A DEATH IN THE FAMILY

It was past ten o'clock, and one by one, with a sudden, swift collapse, each shop in Botany Road extinguished its lights, leaving a blank gap in the shining row of glass windows. Mrs Yabsley turned into Cardigan Street and, taking a firmer grip of her parcels, mounted the hill slowly on account of her breath. She still continued to shop at the last minute, in a panic, as her mother had done before her, proud of her habit of being the last customer at the butcher's and the grocer's. She looked up at the sky and, being anxious for the morrow, tried to forecast the weather. A sharp wind was blowing, and the stars winked cheerfully in a windswept sky. There was every promise of a fine day, but to make sure, she tried the corn on her left foot. The corn gave no sign, and she thought with satisfaction of her new companion, Miss Perkins.

For years she had searched high and low for some penniless woman to share her cottage and Jonah's allowance, and her pensioners had gone out of their way to invent new methods of robbing her. But Miss Perkins (whom she had found shivering and hungry on the doorstep as she was going to bed one night and had taken in without asking questions, as was her habit) guarded Mrs Yabsley's property like a watchdog. For Cardigan Street, when it learned that Mrs Yabsley only worked for the fun of the thing, had leaped to the conclusion that she was rolling in money. They knew that she had given Jonah his start in life, and felt certain that she owned half of the Silver Shoe.

So the older residents had come to look on Mrs Yabsley as their property, and they formed a sort of club to sponge on her methodically. They ran out of tea, sugar and flour, and kept the landlord waiting while they ran up to borrow a shilling. They each had their own day, and kept to it, respecting the rights of their friends to a share of the plunder. None went away empty-handed, and they looked with unfriendly eyes on any new arrivals who might interfere with their rights. They thought they deceived the old woman, and the tea and groceries had a finer flavour in consequence; but they would have been surprised to know that Mrs Yabsley had herself fixed her allowance from Jonah at two pounds a week and her rent.

"That's enough money fer me to play the fool with, an' if it don't do much good, it can't do much 'arm," she had remarked, with a mysterious smile, when he had offered her anything she needed to live in comfort.

The terrible Miss Perkins had altered all that. She had discovered that Mrs Harris was paying for a new hat with the shilling a week she got for Johnny's medicine; that Mrs Thorpe smelt of drink half an hour after she had got two shillings towards the rent; that Mr Hawkins had given his wife a black eye for saying that he was strong enough to go to work again. Mrs Yabsley had listened with a perplexing smile to her companion's cries of indignation.

"I could 'ave told yer all that meself," she said, "but wot's it matter? Who am I to sit in judgment on 'em? They know I've got more money than I want, but they're too proud to ask fer it openly. People with better shirts on their backs are built the same way, if all I 'ear is true. I've bin poor meself, an' yer may think there's somethin' wrong in me 'ead, but if I've got a shillin', an' some poor devil's got nuthin', I reckon I owe 'im sixpence. It isn't likely fer you to understand such things, bein' brought up in the lap of luxury, but don't yer run away with the idea that poor people are the only ones who are ashamed to beg an' willin' to steal."

Mrs Yabsley had asked no questions when she had found Miss Perkins on the step, but little by little her companion had dropped hints of former glory, and then launched into a surprising tale. She was the daughter of a rich man, who had died suddenly, and left her at the mercy of a stepmother, and she had grown desperate and fled, choosing to earn her own bread till her cousin arrived, who was on his way from England to marry her. On several occasions she had forgotten that her name was Perkins, and when Mrs Yabsley dryly commented on this, she confessed

195

that she had borrowed the name from her maid when she fled. And she whispered her real name in the ear of Mrs Yabsley, who marvelled, and promised to keep the secret.

Mrs Yabsley, who was no fool, looked for some proof of the story, and was satisfied. The girl was young and pretty, and gave herself the airs of a duchess. Mrs Swadling, indeed, had spent so much of her time at the cottage trying to worm her secret from the genteel stranger that she unconsciously imitated her aristocratic manner and way of talking, until Mr Swadling had brought her to her senses by getting drunk and giving her a pair of black eyes, which destroyed all resemblance to the fascinating stranger. Mrs Swadling had learned nothing, but she assured half the street that Miss Perkins's father had turned her out of doors for refusing to marry a man old enough to be her father, and the other half that a forged will had robbed her of thousands and a carriage and pair.

Cardigan Street had watched the aristocracy from the gallery of the theatre with sharp, envious eyes, and reported their doings to Mrs Yabsley, but Miss Perkins was the first specimen she had ever seen in the flesh. In a week she learned more about the habits of the idle rich than she had ever imagined in a lifetime. Her lodger lay in bed till ten in the morning, and expected to be waited on hand and foot. And when Mrs Yabsley could spare a minute, she described in detail the splendours of her father's home. She talked incessantly of helping Mrs Yabsley with the washing, but she seemed as helpless as a child, and Mrs Yabsley, noticing the softness and whiteness of her hands, knew that she had never done a stroke of work in her life. Then,

196

with the curious reverence of the worker for the idler, she explained to her lodger that she only worked for exercise.

When Miss Perkins came, she had nothing but what she stood up in; but one night she slipped out under cover of darkness, and returned with a dress-basket full of finery, with which she dazzled Mrs Yabsley's eyes in the seclusion of the cottage. The basket also contained a number of pots and bottles with which she spent hours before the mirror, touching up her eyebrows and cheeks and lips. When Mrs Yabsley remarked bluntly that she was young and pretty enough without these aids, she learned with amazement that all ladies in society used them.

Mrs Yabsley never tired of hearing Miss Perkins describe the splendours of her lost home. She recognized that she had lived in another world, where you lounged gracefully on velvet couches and life was one long holiday.

"It's funny," she remarked, "'ow yer run up agin things in this world. I never 'ad no partic'lar fancy fer dirty clothes an' soapsuds, but in my time, which ever way I went, I never ran agin the drorin'-room carpet an' the easy-chairs. It was the boilin' copper, the scrubbin' brush, an' the kitchen floor every time."

She was intensely interested in Miss Perkins's cousin, who was on his way from England to marry her. She described him so minutely that Mrs Yabsley would have recognized him if she had met him in the street. His income, his tastes and habits, his beautiful letters to Miss Perkins, filled Mrs Yabsley with respectful admiration. As a special favour Miss Perkins promised to read aloud one of his letters announcing his departure from England, but found that she had mislaid it. She made up for it by consulting Mrs Yabsley on the choice of a husband. Mrs Yabsley, who had often been consulted on this subject, gave her opinion.

"Some are ruled by 'is 'andsome face, an' some by 'ow much money 'e's got, but they nearly all fergit they've got ter live in the same 'ouse with 'im. Women 'ave only one way of lookin' at a man in the long run, an' if yer ask my opinion of any man, I want ter know wot 'e thinks about women. That's more important, yer'll find in the long run, than the shape of his nose or the size of 'is bankin' account."

Mrs Yabsley still hid her money, but out of the reach of rats and mice, and Miss Perkins had surprised her one day by naming the exact amount she had in her possession. And she had insisted on Mrs Yabsley going with her to the Ladies' Paradise and buying a toque, trimmed with jet, for thirty shillings, a fur tippet for twenty-five shillings, and a black cashmere dress, ready-made, for three pounds. Mrs Yabsley had never spent so much money on dress in her life, but Miss Perkins pointed out that the cadgers in Cardigan Street went out better dressed than she on Sunday, and Mrs Yabsley gave in. Miss Perkins refused to accept a fur necklet, slightly damaged by moth, reduced to twelve-and-six, but took a plain leather belt for eighteen pence. They were going out tomorrow for the first time to show the new clothes, and she had left Miss Perkins at home altering the waistband of the skirt and the hooks on the bodice, as there had been some difficulty in fitting Mrs Yabsley's enormous girth.

Mrs Yabsley's thoughts came to a sudden stop as she reached the steep part of the hill. On a steep grade her brain ceased to work, and her body became a huge, stertorous machine, demanding every ounce of vitality to force it an inch farther up the hill. Always she had to fight for wind on climbing a hill, but lately a pain like a knife in her heart had accompanied the suffocation, robbing her of all power of locomotion. The doctor had said that her heart was weak, but, judging by the rest of her body, that was nonsense, and a sniff at the medicine before she threw it away had convinced her that he was merely guessing.

When she reached the cottage she was surprised to find it in darkness, but, thinking no harm, took the key from under the doormat and went in. She lit the candle and looked round, as Jonah had done one night ten years ago. The room was unchanged. The walls were stained with grease and patches of dirt, added, slowly through the years as a face gathers wrinkles. The mottoes and almanacs alone differed. She looked round, wondering what errand had taken Miss Perkins out at that time of night. She was perplexed to see a sheet of paper with writing on it pinned to the table. Miss Perkins knew she was no scholar. Why had she gone out and left a note on the table? The pain eased in her heart, and strength came back slowly to her limbs as the suffocation in her throat lessened. At last she was able to think. She had left Miss Perkins busy with her needle and cotton, and she noticed with surprise that the clothes were gone.

With a sudden suspicion she went into the bedroom with the candle, and looked in the wardrobe made out of six yards of cretonne. The black cashmere dress, the fur tippet, and the box containing the toque with jet trimmings

199

were gone! She shrank from the truth, and, candle in hand, examined every room, searching the most unlikely corners for the missing articles. She came back and, taking the note pinned to the table, stared at it with intense curiosity. What did these black scratches mean? For the first time in her life she wished she were scholar enough to read. She had had no schooling, and when she grew up it seemed a poor way to spend the time reading, when you might be talking. Somebody always told you what was in the newspapers, and if you wanted to know anything else, why, where was your tongue? She examined the paper again, but it conveyed no meaning to her anxious eyes.

And then in a flash she saw Miss Perkins in a new light. The woman's anxiety about her was a blind to save her money from dribbling out in petty loans. Mrs Yabsley, knowing that banks were only traps, still hid her money so carefully that no one could lay hands on it. So that was the root of her care for Mrs Yabsley's appearance. She held up the note, and regarded it with a grimly humorous smile. She knew the truth now, and felt no desire to read what was written there—some lie, she supposed—and dropped it on the floor.

Suddenly she felt old and lonely, and wrapping a shawl round her shoulders, went out to her seat on the veranda. It was near eleven, and the street was humming with life. The sober and thrifty were trudging home with their loads of provisions; gossips were gathered at intervals; sudden jests were bandied, conversations were shouted across the width of the street, for it was Saturday night, and innumerable pints of beer had put Cardigan Street in a good humour.

The doors were opened, and the eye travelled straight into the front rooms lit with a kerosene lamp or a candle. Under the veranda at the corner the Push was gathered, the successors of Chook and Jonah, young and vicious, for the larrikin never grows old.

She looked on the familiar scenes that had been a part of her life since she could remember. The street was changed, she thought, for a new generation had arrived, scorning the old traditions. The terrace opposite, sinking in decay, had become a den of thieves, the scum of a city rookery. She felt a stranger in her own street, and saw that her money had spoilt her relations with her neighbours. Once she could read them like a book, but these people came to her with lies and many inventions for the sake of a few miserable shillings. She wondered what the world was coming to. She threw her thoughts into the past with an immense regret. A group on the kerbstone broke into song:

> "Now, honey, yo' stay in yo' own back yard,
>   Doan min' what dem white chiles do;
> What show yo' suppose dey's a-gwine to gib
>   A little black coon like yo'?
> So stay on this side of the high boahd fence,
>   An', honey, doan cry so hard;
> Go out an' a-play, jes' as much as yo' please,
>   But stay in yo' own back yard."

The tune, with a taking lilt in it, made no impression on the old woman. And she thought with regret that the old tunes had died out with the people who sang them. These people had lost the trick of enjoying themselves in a simple manner. Ah for the good old times, when the street was as good as a play, and the people drank and quarrelled and fought and sang without malice! A meaner race had come in their stead, with meaner habits and meaner vices. Her thoughts were interrupted by a tinkling bell, and a voice that cried "Peas an' pies, all 'ot!—all 'ot!"

It was the pieman, pushing a handcart. He went the length of the street, unnoticed. She thought of Joey, dead and gone these long years, with his shop on wheels and his air of prosperity. His widow lived on the rent of a terrace of houses, but his successor was as lean as a starved cat, for the people's tastes had changed, and the chipped-potato shop round the corner took all their money. She thought with pride of Joey and the famous wedding feast—the peas, the pies, the saveloys, the beer, the songs and laughter. Ah well, you could say what you liked, the good old times were gone for ever. Once the street was like a play, and now. . . . Her thoughts were disturbed again by a terrific noise in the terrace opposite. The door of a cottage flew open, and a woman ran screaming into the road; followed by her husband with a tomahawk. But as the door slammed behind him, he suddenly changed his mind and, turning back, hammered on the closed door with frantic rage, calling on someone within to come out and be killed. Then, as he grew tired of trying to get in, he remembered his wife, but she had disappeared.

The crowd gathered about, glad of a diversion, and the news travelled across the street to Mrs Yabsley on her veranda. Doughy the baker, stepping down unexpectedly from the Woolpack to borrow a shilling from his wife, had found her drinking beer in the kitchen with Happy Jack. And while Doughy was hammering on the front door, Happy Jack had slipped out at the back, and was watching Doughy's antics over the shoulders of his pals.

Presently Doughy grew tired and, crossing the street, sat on the kerbstone in front of Mrs Yabsley's, with his eye on the door. And as he sat, he caressed the tomahawk, and carried on a loud conversation with himself, telling all the secrets of his married life to the street. Cardigan Street was enjoying itself. The crowd dwindled as the excitement died out, and Doughy was left muttering to himself. From the group at the corner came the roar of a chorus:

"*You are my honey, honeysuckle, I am the bee,*
I'd like to sip the honey sweet from those red lips, you see;
I love you dearly, dearly, and I want you to love me;
You are my honey, honeysuckle, I am the bee."

Doughy still muttered, but the beer had deadened his senses and his jealous anger had evaporated. Half an hour later his wife crossed the street cautiously and went inside. Doughy saw her and, having reached the maudlin stage, got up and lurched across the street, anxious to make it up and be friends. Quite like the old times, thought Mrs Yabsley, when the street was as good as a play. And suddenly remembering her dismal thoughts of an hour ago, she saw in a flash that she had grown old and that the street had remained young. The past, on which her mind dwelt so fondly, was not wonderful. It was her youth that was wonderful, and now she was grown old. She recognized that the street was the same, and that she had changed—that the world is for ever beginning for some and ending for others.

It was nearly midnight, and, with a shiver, she pulled the shawl over her shoulders and took a last look at the street before she went to bed. Thirty years ago since she came to live in it, when half the street was an open paddock! If Jim could see it now he wouldn't know it! The thought brought the vision of him before her eyes. She was an old woman now, but in her mind's eye he remained for ever young and for ever joyous, the smart workman in a grey cap, with the brown moustache and laughing eyes, who was nobody's enemy but his own. Something within her had snapped when he died, and she had remained on the defensive against life, expecting nothing, surprised at nothing, content to sit out the performance like a spectator at the play.

She thought of tomorrow, and decided to pay a surprise visit to the Silver Shoe before the people set out for church. There was something wrong with Ada, she felt sure. Jonah had failed to look her in the eye when she had asked news of Ada the last time. Well, she would go and see for herself, and talk Ada into her senses again. She locked the door and went to bed.

She gave Jonah and Ada a surprise, but not in the way she intended. On Sunday morning it happened that Mrs Swadling sent over for a pinch of tea, and, growing impatient, ran across to see what was keeping Tommy. She found that he could make no one hear, and growing suspicious, called the neighbours. An hour later the police forced

204

the door, and found Mrs Yabsley dead in bed. The doctor said that she had died in her sleep from heart failure. Mrs Swadling, wondering what had become of Miss Perkins, found a note lying on the floor, and wondered no more when she read:

Dear Mrs Yabsley,

I am sorry that I can't stay for the outing tomorrow, but my cousin came out of Darlinghurst jail this morning, and we are going to the West to make a fresh start. All I told you about my beautiful home was quite true, only I was the upper housemaid. I am taking a few odds and ends that you bought for the winter, as I could never find out where you hid your money. I have searched till my back ached, and quite agree with you that it is safer than a bank. I left your clothes at Aaron's pawnshop, and will post you the ticket. When you get this I shall be safe on the steamer, which is timed to leave at ten o'clock. I hope someone will read this to you, and tell you that I admire you immensely, although I take a strange way of showing it.

In haste,

May.

17

THE TWO-UP SCHOOL

The silence of sleeping things hung over the Haymarket, and the three long, dingy arcades lay huddled and lifeless in the night, black and threatening against a cloudy sky. Presently, among the odd nocturnal sounds of a great city, the vague yelping of a dog, the scream of a locomotive, the furtive step of a prowler, the shrill cry of a feathered watchman from the roost, the ear caught a continuous rumble in the distance that changed as it grew nearer into the bumping and jolting of a heavy cart.

It was the first of a lumbering procession that had been travelling all night from the outlying suburbs—Botany, Fairfield, Willoughby, Smithfield, St Peters, Woollahra and Double Bay—carrying the patient harvest of Chinese gardens laid out with the rigid lines of a chessboard. A sleepy Chinaman, perched on a heap of cabbages, pulled the horse to a standstill, and one by one the carts backed against the kerbstone, forming a line the length of the arcades, waiting patiently for the markets to open. And still, muffled in the distance, or growing sharp and clear, the continuous rumble broke the silence, the one persistent sound in the brooding night.

Presently the iron gates creaked on rusty hinges, the long, silent arcades were flooded with the glow from clusters of electric bulbs, and, with the shuffle of feet on the stone flags, the huge market woke slowly to life, like a man who stretches himself and yawns. Outside, the carters encouraged the horses with short, guttural cries, the heavy vehicles bumped on the uneven flags, the horses' feet clattered loudly on the stones as the drivers backed the carts against the stalls, and the unloading began.

In half an hour the grimy stalls had disappeared under piles of green vegetables, built up in orderly masses by the Chinese dealers. The rank smell of cabbages filled the air, the attendants gossiped in a strange tongue, and the arcades formed three green lanes, piled with the fruits of the earth. Here and there the long green avenues were broken with splashes of colour where piles of carrots, radishes and rhubarb, the purple bulbs of beetroot, the creamy white of cauliflowers, and the soft green of eschalots and lettuce broke the dominant green of the cabbage.

The markets were transformed; it was an invasion from the East. Instead of the sharp, broken cries of the dealers on Saturday night, the shuffle of innumerable feet, the murmur of innumerable voices in a familiar tongue, there was a silence broken only by strange guttural sounds

207

dropping into a sing-song cadence, the language of the East. Chinamen stood on guard at every stall, slant-eyed and yellow, clothed in the cheap slops of Sydney, their impassive features carved in fantastic ugliness, surveying the scene with inscrutable eyes that had opened first on rice-fields, sampans, junks, pagodas, and the barbaric trappings of the silken East.

At four o'clock the sales began, and the early buyers arrived with the morose air of men who have been robbed of their sleep. There were small dealers, Dagoes from the fruit shops, greengrocers from the suburbs, with a chaff-bag slung across their arm, who buy by the dozen. They moved silently from stall to stall, pricing the vegetables, feeling the market, calculating what they would gain by waiting till the prices dropped, making the round of the markets before they filled the chaff-bags and disappeared into the darkness doubled beneath their loads.

Chook and Pinkey reached the markets by the first workman's tram in the morning. As the rain had set in, Chook had thrown the chaff-bags over his shoulders, and Pinkey wore an old jacket that she was ashamed to wear in the daytime. By her colour you could tell that they had been quarrelling as usual, because she had insisted on coming with Chook to carry one of the chaff-bags. And now, as she came into the light of the arcades, she looked like a half-drowned sparrow. The rain dripped from her hat, and the shabby thin skirt clung to her legs like a wet dishcloth. Chook looked at her with rage in his heart. These trips to the market always rolled his pride in the mud, the pride of the male who is willing to work his fingers to the bone to provide his mate with fine plumage.

The cares of the shop had told on Pinkey's looks, for the last two years spent with Chook's mother had been like a long honeymoon, and Pinkey had led the life of a lady, with nothing to do but scrub and wash and help Chook's mother keep her house like a new pin. So she had grown plump and pert like a well-fed sparrow, but the care and worry of the new shop had sharpened the angles of her body. Not that Pinkey cared. She had the instinct for property, the passionate desire to call something her own, an instinct that lay dormant and undeveloped while she lived among other people's belongings. Moreover, she had discovered a born talent for shopkeeping. With her natural desire to please, she enchanted the customers, welcoming them with a special smile, and never forgetting to remember that it was Mrs Brown's third child that had the measles, and that Mrs Smith's case puzzled the doctors. They only wanted a horse and cart, so that she could mind the shop while Chook went hawking about the streets, and their fortunes were made. But this morning the rain and Chook's temper had damped her spirits, and she looked round with dismay on the cold, silent arcades, recalling with a passionate longing the same spaces transformed by night into the noisy, picturesque bazaar through which she had been accustomed to saunter as an idler walks the block on a Saturday morning.

Pinkey waited, shivering in a corner, while Chook did the buying. He walked along the stalls, eyeing the sellers and their goods with the air of a freebooter, for, as he always had more impudence than cash, he was a redoubtable customer. There was always a touch of comedy in Chook's buying, and the Chinamen knew and dreaded him, instantly on the defensive, guarding their precious cabbages against his predatory fingers, while Chook parted with his shillings as cheerfully as a lioness parts with her cubs. A pile of superb cauliflowers caught his eye.

"'Ow muchee?" he inquired.

"Ten shilling," replied the Chinaman.

"Seven an' six," answered Chook, promptly.

"No fear," replied the seller, relapsing into Celestial gravity and resuming his dream of fan-tan and opium.

Chook walked the length of the arcade and then came back. These were the pick of the market, and he must have them. Suddenly he pushed a handful of silver into the Chinaman's hand and began to fill his bag with the cauliflowers. With a look of suspicion the seller counted the money in his hand; there were only eight shillings.

"'Ere, me no take you money," cried he, frantic with rage, trying to push the silver into Chook's hand. And then Chook overwhelmed him with a torrent of words, swearing that he had taken the money and made a sale. The Chinaman hesitated and was lost.

"All li, you no pickum," he said, sullenly.

"No fear!" said Chook, grabbing the largest he could see.

In the next arcade he bought a dozen of rhubarb, Chin Lung watching him suspiciously as he counted them into the bag.

"You gottum more'n a dozen," he cried.

"What a lie!" cried Chook, with a stare of outraged

210

virtue. "I'll push yer face in if yer say I pinched yer rotten stuff," and he emptied the rhubarb out of the bag, dexterously kicking the thirteenth bunch under the stall.

"Now are yez satisfied?" he cried, and began counting the bunches into the bag two by two. As the Chinaman watched sharply, he stooped to move a cabbage that he was standing on, and instantly Chook whipped in two bunches without counting.

"Twelve," said Chook, with a look of indignation. "I 'ope ye're satisfied: I am."

When the bags were full, Pinkey was blue with the cold, and the dawn had broken, dull and grey, beneath the pitiless fall of rain. It was no use waiting for such rain to stop, and they quarrelled again because Chook insisted that she should wait in the markets till he went home with one chaff-bag and came back for the other. Each bag, bulging with vegetables, was nearly the size of Pinkey, but the expert in moving furniture was not to be dismayed by that. She ended the dispute by seizing a bag and trudging out into the rain, bent double beneath the load, leaving Chook to curse and follow.

Halfway through breakfast Pinkey caught Chook's eye fixed on her in a peculiar manner.

"Wot are yer thinkin' about?" she asked, with a smile.

"Well, if yer want ter know, I'm thinkin' wot a fool I was to marry yer," said Chook, bitterly.

A cold wave swept over Pinkey. It flashed through her mind that he was tired of her; that he thought she wasn't strong enough to do her share of the work. Well, she could take poison or throw herself into the harbour.

"Ah!" she said, cold as a stone. "Anythin' else?"

"I mean," said Chook, stumbling for words, "I ought to 'ave 'ad more sense than ter drag yer out of a good 'ome ter come 'ere an' work like a bus 'orse."

"Is that all?" inquired Pinkey.

"Yes; wot did yer think?" said Chook, miserably. "It fair gives me the pip ter see yer 'umpin' a sack round the stalls, when I wanted ter make yer 'appy an' comfortable."

Pinkey took a long breath of relief. She needn't drown herself, then; he wasn't tired of her.

"An' who told yer I wasn't 'appy an' comfortable?" she inquired, "'cause yer can go an' tell 'em it's only a rumour. An' while ye're about it, yous can tell 'em I've got a good 'ome, a good 'usband, an' everythin' I want." Here she looked round the dingy room as if daring it to contradict her. "An' as fer the good 'ome I came from, I wasn't wanted there, an' was 'arf starved; an' now the butcher picks the best joint, an' if I lift me finger, a big 'ulkin' feller falls over 'imself ter run an' do wot I want."

Chook listened without a smile. Then his lips twitched and his eyes turned misty. Pinkey ran at him, crying, "Yer silly juggins, if I've got yous, I've got all I want." She hung round his neck, crying for pleasure, and Mrs Higgs knocked on the counter till she was tired before she got her potatoes.

The wet morning gave Pinkey a sore throat, and that finished Chook. The shop gave them a bare living, but with a horse and cart he could easily double their takings, and Pinkey could lie snug in bed while he drove to Paddy's Market in the morning. He looked round in desperation for some way of making enough money to buy Jack Ryan's horse and cart, which were still for sale. He could think of nothing but the two-up school, which had swallowed all his spare money before he was married. Since his marriage he had sworn off the school, as he couldn't spare the money with a wife to keep.

All his life Chook had lived from hand to mouth. He belonged to the class that despises its neighbours for pinching and scraping, and yet is haunted by the idea of sudden riches falling into its lap from the skies. Certainly Chook had given Fortune no excuse for neglecting him. He was always in a shilling sweep, a sixpenny raffle, a hundred to one double on the Cup. He marked pak-a-pu tickets, took the kip at two-up, and staked his last shilling more readily than the first. It was always the last shilling that was going to turn the scale and make his fortune. Well, he would try his luck again unknown to Pinkey, arguing with the blind obstinacy of the gambler that after his abstinence fate would class him as a beginner, the novice who wins a sweep with the first ticket he buys, or backs the winner at a hundred to one because he fancies its name.

Chook and Pinkey had been inseparable since their marriage, and he spent a week trying to think of some excuse for going out alone at night. But Pinkey, noticing his gloomy looks, decided that he needed livening up, and ordered him to spend a shilling on the theatre. Instantly Chook declined to go alone, and Pinkey fell into the trap. She had meant to go with him at the last moment, but now she declared that the night air made her cough. Chook could tell her all about the play when he came home. This in itself was a good omen, and when two black cats crossed his

213

path on the way to the tram, it confirmed his belief that his luck was in.

When Chook reached Castlereagh Street, he hesitated. It was market-day on Thursday, and the two sovereigns in his pocket stood for his banking account. They would last for twenty minutes, if his luck were out, and he would never forgive himself. But at that moment a black cat crossed the footpath rapidly in front of him, and his courage revived. That made the third tonight. Men were slipping in at the door of the school, which was guarded by a sentinel. Chook, being unknown, waited till he saw an acquaintance, and was then passed in. The play had not begun, and his long absence from the alley gave his surroundings an air of novelty.

The large room, furnished like a barn, gave no sign of its character, except for the ring, marked by a huge circular seat, the inner circle padded and covered with canvas to deaden the noise of falling coins. Above the ring the roof rose into a dome where the players pitched the coins. The gaffers, a motley crowd, were sitting or standing about, playing cards or throwing deck quoits to kill time till the play began. The money-changer, his pockets bulging with silver, came up, and Chook turned his sovereigns into half-crowns. Chook looked with curiosity at the crowd; they were all strangers to him.

The cards and quoits were dropped as the boxer entered the ring. It was Paddy Flynn himself, a retired pugilist, with the face and neck of a bull, wearing a sweater and sandshoes, his arms and legs bared to show the enormous muscles of the ancient athlete. He threw the kip and the

214

pennies into the centre, and took his place on a low seat at the head of the ring.

The gaffers scrambled for places, wedged in a compact circle, the spectators standing behind them to advise or take a hand as occasion offered. Chook looked at the kip, a flat piece of wood, the size of a butter-pat, and the two pennies, blackened on the tail and polished on the face. A gaffer stepped into the ring and picked them up.

"A dollar 'eads! A dollar tails! 'Arf a dollar 'eads!" roared the gamblers, making their bets.

"Get set!—get set!" cried the boxer, lolling in his seat with a nonchalant air; and in a twinkling a bright heap of silver lay in front of each player, the wagers made with the gaffers opposite. The spinner handed his stake of five shillings to the boxer, who cried "Fair go!"

The spinner placed the two pennies face down on the kip, and then, with a turn of the wrist, the coins flew twenty feet into the air. For a second there was a dead silence, every eye following the fall of the coins. One fell flat, the other rolled on its edge, every neck craned to follow its movements. One head and one tail lay in the ring.

"Two ones!" cried the boxer; and the stakes remained untouched.

The spinner tossed the coins again, and, as they fell, the gaffers cried "Two heads!"

"Two heads," repeated the boxer, with the decision of a judge.

The next moment a shower of coins flew like spray across the ring; the tails had paid their dollars to the winning heads. Three times the spinner threw heads, and the pile of silver in front of Chook grew larger. Then Chook, who was watching the spinner, noticed that he fumbled the pennies slightly as he placed them on the kip. Success had shaken his nerve, and instantly Chook changed his cry to "A dollar tails—a dollar tails!"

The coins spun into the air with a nervous jerk, and fell with the two black tails up. The spinner threw down the kip, and took his winnings from the boxer—five pounds for himself and ten shillings for the boxer.

As another man took the kip, the boxer glared at the winning players. "How is it?" he cried with the voice of a footpad demanding charity, and obeying the laws of the game, the winners threw a dollar or more from their heap to the boss.

For an hour Chook won steadily, and then at every throw the heap of coins in front of him lessened. A trot or succession of seven tails followed, and the kip changed hands rapidly, for the spinner drops the kip when he throws tails. Chook stopped betting during the trot, obeying an instinct. Without counting, his practised eye told him that there were about five pounds in the heap of coins in front of him. The seventh man threw down the kip, and Chook, as if obeying a signal, rose from his seat and walked into the centre of the ring. He handed five shillings to the boxer, and placed the pennies tail up on the kip. His stake was covered with another dollar, the betting being even money.

"Fair go!" cried the boxer.

Chook jerked the coins upward with the skill of an old gaffer; they flew into the dome, and then dropped spinning.

As they touched the canvas floor, a hundred voices cried "Two heads!"

"Two heads!" cried the boxer, and a shower of coins flew across the ring to the winners.

"A dollar or ten bob heads!" cried the boxer, staking Chook's win. Chook spun the coins again, and as they dropped heads, the boxer raked in one pound.

"Wot d'ye set?" he cried to Chook.

"The lot," cried Chook, and spun the coins. Heads again, and Chook had two pounds in the boxer's hands, who put ten shillings aside in case Chook "threw out", and staked thirty. Chook headed them again, and was three pounds to the good. The gaffers realized that a trot of heads was coming, and the boxer had to offer twelve to ten to cover Chook's stake. For the seventh time Chook threw heads, and was twelve pounds to the good. This was his dream come true, and with the faith of the gambler in omens, he knew that was the end of his luck. He set two pounds of his winnings, and tossed the coins.

"Two ones!" cried the gamblers, with a roar.

Chook threw again. One penny fell flat on its face; the other rolled on its edge across the ring. In a sudden, deadly silence, a hundred necks craned to follow its movements. Twenty or thirty pounds in dollars and half-dollars depended on the wavering coin. Suddenly it stopped, balanced as if in doubt, and fell on its face.

"Two tails!" cried the gaffers, and the trot of heads was finished. Chook's stake was swept away, and the boxer handed him ten pounds. Chook tossed a pound to him for commission. He acknowledged it with a grunt, and looking round the ring at the winning players cried out "How is it?—how is it?"

With his other winnings Chook had over fifteen pounds in his pocket, and he decided to go, although the night was young. As he went to the stairs, the boxer cried out, "No one to leave for five minutes!" following the custom when a big winner left the room, to prevent a swarm of cadgers, lug-biters, and spielers begging a tram fare, a bed, a cup of coffee from the winner. When Chook reached the top of the staircase, the G.P.O. clock began to strike, and Chook stopped to listen, for he had forgotten the lapse of time. He counted the last stroke, eleven, and then, as if it had been a signal, came the sound of voices and a noise of hammering from the front door. The next moment the doorkeeper ran up the narrow staircase crying "The Johns are here!"

For a moment the crowd of gamblers stared, aghast; then the look of trapped animals came into their faces, and with the noise of splintering wood below, they made a rush at the money on the floor. The boxer ran swearing into the ring to hide the kip and the pennies, butting with his bull shoulders against a mob of frenzied gaffers mad with fear and greed, grabbing at any coins they could reach in despair of finding their own. The news spread like fire. The school was surrounded by a hundred policemen in plain clothes and uniform; every outlet from the alley was watched and guarded. A cold scorn of the police filled Chook's mind. For months the school ran unmolested, and then a raid was planned in the spirit of sportsmen arranging a drive of rabbits for a day's outing. This raid meant capture by the police, an ignominious procession two by two to the lock-up, a night in the cells unless bail was found, and a fine and a lecture from the magistrate in the morning. To some it meant more. To the bank clerk it meant the sack; to the cashier who was twenty pounds short in his cash, an examination of his books and discovery; to the spieler who was wanted by the police, scrutiny by a hundred pair of official eyes.

The gaffers ran here and there bewildered, cursing and swearing in an impotence of rage. Like trapped rats the men ran to the windows and doors, but the room, fortified with iron bars and barbed wire, held them like a trap. The boxer cried out that bail would be found for the captured, but his bull roar was lost in the din.

There was a rush of heavy police boots on the stairs, the lights were suddenly turned out, and in the dark a wild scramble for liberty. Someone smashed a window that was not barred, and a swarm of men fought round the opening, dropping one by one on to the roof of some stables. The first man through shouted something and tried to push back, but a frenzied stream of men pushed him and the others into the arms of the police, who had marked this exit beforehand. Chook found himself on the roof, bleeding from a cut lip, and hatless. Below him men were crouching on the roofs like cats, to be picked off at the leisure of the police.

He could never understand how he escaped. He stood on the roof awaiting capture quietly, as resistance was useless, picked up a hat two sizes too large for him, and, walking slowly to the end of the roof, ducked suddenly under an old signboard that was nailed to a chimney. Every moment he expected a John to walk up to him, but, to his

219

amazement, none came. As a man may walk unhurt amid a shower of bullets, he had walked unseen under twenty policemen's eyes. From Castlereagh Street came a murmur of voices. The theatres were out, and a huge crowd, fresh from the painted scenes and stale odours of the stalls and gallery, watched with hilarious interest the harlequinade on the roofs. In half an hour a procession was formed, two deep, guarded by the police, and followed by a crowd stumbling over one another to keep pace with it, shouting words of encouragement and sympathy to the prisoners. Five minutes later Chook slithered down a veranda post, a free man, and walked quietly to the tram.

18

THE ANGEL LOSES A CUSTOMER

Six months after the death of Mrs Yabsley, Ada and Mrs Herring sat in the back parlour of the Angel sipping brandy. They had drunk their fill and it was time to be going, but Ada had no desire to move. She tapped her foot gently as she listened to the other woman's ceaseless flow of talk, but her mind was elsewhere. She had reached the stage when the world seemed a delightful place to live in; when it was a pleasure to watch the people moving and gesticulating like figures in a play, without jar or fret, as machines move on well-oiled cogs.

There was nothing to show that she had been drinking, except an uncertain smile that rippled over her heavy features as the wind breaks the surface of smooth water. Mrs Herring was as steady as a rock, but she knew without looking that the end of her nose was red, for drink affected

221

that organ as heat affects a poker. Ada looked round with affection on the small room with the sporting prints, the whisky calendar, and the gong. For months past she had felt more at home there than at the Silver Shoe.

She had never forgotten the scene that had followed her first visit to this room, when Jonah, surprised by her good humour, had smelt brandy on her breath. The sight of a misshapen devil, with murder in his eyes, spitting insults, had sobered her like cold water. She had stammered out a tale of a tea-room where she had been taken ill, and brandy had been brought in from the adjoining hotel. Mrs Herring, who had spent a lifetime in deceiving men, had prepared this story for her as one teaches a lesson to a child, but she had forgotten it until she found herself mechanically repeating it, her brain sobered by the shock. For a month she had avoided the woman with the hairy lip, and then the death of her mother had removed the only moral barrier that stood between her and hereditary impulse.

Since then she had gone to pieces. Mrs Herring had prescribed her favourite remedy for grief, a drop of cordial, and Jonah for once found himself helpless, for Mrs Herring taught Ada more tricks than a monkey. Privately she considered Ada a dull fool, but she desired her company, for she belonged to the order of sociable drunkards, for whom drink has no flavour without company, and who can no more drink alone than men can smoke in the dark. Ada was an ideal companion, rarely breaking the thread of her ceaseless babble, and never forgetting to pay for her share. It was little enough she could squeeze out of Aaron, and often she drank for the afternoon at Ada's expense.

She looked anxiously at Ada, and then at the clock. For she drank with the precision of a patient taking medicine, calculating to a drop the amount she could carry, and allowing for the slight increase of giddiness when she stepped into the fresh air of the streets. But today she felt anxious, for Ada had already drunk a glass too much, and turned from her coaxings with an obstinate smile. The more she drank, she thought, the less she would care for what Jonah said when she got home. Mrs Herring felt annoyed with her for threatening to spoil a pleasant afternoon, but she talked on to divert her thoughts from the brandy.

"And remember what I told you, dearie. Every woman should learn to manage men. Some say you should study their weak points, but that was never my way. They all like to think their word is law, and you can do anything you please if you pretend you are afraid to do anything without asking their permission. And always humour them in one thing. Now Aaron insists on punctuality. His meals must be ready on the stroke, and once he is fed, I can do as I please. Now, do be ruled by me, dearie, and come home."

But Ada had turned unmanageable, and called for more drink. Mrs Herring could have slapped her. Her practised eye told her that Ada would soon be too helpless to move, and she thought, with a cringing fear, of Aaron the Jew, and her board and lodging that depended on his stomach.

Outside it had begun to rain, and Joe Grant, a loafer by trade and a lug-biter by circumstance, shifted from one foot to another, and stared dismally at the narrow slit between the swinging doors of the Angel, where he knew there was warmth, and light, and comfort—everything that he

223

desired. The rain, fine as needle-points, fell without noise, imperceptibly covering his clothes and beard with moisture. The pavements and street darkened as if a shadow had been thrown over them, and then shone in irregular streaks and patches of light, reflected from the jets of light that suddenly appeared in the shop windows. Joe looked at the clock through the windows of the bar. It was twenty to six. The rain had brought the night before its time, and Joe wondered what had become of Mrs Jones and her pal. He had had the luck to see her going in at the side door, and she was always good for a tray bit when she came out. Failing her, he must depend on the stream of workmen, homeward bound, who always stopped at the Angel for a pint on their way home.

Suddenly the huge white globes in front of the hotel spluttered and flashed, piercing the darkness and the rain with their powerful rays. The bar, as suddenly illumined, brilliant with mirrors and glass, invited the weary passenger in to share its comforts. Joe fingered the solitary coin in his pocket—threepence. It was more than the price of a beer to him; it was the price of admission to the warm, comfortable bar every night, for the landlord was the friend of every man with the price of a drink in his pocket, and once inside, he could manage to drink at other people's expense till closing time. He kept an eye on the side door for Ada and Mrs Herring, at the same time watching each pedestrian as he emerged from the darkness into the glare of the electric lights.

The fine points of rain had gradually increased to a smart downfall, that drummed on the veranda overhead and gurgled past his feet in the gutter. Behind him, from a leak in the pipe, the water fell to the ground with a noisy splash as if someone had turned on a tap. Joe felt that he hated water like a cat. His watery blue eyes, fixed with a careless scrutiny on every face, told him in an instant whether the owner was a likely mark that he could touch for a drink, but his luck was out. He decided that the two women must have slipped out by another door.

Jonah, who had been caught in the shower, stopped for a moment under the veranda, anxious to get back to the Silver Shoe before closing time. Joe let him pass without stirring a muscle; he knew him. If you asked him for a drink, he offered you work. But, as Jonah hesitated before facing the rain again, a sudden anger flamed in his mind at the sight of Jonah's gold watch-chain and silver-mounted umbrella. Cripes, he knew that fellow when he knocked about with the Push, and now he was rolling in money! And with the sudden impulse of a suicide who throws himself under a train, he stepped up to Jonah.

"Could I 'ave a word with yer, Mr Jones?" he mumbled.

"'Ello, Smacker! Just gittin' 'ome, like myself?" said Jonah.

"Not much use gittin' 'ome to an empty 'ouse," said Joe, with a doleful whine, "an' I've earned nuthin' this week."

"'Ow do yer expect to find work, when the only place yer look fer it is in the bottom of a beer-glass?" said Jonah.

"I 'ave me faults, none knows better than meself," said Joe humbly, "but thinkin' of them won't fill me belly on a night like this."

"Now look 'ere," said Jonah, "I'm in a 'urry. I won't give yer any money, but if ye're 'ungry, come across the street, an' I'll buy yer a meal."

Joe hesitated, but the thought of good money being wasted on food was too much for him, and he played his last card.

"Look, I'll tell yer straight, Mr Jones; it's no use tryin' to pull yer leg. I can git all the tucker I want for the askin', but I'm dyin' for a beer to cheer me up an' keep out the cold."

He smiled at Jonah with an air of frankness, hoping to play on Jonah's vanity by this cynical confession, but his heart sank as Jonah replied "No, not a penny for drink," and prepared to dive into the rain.

"'Orl right, boss," muttered Joe; and then, half to himself, he added "'Ard luck, to grudge a man a pint, with 'is own missis inside there gittin' as full as a tick."

"What's that yer say?" cried Jonah, turning pale.

"Nuthin'," muttered Joe, conscious that he had made a mistake.

But a sudden light flashed on Jonah. Ada had lied to him from the beginning. She had told him that she got the drink at Paddy Boland's in the Haymarket, a notorious drinking-den for women, where spirits were served to customers, disguised as light refreshments. The fear of a public scandal in a room full of women had alone prevented him from going there to find her. It was Mrs Herring's craft to throw Jonah on the wrong scent, and sip comfortably in the back parlour of the Angel, safe from detection, a stone's throw from the Silver Shoe. Jonah turned and walked in at the side door, leaving Joe with the uneasy feeling of the man who killed the goose to get the golden eggs.

Ada had just rung the gong, insisting on another drink with the fatuous obstinacy of drunkards. She lolled in her chair, her hat tilted over one ear, watching the door for the return of Cassidy with the tray and glasses, and wondering dimly why Mrs Herring's voice sounded far away, as if she were speaking through a telephone. Mrs Herring, the tip of her nose growing a brighter red with drink and vexation, was scolding and coaxing by turns in a rapid whisper. Suddenly she stopped, her eyes fixed in a petrified stare at an apparition in the doorway. It was the devil himself, Ada's husband, the hunchback. As he stood in the doorway, his eyes travelled from her to his wife. His face turned white, a nasty greyish white, his eyes snapped like an angry cat's, and then his face hardened in a sneer. But Ada, who was fast losing consciousness of her identity, stared at her husband without fear or surprise. The deadly silence was broken by the arrival of Cassidy, who nearly ran into Jonah with the tray.

"Beg pardon," said he, briskly, and looking down found himself staring into the face of a grinning corpse.

"Don't mind me, Cassidy," said the corpse, speaking. "She can stand another glass, I think."

Cassidy put the tray down with a jerk that upset the glasses.

"I'm very sorry this should have happened, Mr Jones," he stammered. 'I'm sorry—"

"Of course you are," cried Jonah. "Ye're sorry fer anythin' that interferes with yer business of turning men and women into swine."

"Come now," said Cassidy, making a last stand on his dignity, "this is a public house, and I am bound to serve drink to anyone that asks for it. As a matter of fact, I didn't know the lady was in this condition till the barman sent me in to see what could be done."

"You're a liar, an' a fat liar. I hate fat liars—I don't know why—an' if yer tell another, I'll ram yer teeth down yer throat. She's been comin' 'ere for months, an' you've been sending her home drunk for the sake of a few shillings, to poison my life and make her name a byword in the neighbourhood. Now, listen to me! You'll not serve that woman again with drink under any pretext whatever."

"I should be glad to oblige you; but this is a public house, as I said before—"

He stopped as Jonah took a step forward, his fists clenched, transformed in a moment into Jonah the larrikin, king of the Cardigan Street Push.

"D'ye remember me, Cassidy?" he cried. "I've sent better men than you to the 'orspital in a cab. D'ye remember w'en yer were a cop with one stripe, an' we smashed every window in Flanagan's pub for laggin'? D'ye remember the time yer used ter turn fer safety down a side street w'en yer saw us comin'?"

Cassidy's face stiffened for a moment, the old policeman coming to life again at the sight of his natural enemy, the larrikin. But years of ease had buried the guardian of the law under layers of fat. He stepped hastily back from Jonah's fists.

"No, I won't hit yer; yer might splash," cried Jonah bitterly.

And Cassidy, forgetting that the dreaded Push was scattered to the winds, and trembling for the safety of his windows, spoke in a changed voice.

"I'll do anything to meet your wishes, Mr Jones. There's no call to rake up old times. We've both got on since then, and it won't pay us to be enemies. I promise you faithfully that your wife shan't be served with drink here.'

"I'm glad to 'ear it," said Jonah; "an' now yer better 'elp me ter git 'er 'ome."

He looked round the room. There were only himself, Cassidy, and Ada. Mrs Herring, who had been paralysed by the sight of the devil in the shape of a hunchback, had found herself on the footpath, sober as a judge, without very well knowing how she got there.

Ada, stupefied with brandy, and tired over the long conversation, had fallen asleep on the table. Jonah went to the door and called Joe, who was listening dismally to the hum of voices raised in argument and the pleasant clink of glasses in the bar, now filled with workmen carrying their bags of tools, their faces covered with the sweat and grime of the day.

"Fetch me a cab, Smacker," he said. "My wife's been taken ill. She fainted in the street, and they brought her here to recover."

"Right y'are, boss," cried Joe. "She turned giddy as she was walkin' past, an' yer tried to pull 'er round with a drop of brandy."

He repeated the words like a boy reciting a lesson, feeling anxiously with his thumb as he spoke, wondering if the coin Jonah had pushed into his hand was a florin or a half-dollar.

Cassidy and Joe, one on each side, helped Ada into the cab. Her feet scraped helplessly over the flagged pavement, her head lolled on her shoulder, and the baleful white gleam of the huge electric lamps fell like limelight on her face contracted in an atrocious leer.

The Silver Shoe was closed and in darkness, and Jonah drew a breath of relief. The neighbours were at their tea, and he could get his shameful burden in unseen. Prendergast, the cabman, helped him to drag Ada across the shop to the foot of the stairs, where with an oath he threw her across his shoulder, and ran up the winding staircase as if he were carrying a bag of chaff.

Suddenly the door on the landing opened, throwing a flood of light on their faces, and Jonah was astonished to see Miss Grimes, trim and neat, looking in alarm from him to the cabman and his burden. As Prendergast dropped Ada on the couch, she took a step forward.

"What has happened? Is she hurt?" she asked, bending over Ada; but the next moment she turned away.

This unconscious movement of disgust maddened Jonah. What was she doing there to see his humiliation?

"No, she's not hurt," said Jonah dryly. "But wot are you doing 'ere?" he added.

His tone nettled the young woman, and she coloured.

"I'm sorry I'm in the way," she said stiffly, "but Mr Johnson locked up, and was anxious to get away, and as I was giving Ray his lesson, I offered to stay with him till someone came."

"I beg yer pardon," said Jonah. "I'm much obliged to yer fer mindin' the kid, but I didn't want yer to see this."

"I've known it all the time," said Clara, quietly.

"Ah," said Jonah, understanding many things in a flash.

He caught sight of Ray, staring open-mouthed at his mother lying so strangely huddled on the couch.

"Yer mother's tired, Ray," he said. "Go an' boil the kettle; she'll want some tea when she wakes up."

"That's 'ow I 'ave ter lie to everybody; an' I suppose they all know the truth, an' nod an' wink behind my back," he cried bitterly. "I've tried all I know; but now 'er mother's gone, I'm fair beat. People envy me because I've got on, but they little know wot a millstone I've got round my neck."

He lifted his head, and look steadily at Ada snoring in a drunken sleep on the couch. And to Clara's surprise, his face suddenly changed; tears stood in his eyes.

"Poor devil! I don't know that she's to blame altogether. It's in her blood. Her father went the same way. My money's done 'er no good. She'd 'ave been better off in Cardigan Street on two pounds a week."

Clara was surprised at the pity in his voice. She thought that he loathed and despised his wife. Suddenly Jonah looked up at her.

"Will yer meet me tomorrow afternoon?" he asked abruptly.

"Why?" said Clara, alarmed and surprised.

"I want yer to 'elp me. Since 'er mother died, she's gone from bad to worse. I've got no one to 'elp me, an' I feel I'll burst if I don't talk it over with somebody."

"I hardly know," replied Clara, taken by surprise.

"Say the Mosman boat at half past two, an' I'll be there," said Jonah brusquely.

"Very well," said Clara.

19

THE PIPES OF PAN

Circular Quay, shaped like a bite in a slice of bread, caught the eye like a moving picture. The narrow strip of roadway, hemmed in between the Customs House and the huge wool stores, was alive with the multitudinous activity of an ant-hill. A string of electric cars slid past the jetties in parallel lines or climbed the sharp curve to Phillip Street; and every minute cars, loaded with passengers from the dusty suburbs, swung round the corners of the main streets and stopped in front of the ferries. And as the cars stopped, the human cargo emptied itself into the roadway and hurried to the turnstiles, harassed by the thought of missing the next boat.

From the waterside, where the great mail steamers lay moored along the Quay, came the sudden rattle of winches, the cries of men unloading cargo, and the shrill hoot of small steamers crossing the bay. Where the green waters licked the piles and gurgled under the jetties, waterside loafers sat on the edge of the wharves intently watching a fishing-line thrown out. Men in greasy clothes and flannel shirts, with the look of the sea in their eyes, smoked and spat as they watched the ships in brooding silence. For of all structures contrived by the hands of man, a ship is the most fascinating. It is so complete, so perfect in its devices and ingenuity, a house and a habitation for men set adrift on the waste of waters, plunging headlong into danger and romance with its long spars and coiled ropes, its tarry sailors roaring a sea-chanty, and the common habits of eating and sleeping accomplished in a spirit of adventure.

Two streams, mainly women, met at the turnstiles—mothers and children from the crowded, dusty suburbs, drawn by the sudden heat of an autumn sun in a cloudless sky to the harbour for a day in the open air, and the leisured ladies of the North Shore, calm and collected, dressed in expensive materials, crossing from the fashionable waterside suburbs to the Quay to saunter idly round the Block, look in the shops, and drink a cup of tea.

Jonah, who had been standing outside the Mosman ferry for the last half-hour, looked at the clock in the Customs House opposite, and swore to himself. It was on the stroke of three, and she would miss the boat, as usual. It was always the same—she was always late; and when he had worked himself into a fury, deciding to wait another minute, and then to go home, she would suddenly appear breathless, with a smile and an apology that took the words out of his mouth.

He watched each tram as it stopped, looking for one face and figure among the moving crowd, for he had learned to know her walk in the distance while her features were a blur. For months past he had endured that supreme tyranny —the domination of the woman—till his whole life seemed to be spent between thinking about her and waiting for her at appointed corners. The hours they spent together fled with incredible speed, and she always shortened the flying minutes by coming late, with one of half a dozen excuses that he knew by heart.

Their first meeting had been at the Quay the day after he had brought Ada home drunk from the Angel, and since then a silent understanding had grown between them that they should always meet there and cross the water, as Jonah's conspicuous figure made recognition very likely in the streets and parks of the city.

The first passion of his life—love of his child—had for ever stamped on his brain the scenes and atmosphere of Cardigan Street, the struggle for life on the Road, and the march of triumph to the Silver Shoe. And this, the second passion of his life—love of a woman—was set like a stage-play among the wide spaces of sea and sky, the flight of gulls, the encircling hills, and the rough, salt breath of the harbour.

Suddenly he saw her crossing the road, threading her way between the electric cars, and noted with intense satisfaction the distinction of her figure, clothed in light tweed, with an air of scrupulous neatness in which she could hold her own with the rich idlers from the Shore. She smiled at him with her peculiar, intense look, and then

235

frowned slightly. Jonah knew that something was wrong, and remembered that he had forgotten to raise his hat, an accomplishment that she had taught him with much difficulty.

"So sorry to be late, but I couldn't really help it. I'll tell you presently," she said, as they passed the turnstiles.

Jonah knew by her voice that she was in a bad temper, and his heart sank. The afternoon that he had waited for and counted on for nearly a week would be spoiled. Never before in his life had his pleasures depended on the humour or caprice of anyone, but he had learned with dismal surprise that a word or a look from this woman could make or mar the day for him. He gave her a sidelong look, and saw she was angry by a certain hardness in her profile, and, as he stared moodily at the water, he wondered if all women were as mutable and capricious. In his dealings with women—shophands who moved at his bidding like machines—he had never suspected these gusts of emotion that ended as suddenly as they began. Ada had the nerves of a cow.

Over the way the Manly boat was filling slowly with mothers and children and stray couples. A lamentable band on the upper deck mixed popular airs with the rattle of winches. The Quay was alive with ferry-boats, blunt-nosed and squat like a flat-iron, churning the water with invisible screws. A string of lascars from the P. & O. boat caught his eye with a patch of colour, the white calico trousers, the gay embroidered vests, and the red or white turbans bringing a touch of the East to Sydney. Suddenly the piles of the jetty slipped to the rear, and the boat moved out past

236

the huge mail-steamers from London, Marseilles, Bremen, Hongkong, and Yokohama lying at the wharves.

As they rounded the point the warships swung into view, grim and forbidding, with the ugly strength of bull-dogs. A light breeze flicked the waters of the harbour into white flakes like the lash of a whip, and Jonah felt the salt breath of the sea on his cheeks. His eye travelled over the broad sheet of water from the South Head, where the long rollers of the Pacific entered and broke with a muscular curve, to the shores broken by innumerable curves into bays where the moving waters, already tamed, lost their beauty like a caged animal, and spent themselves in fretful ripples on the sand. Overhead the sky, arched in a cloudless dome of blue, was reflected in the turquoise depths of the water.

Then Mosman came in sight with its shaggy slopes and terra-cotta roofs, the houses, on the pattern of a Swiss chalet, standing with spaces between, fashionable and reserved. Jonah thought of Cardigan Street, and smiled. They walked in silence along the path to Cremorne Point, the noise of birds and the rustling of leaves bringing a touch of the country to Jonah.

"Had you been waiting long?" asked Clara, suddenly.

"Since twenty past two," replied Jonah.

"The impudence of some people is incredible," she said. "I've just lost a pupil and a guinea a quarter—it's the same thing. The mother thought I should buy the music for the child out of the guinea. That means a hat and a pair of gloves or a pair of boots less through no fault of my own...You don't seem very sympathetic," she cried, looking sharply at Jonah.

237

"I ain't," said Jonah, calmly.

"Well, I must say you don't pick your words. A guinea may be nothing to you, but it means a great deal to me."

"It ain't that," said Jonah, "but I hate the thought of yer bein' at the beck an' call of people who ain't fit to clean yer boots. Ye're like a kid 'oldin' its finger in the fire an' yellin' with pain. There's no need fer yer to do it. I've offered ter make yer cashier in the shop at two pounds a week, if yer'd put yer pride in yer pocket."

"And throw a poor girl out of work to step into her shoes."

"Nuthin' of the sort, as I told yer. She's been threatenin' fer months to git married, but it 'urts 'er to give up a good billet an' live on three pounds a week. Yer'd do the bloke a kindness, if yer made me give 'er the sack."

"It's no use. My mother wouldn't listen to it. For years she's half starved herself to keep me out of a shop. She can never forget that her people in England are gentry."

"I don't know much about gentry, but I could teach them an' yer mother some common sense," said Jonah.

"We won't discuss my mother, if you please," said Clara, and they both fell silent.

They had reached the end of Cremorne Point, a spur of rock running into the harbour. Clara ran forward with a cry of pleasure, her troubles forgotten as she saw the harbour lying like a map at her feet. The opposite shore curved into miniature bays, with the spires and towers of the city etched on a filmy blue sky. The mass of bricks and mortar in front was Paddington and Woollahra, leafless and dusty where they had trampled the trees and green grass beneath their feet; the streets cut like furrows in a field of brick. As the eye travelled eastward from Double Bay to South Head the red roofs became scarcer, alternating with clumps of sombre foliage. Clara looked at the scene with parted lips as she listened to music. This frank delight in scenery had amused Jonah at first. It was part of a woman's delight in the pretty and useless. But, as his eyes had become accustomed to the view, he had begun to understand. There was no scenery in Cardigan Street, and he had been too busy in later years to give more than a hasty glance at the harbour. There was no money in it.

From where they sat they could see a fleet of tramps and cargo-boats lying at anchor on their right. Jonah examined them attentively, and then his eyes turned to the city, piled massively in the sunlight, studded with spires and towers and tall chimneys belching smoke into the upper air. It was this city that had given him life on bitter terms, a misshapen and neglected street-arab, scouring the streets for food, of less account than a stray dog.

His eye softened as he looked again at the water. As the safest place for their excursions they had picked by chance on the harbour with its fleet of steamers that threaded every bay and cove, and little by little, in the exaltation of the senses following his love for this woman, the swish of the water slipping past the bows, the panorama of rock and sandy beach, and the salt smell of the sea were for ever part of this strange, emotional condition where reality and dream blended without visible jar or shock.

He turned and looked at the woman beside him. She was silent, looking seaward. He stared at her profile, cut like a cameo, with intense satisfaction. The low, straight forehead, the straight nose, the full curving chin, satisfied his eye like a carved statue. About her ear, exquisitely small and delicate, the wind had blown a fluff of loose hair, and on this insignificant detail his eye dwelt with rapture. This woman's face pleased him like music. And as he looked, all his desires were melted and confounded in a wave of tenderness, caressing and devotional, the complete surrender of strength to weakness. He wanted to take her in his arms, and dared not even touch her hand. There had been no talk of love between them, and she had kept him at a distance with her air of distinction and superficial refinements. She seemed to spread a silken barrier between them that exasperated and entranced him. Some identity in his sensations puzzled him, and as he looked, with a flash he was in Cardigan Street again, stooping over his child with a strange sensation in his heart, learning his first lesson in pity and infinite tenderness. Another moment and he would have taken her in his arms. Instead of that, he said "I'm putting that line of patent leather pumps in the catalogue at seven and elevenpence, post free."

Instantly Clara became attentive.

"You mean those with the buckles and straps? They'll go like hot cakes!"

"They ought to," said Jonah, dryly. "Post free brings them a shade below cost price."

"A shade below cost?" said Clara in surprise. "I thought you bought them at seven and six?"

"So I do," replied Jonah; "but add twelve per cent for working expenses, an' where's the profit? Packard's manager puts them in the window at eight an' six, an' wonders why they don't sell. His girls come straight from the factory and buy them off me. They're the sort I want—waitresses, dressmakers, shop-hands, bits of girls that go without their meals to doll themselves up. They want the cheapest they can get, an' they're always buying."

And at once they plunged into a discussion on the business of the Silver Shoe. Clara always listened with fascination to the details of buying and selling. Novelettes left her cold, but the devices to attract customers, the lines that were sold at a loss for advertisement, the history of the famous Silver Shoe that Jonah sold in thousands at a halfpenny a pair profit, astonished her like a fairy-tale that happened to be real.

One day, while shopping at Jordan's mammoth cash store, her ear had caught the repeated clink of metal, and turning her head, she stood on the stairs, thunderstruck. She saw a square room lit with electric bulbs in broad daylight. It was the terminus of a multitude of shining brass tubes leading from counters the length of a street away, and, with an incessant popping, the tubes dropped a cascade of gold and silver before the cashiers, silent and absorbed in this river of coin. She felt that she was looking at the heart of this huge machine for drawing money from the pockets of the multitude. The Silver Shoe, that poured a stream of golden coins into the pockets of the hunchback, fascinated her in a like manner.

They had talked for half an hour, intent on figures which Jonah dotted on the back of an envelope, when they were surprised by a sudden change in the light. The sun was low in the sky, dipping to the horizon, where its motion seemed more rapid, as if it had gathered speed in the descent. The sudden heat had thrown a haze over the sky, and the city with its spires and towers was transformed. The buildings floated in a liquid veil with the unreality of things seen in a dream. The rays of the sun, filtered through bars of crystal cloud, fell not crimson nor amber nor gold, but with the mystic radiance of liquid pearls, touching the familiar scene with Eastern magic. In the silvery light a dome reared its head that might have belonged to an Eastern mosque with a muezzin calling the faithful to prayers. Minarets glistered, remote and ethereal, and tall spires lifted themselves like arrows in flight. On the left lay low hills softly outlined against the pearly sky; hills of fairyland that might dissolve and disappear with the falling night; hills on the borderland of fantasy and old romance.

And as they watched, surprised out of themselves by this magic play of light, the sun's rim dipped below the skyline, a level lake of blood, and the fantastic city melted like a dream. The pearly haze was withdrawn like a net of gossamer, and the magic city had vanished at a touch. The familiar towers and spires of Sydney reappeared, silhouetted against the amber rim of night; the hills, robbed of their pearly glamour, huddled beneath a belt of leaden cloud; the harbour waters lay flat and grey like a sheet of polished metal; light clouds were pacing in from the sea.

They stared across the water, silent and thoughtful, touched for a moment with the glamour of a dream. The sound of a cornet, prolonged into a wail, reached them from the deck of a Manly steamer. At intervals the full strength of the band, cheerful and vulgar, was carried by a gust of wind to their ears.

"Oh, I would like to hear some music!" cried Clara. "Something slow and solemn, a dirge for the dying day."

Jonah turned and looked at her curiously, surprised by the gush of emotion in her voice. He started to speak, and hesitated. Then the words came with a rush.

"I could give yer a tune meself, but I suppose yer'd poke borak."

"Give me a tune? I never knew you could sing," said Clara, in surprise.

"Sing!" said Jonah, in scorn. "I can beat any singin' w'en I'm in good nick."

"Whatever do you mean?" said Clara. She was surprised to see that the habitual shrewd look had gone out of his eyes. He looked half ashamed and defiant.

"Yer remember w'en I first met yer in the shop I mentioned that I could do a bit with the mouth-organ?"

"The mouth-organ?" said Clara, smiling. "I thought only boys amused themselves with that."

"No fear!" cried Jonah. "I 'eard a bloke at the Tiv. play a fair treat. That's 'ow I come to git this instrument," and he tapped something in his breast pocket. "Kramer's 'ad to send 'ome for it, an' I only got it this afternoon. I've bin dyin' to 'ave a go at it, but I always wait till I git the place to meself. It wouldn't do for the 'ands to see the boss playin' the mouth-organ."

He took the instrument out of his pocket, and handed it to Clara with the pride of a fiddler showing his Strad.

243

Clara looked carelessly at the flat row of tubes cased in nickel-silver.

"Exhibition concert organ with forty reeds," said Jonah.

Again Clara looked at the instrument with a slightly disdainful air, as an organist would look at a penny whistle.

"Well, play something," she said with a smile.

Jonah breathed slowly into the reeds, up and down the scale, testing the compass of the instrument. It was full and rich, unlike any that she had heard in the streets. Presently he struck into a popular ballad from the music-hall, holding the organ to his mouth with the left hand. With his right he covered the pipes to control the volume of sound as a pianist uses the pedals. When he had finished, Clara smiled in encouragement, with a secret feeling that he was making himself ridiculous. She looked across the water, wishing he would put the thing away and stop this absurd exhibition. But Jonah had warmed up to his work. He was back in Cardigan Street again, when the Push marched through the streets with him in the lead, playing tunes that he had learned at the music-halls.

In five minutes Clara's uneasiness had vanished, and she was listening to the music with a dreamy languor quite foreign to her usual composure. Her mind was filled with the fantastic splendour of the sunset; the fresh salt air had acted like a drug; and the sounds breathed into the reeds made her nerves vibrate like strings. Strange, lawless thoughts floated in her mind. The world was meant for love, and passionate sadness, and breaking hearts that healed at the glance of an eye. And as her ear followed the tune,

244

her eyes were drawn with an irresistible movement to the musician. She found him staring at her with a magnetic look in his eyes.

He was no longer ridiculous. The large head, wedged beneath the shoulders, the projecting hump, monstrous and inhuman, and the music breathed into the reeds set him apart as a sinister, uncanny being. She frowned in an effort to think what the strange figure reminded her of, and suddenly she remembered. It was the god Pan, the goat-footed lord of rivers and woods, sitting beside her, who blew into his pipes and stirred the blood of men and women to frenzies of joy and fear. There was fear and exultation in her heart. A pagan voluptuousness spread through her limbs. Jonah paused for a moment, and then broke into the pick of his repertory. And Clara listened, hypnotized by the sounds, her brain mechanically fitting the words to the tune:

> *"Come to me, sweet Marie, sweet Marie, come to me!*
> *Not because your face is fair, love, to see;*
> *But your soul, so pure and sweet,*
> *Makes my happiness complete,*
> *Makes me falter at your feet, sweet Marie."*

The vulgar, insipid words rang as plainly in her ears as if a voice were singing them. Jonah stopped playing, and stared at her with a curious glitter in his eyes. She felt, in a dazed, dreamy fashion, that this was the hunchback's declaration of love. The hurdy-gurdy tune and the unsung words had acted like a spell. For a space of seconds she gazed with a fixed look at Jonah, waiting for him to move or

245

speak. She seemed to be slipping down a precipice without the power or desire to resist. Then, like a fit of giddiness, the sensation passed. She stumbled to her feet and ran wildly down the rocky path to the wharf where the ferry-boat, glittering with electric lights, like a gigantic firefly, was waiting at the jetty.

Chook caught the last tram home, and found Pinkey asleep in bed with a novelette in her hand. She had fallen asleep reading it. The noise of Chook's entry roused her, and she stared at him, uncertain of the hour. Then, seeing him fully dressed, she decided that it was four o'clock in the morning, and that he was trying to sneak off to Paddy's Market without her. She was awake in an instant, and her face flushed pink with anger as she jumped out of bed, indignant at being deprived of her share of the unpleasant trip to the markets. Three times a week she nerved herself for that heartbreaking journey in the raw morning air, resolved never to let Chook see her flinch from her duty. As she started to dress herself with feverish haste, Chook recovered enough from his astonishment to ask her where she was going.

247

"To Paddy's, of course," she replied fiercely. "Yer sneaked off last week on yer own, an' cum 'ome so knocked out that yer couldn't eat yer breakfast."

A cold shiver ran through Chook. Her mind was affected, and in a flash he saw his wife taken to the asylum and himself left desolate. Then he understood, and burst into a roar.

"Git into bed again, Liz," he cried. "Ye're walkin' in yer sleep."

"Wot's the time?" she asked, with a suspicious look.

"Five past twelve," said Chook, reluctantly.

"An' ye're only just come 'ome! Wot d'ye mean by stoppin' out till this time of night?" she cried, turning on him furiously, but secretly relieved, like a patient who finds the dentist is out.

"The play was out late, an' we…" stammered Chook.

As he stammered, Pinkey caught sight of a rip in his sleeve, and looking at him intently, was horrified to see his lip cut and bleeding. She gave a cry of terror and burst into tears.

"Yer never went to no play; yer've bin fightin'," she sobbed.

"No, I ain't, fair dinkum," cried Chook. "I'll tell yer 'ow I come by this, if yer wait a minute."

"Yer never cut yer lip lookin' at the play; yer've gone back ter the Push, as Sarah always said yer would."

"I'll screw Sarah's neck when I can spare the time," said Chook, savagely.

Chook, the old-time larrikin, had turned out a model husband, but, for years after his marriage, Mrs Partridge had taken a delight in prophesying that he would soon tire of Pinkey's apron-strings and return to the Push and the streets. And now, although Waxy Collins and Joe Crutch were in jail for sneak-thieving, their places taken by younger and more vicious scum, Pinkey thought instantly of the dread Push when Chook grew restive.

"No," said Chook, deciding to cut it short, "I tore me coat an' cut me lip gittin' away from the Johns at Paddy Flynn's alley."

Pinkey turned sick with fear. The two-up school was worse than the Push, and they were ruined.

"I knew it the moment I set eyes on yer. Yer've been bettin' again, an' lost all yer money. Yer've got nothing left for the markets, an' the landlord'll turn us out," she cried, seeing herself already in the gutter.

"Yes, I lost a bit, but I pulled up, an' I'm a couple of dollars to the good," said Chook, feeling in his pocket for some half-crowns.

"Well, give it to me," said Pinkey, "an' I'll go straight termorrer and pay ten shillings on a machine."

"Wot would yer 'ave said if I'd won ten or fifteen quid?" asked Chook.

"I should 'ave said 'Buy Jack Ryan's 'orse an' cart, an' never go near a two-up school again'," said Pinkey, thinking of the impossible.

"Well, I won the dollars, an' I'll do as yer say," cried Chook, emptying his pockets on the counterpane.

As Chook poured the heap of gold and silver on to the bed, Pinkey gasped, and turned deadly white. Chook thought she was going to faint.

249

"It's all right, Liz," he cried. "I've 'ad a good win, an' we're set up fer life."

He was busy sorting the gold and silver into heaps, first putting aside his stake, two pounds ten. There were fifteen pounds twelve shillings and sixpence left. Pinkey stared in amazement. It seemed incredible that so much money could belong to them. And suddenly she thought, with a pang of joy, that no longer would she need to nerve herself for the cruel journey to the markets in the morning. Chook would drive down in his own cart, and she would be waiting on his return with a good breakfast. They had gone up in the world like a rocket.

The marriage of Pinkey, three years ago, had affected Mrs Partridge like the loss of a limb. For over two years she had been chained to the same house, in the same street, with the desire but not the power to move. Only once had she managed to change her quarters with the aid of William, and the result had been disastrous. For the first time in his life William had lost a day at Grimshaw's to move the furniture, and for six months he had brooded over the lost time. This last move had planted them in Botany Street, five minutes' walk from Chook's shop. At first Mrs Partridge had fretted, finding little consolation in the new ham-and-beef shop on Botany Road; and then, little by little, she had become attached to the neighbourhood. She had been surprised to find that entertainment came to her door unsought, in the form of constant arrivals and departures among the neighbours. And each of them was the beginning or the end of a mystery, which she probed to the bottom with the aid of the postman, the baker, the butcher, and the tradesmen who were left lamenting with their bills unpaid. Never before in her wanderings had she got so completely in touch with her surroundings.

But from habit she always talked of moving. She could never pass an empty house without going through it, sniffing the drains, and requesting the landlord to make certain improvements, with the mania of women who haunt the shops with empty purses, pricing expensive materials. Every week she announced to Chook and Pinkey that she had found the very house, if William would take a day off to move. But in her heart she had no desire to leave the neighbourhood. It was an agreeable and daily diversion for her to run up to the shop, and prophesy ruin and disaster to Chook and Pinkey for taking a shop that had beggared the last tenant, ignoring the fact that Jack Ryan had converted his profits into beer. Chook's rough tongue made her wince at times, but she refused to take offence for more than a day. She had taken a fancy to Chook the moment she had set eyes on him, and was sure Pinkey was responsible for his sudden bursts of temper. She thought to do him a service by dwelling on Pinkey's weak points, and Chook showed his gratitude by scowling. Pinkey, who had been a machinist in the factory, was no hand with a needle, and Mrs Partridge commented on this in Chook's hearing.

"An' fancy 'er 'ardly able to sew on a button, which is very dangerous lyin' about on the floor, as children will eat any-thin', not knowin' the consequences," she cried.

Chook pointed out that there were no children in the house to eat stray buttons.

"An' thankful you ought to be for that," she cried.

"There's Mrs Brown's baby expectin' to be waited on 'and an' foot, an' thinks nothin' of wakin' 'er up in the night, cryin' its heart out one minute, an' cooin' like a dove the next, though I don't 'old with keepin' birds in the 'ouse as makes an awful mess, an' always the fear of a nasty nip through the bars of the cage, which means a piece of rag tied round your finger."

Here she stopped for breath, and Chook turned aside the torrent of words by offering her some vegetables, riddled with grubs, for the trouble of carrying them home. She considered herself one of Chook's best customers, having dealt off him since their first meeting. Every market-day she came to the shop, picked out everything that was damaged or bruised, and bought it at her own price. She often wished that Pinkey had married a grocer.

Chook had said nothing to her of his win at the two-up school, and she only heard of it at the last moment through a neighbour. She put on her hat, and just reached the shop in time to see Chook drive up to the door in his own horse and cart. Pinkey was standing there, radiant, her dreams come true, already feeling that their fortunes were made. Mrs Partridge looked on with a choking sensation in her throat, desiring nothing for herself, but angry with Fortune for showering her gifts on others. Then she stepped up briskly, and cried out:

"I 'eard all about yer luck, an' I sez to myself, 'it couldn't 'ave 'appened to a more deservin' young feller.' You'll ride in yer carriage yet, mark my words."

She came nearer and stared at the mare, anxious to find fault, but knowing nothing of the points of a horse.

252

She decided to make friends with it, and rubbed its nose. The animal, giving her an affectionate look, furtively tried to bite her arm, and then threw back its head, expecting the rap on the nose that always followed this attempt. Mrs Partridge trembled with fear and rage.

"Well, I never!" she cried. "The sly brute! Looked at me like a 'uman being, an' then tried to eat me, which I could never understand people preachin' about kindness to dumb animals, an' 'orses takin' a delight in runnin' over people in the street every day."

"It's because they've got relations that makes 'em thankful animals are dumb," said Chook.

"Meaning me?" cried Mrs Partridge, smelling an insult.

"You?" said Chook, affecting surprise. "I niver mind yous talkin'. It goes in one ear an' out of the other."

Mrs Partridge bounced out of the shop in a rage, but next day she came back to tell Pinkey that she had found the very house in Surry Hills for a shilling a week less rent. She stayed long enough to frighten the life out of Pinkey by telling her that she had heard that Jack Ryan was well rid of the horse, because it had a habit of bolting and breaking the driver's neck. Chook found Pinkey trembling for his safety, and determined to put a stop to these annoyances. He disappeared for a whole day, and when Pinkey wanted to know where he had been, he told her to wait and see. They nearly quarrelled. But the next morning he gave her a surprise. After breakfast he announced that he was going to take her to the Druids' picnic in his own cart, and that Mrs Partridge had consented to mind the shop in their absence.

When Chook asked Mrs Partridge to mind the shop for the day, she jumped at the idea. She felt that she had a gift for business which she had wasted by not marrying the greengrocer; and now, with the shop to herself, she would show them how to deal with the customers, and find time in between to run her eye through Pinkey's boxes. She, too, would have a holiday after her own heart. She decided to wear her best skirt and blouse, to keep the customers in their place and remind them that she was independent of their favours. She found everything ready on her arrival. The price of every vegetable was freshly painted on the window by Chook in white letters, and there were five shillings in small change in the till. Lunch was set for her on the kitchen table, a sight to make the mouth water, for Chook, remembering the days of his courting, had ransacked the ham-and-beef shop for dainties—sheep's trotters, brawn, pig's cheek, ham-and-chicken sausage, and a bottle of mixed pickles. Nothing was wanting. As Chook drove off with Pinkey, she waved her hand to them, and then, surveying the street with the air of a proprietor, entered the shop and took possession.

They were going to Sir Joseph Banks's for the picnic; but, to Pinkey's surprise, the cart turned into Botany Street and pulled up in front of Sarah's cottage.

"Wotcher stoppin' 'ere for?" she inquired.

"'Cause we're goin' ter git out," said Chook, with a grin.

"Git out? Wot for? There's nobody at 'ome, Dad's at work."

"I know; that's w'y I came," said Chook, tying the reins to the seat. "Git down, Liz; yer've got a 'ard day in front of yer."

"'Ard day? Wotcher mean?" cried Pinkey, suspiciously.

"We're goin' ter move Sarah's furniture to the new 'ouse she found in Surry Hills," replied Chook.

"She never took no 'ouse," said Pinkey.

"No, I took it yesterday in 'er name," said Chook, grinning at Pinkey's perplexed frown. "I wanted ter give 'er a pleasant surprise fer' 'er birthday."

"Wot about the picnic?" exclaimed Pinkey, suddenly.

"There ain't no picnic," said Chook. "It's next Monday; the date must 'ave slipped me mind."

"An' yer mean ter move 'er furniture in without 'er knowin'?"

"That's the dart," said Chook, with a vicious smile. "If Sarah's tongue don't git a change of air, I'll git three months fer murder. So 'urry up, Liz, an' put this apron over yer skirt."

The impudence of Chook's plan took her breath away, but when he insisted that there was no other way of getting rid of Mrs Partridge, she consented, with the feeling that she was taking part in a burglary. Chook took the key from under the flower-pot and went in. They found the place like a pigsty, for in the excitement of dressing for her day behind the counter, Sarah had wasted no time in making the bed or washing up, and Pinkey, trained under the watchful eye of Chook's mother, stood aghast. She declared that nothing could be done till that mess was cleared away, and tucked up her sleeves.

The appearance of the cart had roused the neighbours' curiosity, and Chook engaged them in conversation over the back fence. He explained that Mrs Partridge had begged him to come down and move her furniture while she minded the shop. There was a general sigh of relief. Nothing had escaped her eye or tongue. Mrs King, who was supposed to be temperance, did wonders with the bottle under her apron, but was caught. Then she found out that Mrs Robinson's brother, who was supposed to be doing well in the country, was really doing seven years. Chook refused half a dozen offers of help before Pinkey had finished washing up.

As Chook lacked the professional skill of Jimmy the van-man, Pinkey was obliged to make two loads of the furniture; but by twelve o'clock the last stick was on the cart, and Pinkey, sitting beside her husband on a plank, carried the kerosene lamp in her lap to prevent breakage. By sunset everything was in its place, and Chook and Pinkey, aching in every joint, locked the door and drove home.

Meanwhile, Mrs Partridge had spent a pleasant day conducting Chook's business on new lines. She had always suspected that she had a gift for business, and here was an opportunity to prove it. The first customer was a child, sent for three penn'orth of potatoes. As children are naturally careless, Mrs Partridge saw here an excellent opportunity for weeding out the stock, and went to a lot of trouble in picking out the small and damaged tubers, reserving the best for customers who came to choose for themselves. Five minutes later she was exchanging them for the largest in the sack under the direction of an infuriated mother.

This flustered her slightly, and when Mrs Green arrived, complaining of rheumatic twinges in her leg, she decided to try Pinkey's sympathetic manner.

"Ah, if anybody knows what rheumatism is, I do," she cried. "For years I suffered cruelly, an' then I was persuaded to carry a new pertater in me pocket, an' I've never 'ad ache or pain since; though gettin' cured, to my mind, depends on the sort of life you've led."

Mrs Green, a woman with a past, flushed heavily.

"'Oo are yer slingin' off at?" she cried. "You and yer new pertater. I'd smack yer face for two pins," and she walked out of the shop.

This made Mrs Partridge careful, and she served the next customers in an amazing silence. Then she dined royally on the pick of the ham-and-beef shop, and settled down for the afternoon. But she recovered her tongue when Mrs Paterson wanted some lettuce for a salad.

"Which I could never understand people eatin' salads, as I shall always consider bad for the stomach, an' descendin' to the lower animals," she cried. "Nothing could make me believe I was meant to eat vegetables raw when I can 'ave them boiled an' strained for 'alf an 'our."

In her eagerness to convert Mrs Paterson to her views, she forgot to charge for the lettuce. When Chook and Pinkey arrived, she had partially destroyed the business, and was regretting that she had been too delicate to marry the greengrocer. She showed Chook the till bulging with copper and silver.

"Yer've done us proud," cried Chook, staring.

Mrs Partridge sorted out ten shillings from the heap.

"That's Mrs Robins's account," she remarked.

"Wot made 'er pay?" inquired Pinkey, suspiciously. "Yer didn't go an' ask 'er for it, did yer?"

"Not likely," said Mrs Partridge; "but when she complained of the peas bein' eighteenpence a peck, I pointed out that if she considered nothing too dear for 'er back, she should consider nothing too dear for 'er stomach, an' she ran 'ome to fetch this money an' nearly threw it in my face."

"Me best customer," cried Pinkey in dismay. "She pays at the end of the month like clockwork."

Mrs Partridge stared at the heap of silver, and changed the subject.

"It 'ud give me the creeps to sleep in the 'ouse with all that money," she remarked, "after readin' in the paper as 'ow burglars are passionate fond of silver, an' avin' no reg'lar 'ours for callin', like to drop in when least expected." She noted with satisfaction that Pinkey changed colour, and shook the creases out of her skirt. "Well, I must be goin'," she added. "I never like to keep William waitin' for 'is tea."

A cold wave swept over Chook. He had clean forgotten William, who would go home to Botany Street and find an empty house. Pinkey dived into the bedroom, and left Chook to face it out.

"'Ere's yer key," he said helplessly, to make a beginning.

"This is my key," said Mrs Partridge, feeling in her pocket, "an' the other one is under the flower-pot for William, if I'm out. I dunno what you mean."

"I mean this is the key of yer new 'ouse in Surry Hills,"

said Chook, fumbling hopelessly with the piece of iron.

"You've bin drinkin', an' the beer's gone to yer 'ead," said Mrs Partridge, unwilling to take offence.

"I tell yer I'm as dry as a bone," cried Chook, losing patience. "Yer think yer live in Botany Street, but yer don't. Yer live in Foveaux Street, an' this is the key of the 'ouse."

"I think I live in Botany Street, but I've moved to Foveaux Street," repeated Mrs Partridge, but the words conveyed no meaning to her mind.

She came closer to Chook. He looked and smelt sober, and suddenly a horrid suspicion ran through her mind that her brain was softening. She was older than they thought, for she had taken five years off her age when she had married William. In an agony of fear she searched her memory for the events of the past month, trying to recall any symptom of illness that should have warned her. She could remember nothing, and turned to Chook with a wild fear in her eyes. Something must be wrong with him.

"Can you understand what you're sayin'?" she asked.

"Yes," said Chook, anxious to get it over. "Yer lived in Botany Street this morning, but yer moved today, an' now yer live in Foveaux Street in the 'ouse yer picked on Monday."

"Do you expect me to believe that?" cried Mrs Partridge.

"No," said Chook; "but yer will w'en yer go 'ome an' find your 'ouse empty."

"An' who moved me?"

"Me an' Liz," said Chook. "The picnic wasn't till next week, an' Liz an' me thought we'd give yer a surprise."

For the first time in her life Mrs Partridge was speechless. She saw that she had been tricked shamefully. They had ransacked her house, and laid bare all the secrets of her little luxuries. She quailed as she remembered what they had found in the cupboard and the bottom drawer of the wardrobe. Never again could she face Chook and Pinkey, knowing what they did, and take her pickings of the shop. Suddenly she recovered her tongue, and turned on Chook, transformed with rage.

"William will break every bone in yer body when 'e 'ears what you've done," she cried, "mark my words. An' in case I never see yer again, let me tell yer somethin' that's been on my mind ever since I first met you. If that ginger-headed cat 'idin' behind the bedroom door 'adn't married yer, nobody else would, for you're that ugly it 'ud pay yer to grow whiskers an' 'ide yer face."

And with this parting shot she marched out of the shop and disappeared in the darkness.

21

DAD WEEPS ON A TOMBSTONE

The scene at Cremorne Point had suddenly reminded Clara that she was playing with fire. In the beginning she had consented to these meetings to humour the parent of her best pupil, and gradually she had drifted into an intimacy with Jonah without the courage to end it. To her fastidious taste his physical deformity and the flavour of Cardigan Street that still clung about his speech and manners put him out of court as a possible lover; but it had gratified her pride to discover that he was in love with her, and as he never expressed himself more plainly than by furtive glances and sudden inflections in his voice, she felt sure of her power to keep him at a distance.

These outings, indeed, had nearly fallen through, when Jonah, fumbling for words and afraid to say what was on his mind, had touched on a detail of his business. To his surprise, Clara caught fire like straw, fascinated at being shown the inner workings of the Silver Shoe. And from that time a curious attitude had grown between them. Jonah talked of his business, and stared at Clara as she listened, forgetful of him, her mind absorbed in details of profit and loss. She found the position easy to maintain, for Jonah, catching at straws, demanded no positive encouragement. A chance word or look from her was rich matter for a week's thought, twisted and turned in his mind till it meant all he desired.

She saw clearly and coldly that Jonah had placed her on a pedestal, and she determined never to step down of her own accord, recognizing with the instinct for business that had surprised Jonah that she would lose more than she would gain. And yet the sudden glimpse of passion in Jonah had whetted her appetite for more. It had recalled the days of her engagement with a singular bitterness and pleasure. She thought with a hateful persistence of her first love, the man who had accustomed her to admiration and then shuffled out of the engagement, forced by the attitude of his relatives to her father. But for weeks after the scene at Cremorne Jonah had retired within himself terrified lest he should alarm her and put an end to their outings. So far she had timed their meetings for the daylight out of prudence, but, pricked on by curiosity, she had begun to dally on the return journey, desiring and fearing some token of his adoration.

Meanwhile Jonah swung like a pendulum between hope and despair. He dimly suspected that a bolder man would have had his declaration out and done with long

262

ago, and he waited for a favourable opportunity; but it came and went, and left him speechless. He had accepted Ada as the typical woman, and now found himself as much at sea as if he had discovered a new species, for he never suspected that any other woman had it in her power, given a favourable opportunity, to lead him to this new world of sensation. Women had always been shy of him, and with his abnormal shape and his absorption in business it had been easy for him to miss what lay beneath the surface. But for the accident of his meeting with Clara, his temperament would have carried him through life, unconscious of love from his own experience and regarding it as a fable of women and poets.

Jonah never spent money willingly, except where Ray was concerned, and Clara in their first meetings had been surprised and chilled by his anxiety to get the value of his money. He had informed her, bluntly, that money was not made by spending it; but for some months he had been surprised by a desire to spend his money to adorn and beautify this woman. Clara, however, maintaining her independence with a wary eye, had refused to take presents from him. He had become more civilized and more human under the weight of his generous emotions, but they could find no outlet.

It was the affair of Hans Paasch that opened his eye to the power for good that she exercised over him. When his shop had closed for want of customers, Paasch found that his failing eyesight and methodical slowness barred him from competing with younger and quicker men, and, his mind weakened and bewildered by disaster, he had turned

263

for help to his first and only love, the violin. For some years he had taught a few pupils who were too poor to pay the fees of the professional teachers, and, persuaded that pupils would flock to him if he gave his whole time to it he took a room and set up as a teacher. In six months he had to choose between starvation by inches or playing dance music in Bob Fenner's hall for fifteen shillings a week. For a while he endured this, playing popular airs that he hated and despised for the larrikins whom he hated and feared, a nightly butt and target for their coarse jests. Then he preferred starvation, and found himself in the gutter with the clothes he stood up in and his fiddle. He had joined the army of mendicant musicians, who scrape a tune in front of hotels and shops, living on charity thinly veiled.

They had passed him one night on their return from Mosman, playing in front of a public-house to an audience of three loafers. The streets had soon dragged him to their level. Unkempt and half starved, he wore the look of the vagrant who sleeps in his clothes for want of bedding. Grown childish in his distress, he had forgotten his lifelong habits of neatness and precision, going to pieces like a man who takes to drink.

Clara, who knew his history, was horrified at the sight. She thought he lived comfortably on a crust of bread by giving lessons. Jonah turned sulky when she reproached him.

"I don't see 'ow I'm ter blame for this any more'n if 'e'd come to the gutter through drink. It was a fair go on the Road, an' if I beat 'im an' the others, it was because I was a better man at the game. I spent nearly all my money

264

in that little shanty where I started, an' 'im an' the others looked on an' 'oped I'd starve. Yer talk about me bein' cruel an' callous. It's the game that's cruel, not me. I knocked 'im out all right, but wot 'ud be the use of knockin' 'im down with one 'and an' pickin' 'im up with the other?"

"You say yourself that he took you off the streets, and gave you a living."

"So 'e did, but 'e got 'is money's worth out of me. I did the work of a man, an' saved 'im pounds for years. Yer wouldn't 'ave such a sentimental way of lookin' at things if yer'd been a street-arab, sellin' newspapers, an' no one ter make it 'is business whether yer lived or starved."

"But surely you can't see him in that condition without feeling sorry for him?"

"Oh yes, I can; 'e's no friend of mine. 'E told everybody on the Road that I went shares with the Devil," said Jonah, with an uneasy grin. "'Ere, I'll show yer wot 'e thinks of me."

He felt in his pocket for a coin, and crossed the street. Paasch had finished his piece, and putting his fiddle under his arm, turned to the loafers with a beseeching air. They looked the other way and discussed the weather. Then Jonah stepped up to him and thrust the coin into his hand. Paasch, feeling something unaccustomed in his fingers, held it up to the light. It was a sovereign, and he blinked in wonder at the coin then at the giver, convinced that it was a trick. Then he recognized Jonah, and a look of passionate fear and anger convulsed his features. He threw down the coin as if it had burnt him, crying "No, I vill not take your cursed moneys. Give me back mine shop and mine business

265

that you stole from me. You are a rich man and ride in your carriage, and I am the beggar, but I would not change with you. The great gods shall mock at you. Money you shall have in plenty while I starve, but never your heart's desire, for like a dog did you bite the hand that fed you."

Suddenly his utterance was choked by a violent fit of coughing, and he stared at Jonah, crazed with hate and prophetic fury. A crowd began to gather, and Jonah, afraid of being recognized, walked rapidly away.

"Now yer can see fer yerself," he cried, sullenly.

"Yes, I see," said Clara, strangely excited; "and I think you would be as cruel with a woman as you are with a man."

"I've given yer no cause ter say that," protested Jonah.

"Perhaps not," said Clara; "but that man won't last through the winter unless he's cared for. And if he dies, his blood will be on your head, and your luck will turn. His crazy talk made me shiver. Promise me to do something for him."

"Ye're talkin' like a novelette," said Jonah, roughly.

But Paasch's words had struck a superstitious chord in Jonah, and he went out of his way to find a plan for relieving the old man without showing his hand. He consulted his solicitors, and then an advertisement in the morning papers offered a reward to anyone giving the whereabouts of Hans Paasch, who left Hassloch in Bavaria in 1860, and who would hear of something to his advantage by calling on Harris & Harris, solicitors. A month later Jonah held a receipt for twelve pounds ten, signed by Hans Paasch, the first instalment of an annuity of fifty pounds a year miraculously left him by a distant cousin in Germany.

He showed this to Clara while they were crossing in the boat to Mosman. She listened to him in silence. Then a flush coloured her cheeks.

"You'll never regret that," she said; "it's the best day's work you ever did."

"I 'ope I'll never regret anythin' that gives you pleasure," said Jonah, feeling very noble and generous, and surprised at the ease with which he turned a compliment.

They had the Point to themselves, as usual, and Clara went to the edge of the rocks to see what ships had come and gone during the week, trying to identify one that she had read about in the papers. Jonah watched her in silence, marking every detail of her tall figure with a curious sense of possession that years of intimacy had never given him with Ada. And yet she kept him at a distance with a skill that exasperated him and provoked his admiration. One day when he had held her hand a moment too long, she had withdrawn it with an explanation that sounded like an apology. She explained that from a child she had been unable to endure the touch of another person; that she always preferred to walk rather than ride in a crowded bus or tram because bodily contact with others set her nerves on edge. It was a nervous affection, she explained, inherited from her mother. Jonah had his own opinion of this malady, but he admitted to himself that she would never enter a crowd or a crush.

The result of her pleading for Paasch had put her in a high good humour. It was the first certain proof of her power over Jonah, and she chattered gaily. She had risen in her own esteem. But presently, to her surprise, Jonah took some papers from his pocket and frowned over them.

"It's very impolite to read in other people's company," she remarked, with a sudden coolness.

"I beg yer pardon," said Jonah, starting suddenly, as if a whip had touched him. She never failed to reprove him for any lapse in manners, and Jonah winced without resentment.

"I thought this might interest yer," he continued. "I'm puttin' Steel in as manager at last, an' this is the agreement."

"Who advised you to do that?" said Clara, with an angry flush.

"Well, Johnson's been complainin' of overwork fer some time, but Miss Giltinan decided me. She's very keen on me openin' up branches in the suburbs."

"You place great weight on Miss Giltinan's opinion," said Clara, jealously.

"Ter tell the truth, I do," said Jonah. "Next ter yerself, she's got the best 'ead fer business of any woman I know."

"I don't agree with it at all," said Clara. "You're the brains of the Silver Shoe, and another man's ideas will clash with yours."

"No fear!" said Jonah. "I've got 'im tied down in black and white by my solicitors."

Clara ran her eye over the typewritten document, reading some of the items aloud.

"'Turn over the stock three times a year'! What does that mean?" And she listened while Jonah explained, the position of pupil and tutor suddenly reversed.

"'Ten and a half per cent bonus, in addition to his salary, if he shows an increase on last year's sales.

268

"'Net profits on the departments not to exceed twenty-five per cent'," read Clara in amazement. "Why, I should have thought the more profit he made, the better for you."

"No fear," said Jonah, with a grin; "I can't 'ave a man puttin' up the price of the Silver Shoe with his eye on his bonus."

Then a long discussion followed that lasted till nightfall. As the night promised to be fine, Jonah persuaded her to take tea at a dilapidated refreshment-room, halfway to the jetty, and they continued the discussion over cups of discoloured water and stale cakes. When they reached the Point again the moon was rising clear in the sky, and they sat and watched in silence the gradual illumination of the harbour. The wind had dropped, and tiny ripples alone broke the surface of the water. On the opposite shore the beaches lay obscured in the faint light of the moon, growing momently stronger, the land and water melted and confounded together in the grey light. The lesser stars fled at the slow approach of the moon, and in an hour she floated alone in the sky, save for the larger planets, flooding the deep abysses of the night with a gleam of silver, tender and caressing, that softened the angles and blotted details in brooding shadows.

Overhead curved the arch of night, a deep, flawless blue with velvety depths, pale and diluted with light as it touched the skyline. On the right, in the farther distance, Circular Quay flashed with the gleam of electric arcs, each contracted into a star of four points. And they glittered on the waterline like clustered gems without visible setting. A fainter glow marked the packed suburbs of the east; and then the lamps, flung like jewels in the night, picked out the line of shore to Rose Bay and the Heads.

Ferry-boats were crossing the harbour, jewelled and glittering with electric bulbs, moving in the distance without visible effort with the motion of swans, the throb of engines and the swirl of water lost in the distance. It was a symphony in light, each detached gleam on the sombre shore hanging

Like a rich jewel in an Ethiop's ear.

Between the moon and the eye the water lay like a sheet of frosted glass; elsewhere the water rippled without life or colour, treacherous and menacing in the night.

Jonah turned and looked at the woman beside him. They were alone on the rocky headland, the city and the world of men seemed remote and unreal, cut off by the silvery light and the brooding shadows. It dawned slowly on him that his relations with this woman were independent of time and space. Of all things visible, it was she alone that mattered. Often enough he had missed his cue, but now, as if answering a question, he began speaking softly, as if he were talking to himself:

"Clara!—Clara Grimes!—Clara! I've wanted ter say that out aloud fer months, but I've never found the place ter say it in. It sounds quite natural 'ere. Yer know that I love yer—I've seen it in yer face; but yer don't know that you're the first woman I ever wanted. No, yer needn't run away. I'm afraid ter touch yer, an' yer know it. Yer thought because I was married that I knew all about women. Why,

I didn't know what women were made for till I met you. I thought w'en I 'ad the shop an' my boy that I had everythin' I wanted, but the old woman was right. There's a lot more in this world than I ever dreamt of. Seein' you opened my eyes. An' now I want yer altogether. I want ter see yer face every 'our of the day, an' tell yer whatever comes into my mind. I spend 'ours talkin' to yer w'en I'm by myself.

"It's only my right," he went on, with increased energy. "I'm a man in spite of my shape, an' I only ask fer what I'm entitled to. I can see that other men 'ave been gittin' these things without me knowin' it. I used ter grin at Chook, but I was the fool. I had everythin' that I could see that was worth 'avin', an' somehow I wasn't satisfied. I never could see much in this life. I often wondered what it was all about. But now I understand. What's this for," and he indicated the dreamy peaceful scene with a sweep of his hand, "if it only leaves yer starin' and wonderin'? I know now. It's ter make me think about yer an' want yer. Well, yer've made a man of me, an' it's up ter yous ter make the best of me." He broke off with a short laugh. "P'raps this sounds funny ter you. I've 'eard old women at the Salvos' meetings talk like this, tellin' of the wonderful things they found out w'en they got converted."

Clara had listened in silence, with an intent, curious expression on her face. Jonah's words were like balm to her pride, lacerated three years ago by her broken engagement. And she listened, immensely pleased and a little afraid, like a mischievous child that has set fire to the curtains. Jonah's face was turned to her, and as she looked at him her curiosity was changed to awe at the sight of passion on

271

fire. She thought of the crazy fiddler's words, and felt in herself an infinite sadness, for she knew that Jonah would never gain his heart's desire.

"I've 'ad my say," he continued, "an' now I'll talk sense. You're a grown woman, an' yer know what all this means. I can give yer anythin' yer like: a house an' servants; everythin' yer want. What do yer say?"

Clara had gone white to the lips. It had come at last, and the Silver Shoe was within her reach, but the gift was incomplete. She must decline it, and take her chances for the future.

"Not quite everything, Joe," she replied gently, afraid of wounding him. "Ever since I was a girl I've had something to be ashamed of through no fault of my own—my drunken father, the street we live in, our genteel poverty; and now, when I seem to have missed all my chances, you come along, and offer me everything I want with the main thing left out. Oh, I know those cottages where the husband is a stranger, and the neighbours watch them behind the curtains, and pump the servant over the back fence! I'm too proud for that sort of thing. Oh, what a rotten world this is!" she cried passionately, and burst into a storm of weeping. It was the most natural action of her life.

Jonah sat and stared at the lights of the Quay, dismayed by her tears but relieved in his mind. He had spoken at last; already he was framing fresh arguments to persuade her. Presently she dried her eyes and looked at him with the ghost of a smile. Then began a discussion which threatened to last all night, neither of them giving way from the position they had taken up, neither yielding an inch to the other's entreaties. Suddenly Jonah looked at his watch with an exclamation. It was nearly ten. In the heat of argument they had forgotten the lapse of time. They scrambled over boulders and through the lantana bushes down to the path, and just caught the boat.

When they reached the Quay they were surprised again by the splendour of the night. The moon, just past the full, flooded the streets with white light that left deep shadows between the buildings like a charcoal drawing. They took a tram to the Haymarket, as they were afraid of being recognized in the Waterloo cars, and reached Regent Street after eleven. The hotels had disgorged their customers, who were talking loudly in groups on the footpath or lurching homeward with uneven steps. Jonah was explaining that he must see Clara all the way home on account of the lateness of the hour, when he was astonished to hear someone sobbing in the monumental mason's yard as if his heart would break. He turned and looked. The headstones and white marble crosses stood in rows with a faint resemblance to a graveyard; the moonlight fell clear and cold on these monuments awaiting a purchaser. Some, already sold, were lettered in black with the name of the departed. Jonah and Clara stared, puzzled by the noise, when they saw an old man in the rear of the yard in a top hat and a frock coat, clinging to a marble cross. He lurched round, and instantly Clara, with a gasp of amazement and shame, recognized her father.

She moved into the shadows of a house, humiliated to her soul by this exhibition; but Jonah laughed, in spite of himself, at the figure cut by Dad among the ready-made

273

monuments. As he laughed, Dad caught sight of him, and clinging to a marble angel with one arm for support, beckoned wildly with the other.

"Come here—come here," he cried between his sobs. "I'm all alone with the dead, and nobody to shed a tear 'cep' meself. Shame on you, shame on you," he cried, raising his voice in bitter grief, "to pass the poor fellows in their graves without sheddin' tear!"

He stopped and stared with drunken gravity at the name on the nearest tombstone, trying to read the words which danced before his eyes in the clear light. Jonah saw them plainly.

SACRED TO THE MEMORY OF
SARAH JAMES,
Aged Eighty-five.

A fresh burst of grief announced that Dad had deciphered the lettering.

"Sam!" he cried bitterly. "Me old fren' Sam! To think of bringing him here without letting me know! Me old fren'."

Here sobs choked his utterance. He stooped and examined the shining marble slab again, lurching from one side to the other with incessant motion.

"An' not a flowersh onsh grave!" he cried. "Sam was awfly fond flowersh."

"Get away 'ome, or the Johns'll pinch yer," said Jonah.

Dad stopped and stared at him with a glimmering of reason in his fuddled brain.

"I know yoush," he cried, with a cunning leer. "An' I know your fren' there. She isn't yer missis. She never is, y' know. Naughty boy!" he cried, wagging his finger at Jonah; "but I won't split on pal."

That reminded him of the deceased Sam, and he turned again to the monument.

"Goo'bye, Sam," he cried suddenly, under the impression that he had been to a funeral. "I've paid me respecks to an ol' fren', an' now we'll both sleep in peace."

"Come away and leave him," whispered Clara, trembling with disgust and mortification.

"No fear!" said Jonah. "The Johns down 'ere don't know 'im, an' they'll lumber 'im. You walk on ahead, an' I'll steer 'im 'ome.

He looked round; there was not a cab to be seen.

He led Dad out of the stonemason's yard with difficulty, as he wanted to wait for the mourning coaches. Then, opposite the mortuary, he remembered his little present for the Duchess, and insisted on going back.

"Wheresh my lil' present for Duchess?" he wailed. "Can't go 'ome without lil' present."

Jonah was in despair. At last he rolled his handkerchief into a bail and thrust it into Dad's hand.

Then Dad, relieved and happy, cast Jonah off, and stood for a moment like the Leaning Tower of Pisa. Jonah watched anxiously, expecting him to fall, but all at once, with a forward lurch Dad broke into a run, safe on his feet as a spinning top. Jonah had forgotten Dad's run, famous throughout all Waterloo, Redfern, and Alexandria.

22

A FATAL ACCIDENT

As Clara crossed the tunnel at Cleveland Street, she found that she had a few minutes to spare, and stopped to admire the Silver Shoe from the opposite footpath. Triumphant and colossal, treading the air securely above the shop, the glittering shoe dominated the street with the insolence of success. More than once it had figured in her dreams, endowed with the fantastic powers of Aaron's rod, swallowing its rivals at a gulp or slowly crushing the life out of the bruised limbs.

Her eye travelled to the shop below, with its huge plate-glass windows framed in brass, packed with boots set at every angle to catch the eye. The array of shining brass rods and glass stands, the gaudy ticket on each pair of boots with the shillings marked in enormous red figures and the pence faintly outlined beside them, pleased her eye like a picture. Today the silver lettering was covered with narrow posters announcing that Jonah's red-letter sale was to begin tomorrow. And as she stared at this huge machine for coining money, she remembered, with a sudden disdain, her home with its atmosphere of decay and genteel poverty. She was conscious of some change in herself. The slight sense of physical repugnance to the hunchback had vanished since his declaration. He and his shop stood for power and success. What else mattered?

Her spirits drooped suddenly as she remembered the obstacle that lay between her and the pride of openly sharing the triumphs of the Silver Shoe as she already shared its secrets. She thought with dismay of the furtive meetings drawn out for years without hope of relief unless the impossible happened. A watched pot never boils, and Ada was a young woman.

She crossed the street and entered the shop, her eye scouting for Jonah as she walked to the foot of the stairs, for since the appointment of a manager, Jonah had found time to slip up to the room after the lesson to ask her to play for him, on the plea that the piano was spoiling for want of use. And he waited impatiently for these stolen moments, with a secret desire to see her beneath his roof in a domestic setting that gave him a keener sense of intimacy than the swish of waters and wide spaces of sea and sky. But today she looked in vain, and Miss Giltinan, seeing the swift look of inquiry, stepped up to her.

"Mr Jones was called away suddenly over some arrangements for our sale that opens tomorrow. He left word with me that he'd be back as soon as possible," she said.

277

Clara thanked her, and flushed slightly. It seemed as if Jonah were excusing himself in public for missing an appointment. As she went up the stairs one shopman winked at the other and came across with a pair of hobnailed boots in his hand.

"This'll never do," he whispered, "the boss missin' his lesson. He'll get behind in his practice."

"Wotcher givin' us?" replied the other. "The boss don't take lessons; it's the kid."

"Of course he don't," said the other with a leer. "He learns a lot here by lookin' on, an' she tells him the rest at Mosman in the pale moonlight. If I won a sweep, I'd take a few lessons meself an' cut him out."

He became aware that Miss Giltinan was standing behind him, and raised his voice.

"I was tellin' Harris that the price of these bluchers ought to be marked down; they're beginning to sweat," he explained, turning to Miss Giltinan and showing her some small spots like treacle on the uppers.

"Mr Jones doesn't pay you good money to talk behind his back; and if you take the trouble to look at the tag, you'll see those boots have already been marked down," she replied indignantly.

The shopman slunk away without a word. Miss Giltinan was annoyed. It was not the first time that she had heard these scandalous rumours, for the shop was alive with whispers, some professing to know every detail of the meetings between Jonah and the music-teacher, naming to a minute the boat they caught on their return from Mosman. Jonah had contrived to avoid the faces that were familiar to him, but he had forgotten that he must be seen and recognized by people unknown to him. Miss Giltinan's clear and candid mind rejected these rumours for lying inventions, incapable of belief that her idol, Jonah, would carry on with any woman. They talked about him going upstairs to hear the piano. What was more natural when he couldn't play it himself? And she dismissed the matter from her mind and went about her business.

Clara gave Ray his lesson, listening between whiles for a rapid step from below, but none came. She decided to go, and picked up her gloves. But as she passed the bedroom door on the landing, a voice that she recognized for Ada's called out "Is that you, Miss Grimes?"

"Yes," said Clara, and paused.

The voice sounded faint and thin, like that of a sick woman.

"'Ow is it y'ain't playin' anythin' today?" she continued.

"Mr Jones is out," replied Clara, annoyed by this conversation through the crack of a door, and anxious to get away.

"Oh, is 'e?" said Ada, with an increase of energy in her voice. "I wish yer'd come in fer a minit, if ye're not in a 'urry."

Clara pushed the door open, and went in. It was her first sight of the bedroom, and she recoiled in dismay. The place was like a pigsty. Ada was lying on the bed, still tossed and disordered from last night, in a dirty dressing-gown. A basin of soapy water stood on the washstand, and the carpeted floor was littered with clothes, a pile of penny novelettes, and a collection of odds and ends on their way

279

to the rag-bag. In spite of the huge bedroom suite with its streaked and speckled mirrors, the room seemed half furnished.

For a moment Clara was puzzled, and then her quick, feminine eye noted a complete absence of the common knick-knacks and trifles that indicate the refinement or vulgarity of the owner. She remembered that Jonah had told her that Ada pawned everything she could lay hands on since he stopped her allowance. But she was more surprised at the change in Ada herself. Months ago Ada had begun to avoid her, ashamed of her slovenly looks, and now Clara scarcely recognized her. Her eyes were sunken, her cheeks had fallen in, and a bluish pallor gave her the look of one recovering from a long illness. The room had not been aired, and the accumulated odours of the night turned Clara sick. She was thinking of some excuse to get away when Ada began to speak with a curious whine, quite unlike her old manner.

"I'm ashamed ter ask yer in, Miss Grimes, the room's in such a state; but I've been very ill, with no one ter talk to fer days past. Not that I'm ter blame. I 'ope it's niver your lot to 'ave a 'usband with thousan's in the bank, an' too mean ter keep a servant. 'Ere am I from mornin' ter night, slavin' an' drudgin', an' me with a leg that bad I can 'ardly stand on it. I'll just show yer wot state I'm in. It's breakin' out all over. Me blood's that bad fer want of proper food an' nourishment." She began to unfasten a dirty bandage below her knee. Clara turned her head in disgust. The flesh was covered with ulcerated sores.

"I don't know 'ow you find 'im, Miss Grimes," she continued, her voice rising in anger, "but if yer believe me, a meaner man niver walked the earth. I've 'ad ter pawn the things in this very room ter pay the baker an' the grocer. That's 'ow 'e makes 'is money. Starvin' 'is own wife ter squeeze a few shillin's for 'is bankin' account. 'E knows I can't go outside the door, 'cause I've got nuthin' ter put on; but 'e takes jolly good care ter go down town an' live on the fat of the land."

From the next room came the fitful, awkward sounds of a five-finger exercise from Ray. Clara listened with silent contempt to this torrent of abuse. She knew that it was false; that the more Jonah gave her, the more she spent on drink. And as she looked at Ada's face, ravaged by alcohol, a stealthy thought crept into her mind that set her heart beating. Suddenly Ada's anger dropped like a spent fire.

"Did yer say Mr Jones was busy in the shop?" she inquired, feebly.

"No," said Clara; "I understand that he went down town on important business, and won't be back till late."

"Thank yer," said Ada, with a curious glitter in her eyes. "Would yer mind callin' Ray in? I want ter send 'im on a message to the grocer's."

Clara went into the next room and sent Ray to his mother, stopping for a minute to shut the keyboard and put the music straight. After every lesson she was accustomed to examine the piano as if it were her own property. When she entered the bedroom again, Ada was whispering rapidly to Ray. She looked up as Clara entered, and gave him some money in a piece of paper.

"An' tell 'im I'll send the rest tomorrer," she added aloud.

281

Ray went down the back stairs, swinging an empty millet-bag in his hand. For another five minutes Clara remained standing, to show that she was anxious to get away, while Ada abused her husband, giving detailed accounts of his meanness and neglect. Suddenly her mood changed.

"I'm afraid I mustn't keep yer any longer, Miss Grimes," she said abruptly; "an' thank yer fer lookin' in ter see 'ow I was."

Clara, surprised and relieved at the note of dismissal in her voice, took her leave.

She went down the winding staircase at the rear of the shop, opposite the cashier's desk. The pungent odour of leather was delightful in her nostrils after the stale smell of the room above, and she halted at the turn of the landing to admire the huge shop, glittering with varnish, mirrors, and brass rods. Then she looked round for Jonah, but he was nowhere to be seen.

The sight of Ada, ravaged by alcohol, had filled her with strange thoughts, and she walked up Regent Street, comparing Ada with her own father, who seemed to thrive on beer. There must be some difference in their constitutions, for Ada was clearly going to pieces, and...the thought entered her mind again that quickened her pulse. She had never thought of that! She was passing the Angel with its huge white globes and glittering mirrors that reflected the sun's rays, when she caught sight of Ray coming out of the side door, swinging an empty millet-bag in his hand. A sudden light flashed on her mind. Ada's invitation into the bedroom, the inquiry about Jonah, and her sudden dismissal all meant this.

"Did you get what your mother wanted?" she asked the child, with a thumping sensation in her heart.

"No," said Ray carelessly; "the man wouldn't give me the medicine. He told me to go home and fetch the rest of the money."

"How much more do you want?" asked Clara, in a curious tone.

"Eighteen pence," said Ray, showing two half-crowns in his hand.

Clara hesitated, with parched lips. She remembered Ada's face, ravaged by brandy. She was a physical wreck, and six months ago...perhaps another bottle...

The thought grazed her mind with a stealthy, horrible suggestion. She felt in her purse with trembling fingers, and found a shilling and a sixpence.

"Go and get your mother's medicine," she whispered, putting the money into Ray's hand; "but don't tell her that you met me, or she may scold you."

Ray turned in at the side door, and Clara, white to the lips, hurried round the corner.

It took Ray half an hour to cover the short distance between the Angel and the Silver Shoe, with a bottle of brandy swinging carelessly in the millet-bag. Cassidy himself, all smiles, had carefully wrapped it in paper. Ray had promised to hurry home with the medicine for his mother, but, as usual, the shop windows were irresistible. Some of his early trips to the Angel had taken half a day.

Meanwhile Ada lay on the bed in an agony of attention, atrociously alert to every sound, hearing with every nerve in her body. Her nerves had collapsed under the repeated debauches, and the scream of an engine shunting in the railway yards went through her like a knife. The confused rumble of carts in Regent Street, the familiar sounds from the shop below, the slamming of a door, a voice raised in inquiry, the monotonous, kindly echoes of life, struck on the raw edges of her nerves, exasperating her to madness.

And through it all her ears sought for two sounds with agonizing acuteness—the firm, rapid step of Jonah mounting the stairs winding from the shop, or the nonchalant, laggard footfall of Ray ascending from the stairs at the rear. Would Cassidy send the bottle and trust her for the other eighteen pence? Would Jonah hurry back to meet Miss Grimes? Presently her ear distinguished the light, uncertain step of Ray. Every nerve in her body leapt for joy when she saw the bottle. She looked at the clock; it was nearly four. She had at least an hour clear, for Jonah would be in no hurry now that he had missed the music-lesson. She snatched the bag from the astonished child.

"Go an' see if yer father's in the shop. If 'e ain't there, yer can go an' play in the lane till 'e comes back," she cried.

Her hands shook as she held the bottle, but with a supreme effort she controlled her muscles and drew the cork without a sound, an accomplishment that she had learned in the back parlour of the Angel. She poured out half a glass, and swallowed it neat. The fiery liquid burnt her throat and brought the tears to her eyes, but she endured it willingly for the sake of the blessed relief that always followed. A minute later she repeated the dose and lay down on the bed. In ten minutes the seductive liquid had calmed her nerves like oil on troubled waters. She listened to the familiar sounds of

284

the shop and the street with a delicious languor and sense of comfort in her body. In an hour she had reached the maudlin stage, and the bottle was half empty.

She felt at peace with the world, and began to think kindly of Jonah. Hazily she remembered her bitter speech to Miss Grimes, and wondered at her violence. There was nothing the matter with him. He had been a good husband to her, working day and night to get on in the world. She felt a sudden desire to be friendly with him. Maudlin tears of self-reproach filled her eyes as she thought how she had stood in his way instead of helping him. She would mend her ways, give up the drink which was killing her and take her proper position, with a fine house and servants. With a fatuous obstinacy in her sodden brain, she decided not to lose a minute, but to go and surprise Jonah with her noble resolutions.

She got to her feet, and saw the brandy bottle. Ah! Jonah must not know that she had been drinking, and with the last conscious act of her clouded brain she staggered into the sitting-room and hid the bottle under the cushions of the sofa. Then, conscious of nothing but her resolve, she lurched to the top of the stairs. It was nearly dark, and she felt for the railing, but the weight of her body sent an atrocious pain through her leg, and to ease it she took a step forward to put her weight on the other. And then, without fear, and without the desire or the power to save herself, she stepped into space and fell headlong down the winding staircase that she had always dreaded, rolling and bumping with a horrible noise on the wooden steps down to the shop, where the electric lights had just been

285

switched on. She rolled sideways, and lay, with a curious slackness in her limbs, in front of the cashier's desk. One of the shopmen, startled by the noise, turned, and then, with a look of horror on his face, ran to the door. He bumped into Jonah, who was coming from the ladies' department.

"Wot the devil's this?" cried Jonah.

The man turned and pointed to the huddled heap at the foot of the stairs.

"It's yer missis. She fell from the top. 'Er face is looking the wrong way."

Jonah ran forward and shouted for a doctor. Then he knelt down and tried to lift Ada into a sitting posture, but her head sagged on one side. And Jonah realized suddenly, with a curious feeling of detachment, that he was free. When the doctor arrived, he told them that death had been instantaneous, as she had broken her neck in the fall.

The next day the Silver Shoe was closed on account of the funeral. The Grimes family sent a wreath, but Jonah looked in vain for Clara among the mourners. He was disappointed but relieved, fearing that the exultation in his heart would betray him in the presence of strangers. He dwelt with rapture on the moment in which he would meet her face to face, free to love and be loved, willing to lose some precious hours for the sake of rehearsing schemes for the future in his mind. He listened without emotion to the conventional regrets of the mourners, agreeing mechanically with their empty remarks on his great loss, a mocking devil in his brain.

The day after the funeral the Silver Shoe returned to business, and Jonah spent the morning in the shop, too nervous to sit idle. He had spent a sleepless night debating whether he should go to Clara or wait till she came to him of her own accord. The shop was alive with customers, drawn by the red-letter sale, but there was no sign of the one woman above all he desired to see. Suddenly he decided, with a certainty that astonished him, that she would come in the afternoon. After dinner he stayed in the sitting-room, fidgeting with impatience. He looked for something to do, and remembered that he had still to clear up the mystery of Ada's drunken bout. All the shop-hands had denied lending her money, and the mystery was increased by his finding no bottle in the usual hiding places. Ray, when questioned about brandy, had stared at him with bewildered eyes. And to calm his nerves he made another search of the rooms.

He turned out the drawers and cupboards, meeting everywhere evidence of Ada's slovenly habits. And at the sight and touch of the tawdry laces and flaring ribbons he was surprised by an emotion of tenderness and pity for his dead wife. He realized that the last link had snapped that bound him to Cardigan Street and the Push. Something vibrated in him as he thought of the woman who had shared his youth, and he understood suddenly that no other woman could disturb her possession of the years that were dead. Clara could share the future with him, but half his life belonged irrevocably to Ada.

He had searched every likely nook and corner of the rooms, and found nothing. The absence of the bottle set him thinking. He became certain that the hand of another was in this. Ada had never left her room; therefore the bottle had been brought to her. And the one who brought it had taken it away again. Clara had been the last one to see her alive, and of course…He stopped with an unshaped thought in his mind, and then smiled at it for an absurdity. Tired with his exertions, he sat on the sofa, digging his elbow into the cushion, and instantly felt something hard underneath. The next moment he was on his feet, holding in his hands the bottle of brandy, half empty. He stared stupidly at the bottle that had sent Ada to her death and set him free, wondering who had paid for it and brought it into the house. As he turned the bottle in his hands, examining it with the morbid interest with which one examines a bloodstained knife, he heard a light tap on the door.

"Come in," he cried, absorbed in his discovery.

He turned with the bottle in his hands, to find Clara standing in the doorway with a tremulous smile on her lips. But, as Jonah turned, her eye fell on the bottle.

"I've been a day findin' this," said Jonah; "but now—"

An extraordinary change in Clara's face stopped the words on his lips. The tremulous smile on her parted lips changed to a nervous grin, and her colour turned to a greyish white as she stared at the bottle, her eyes dilated with horror. For some moments there was a dreadful silence, in which Jonah distinctly heard Miss Giltinan giving an order downstairs. Slowly he looked from Clara to the bottle. Again he stared at the frightened woman, and his mind leapt to a dreadful certainty.

"Come in, an' shut the door," he said. His voice was little more than a whisper.

Clara obeyed him mechanically.

"Sit down," he added, putting the bottle on the table.

For a while each stared at the other, too stunned to move or speak. Jonah's world had fallen about his ears, and Clara's dreams of wealth mocked at her and fled.

Suddenly, in the deadly silence, Jonah began to speak.

"So it was you, was it? I never thought of that. I wonder what brought yer 'ere just as I found this? They say murder will out, an' I believe it now. If this 'appened to anybody else, 'e'd go mad. But I can stand it. I'm tough. I fought my way up from the gutter. An' ye're the woman that I worshipped...For God's sake, woman, speak! Make up something that I can believe. Say yer never 'ad a 'and in this, an' I'll kiss the ground yer walk on. No, it wouldn't be any use. I couldn't believe the angel Gabriel, if he looked at me with that face. Yer paid for that bottle an' brought it 'ere. I saw that the moment yer set eyes on it. Yer thought Ada wasn't goin' ter hell fast enough, an' yer'd give 'er a shove. An' I see now why yer did it. Yer wanted ter step into 'er shoes, an 'andle my money. It wasn't me yer wanted. I might 'ave known that. It was the shop that yer were always talkin' about. An' if yer 'adn't walked in at that door just now, I should never 'ave suspected. Screamin' funny, ain't it? She wasn't much loss, but she was a thousand times better than the ladylike devil that killed her. I don't know 'ow the law stands in a case like this. Yer may be safe from that, but yer've got me ter deal with first. Yer led me on with yer damned airs to believe in things I've never dreamt of before. An' now yer've killed the best in me as sure as yer murdered my wife. Well, yer must pay for that, too."

Clara sat on the chair like one in a trance. She understood in a numbed kind of way that something dreadful was going to happen. O God, she had never meant to do wrong! And if this was the punishment, let it come quickly. Jonah had been walking backwards and forwards with nervous steps, and she noted every detail of his person with a fixed stare. The early repugnance to his deformity returned with horror as she studied the large head, wedged between the shoulders as if a giant's hand had pressed it down, the projecting hump, and the unnaturally long arms ending in the hard, hairy fist of the shoemaker.

She felt that he was going to kill her. She wanted to speak, to cry out that she was not so guilty as he thought, but her tongue was like a rasp. Suddenly Jonah stopped in front of her. Her stony silence had maddened him, and in a moment he was transformed into the old-time larrikin, accustomed to demand an eye for an eye, a tooth for a tooth. He rushed at her with a cry like an animal, and caught her by the throat with his powerful hands. But the contact of his fingers with that delicate flesh that he had never dared to touch before brought him to his senses. A violent shudder shook him like ague, his fingers relaxed, and with a sobbing cry, dreadful to hear, he dragged the fainting woman to her feet and pushed her towards the door, crying "Go, go, for God's sake!"

She walked unsteadily through the shop with a face the colour of chalk, hearing and seeing nothing. The red-letter sale was in full swing. A crowd of customers jostled one another as they passed in and out; the coins clinked merrily in the till. Miss Giltinan caught sight of her face, and wondered. Half an hour later, growing suspicious, she ran upstairs, and knocked at the door on a pretext of business. Hearing nothing, she opened the door, with her heart in her mouth, and looked in. Jonah was crouching motionless on the end of the sofa, his head buried among the cushions, like a stricken animal. Puzzled, but reassured, she closed the door gently and went downstairs.

**

Jonah never saw Clara again. He spent a week in the depths, groping blindly, hating life for its deceptions. Then one day, his passion of hatred and loathing for Clara left him suddenly, as a garrison surrenders without a blow. He took a cab to her house, and knocked at the door. A curtain moved, but the door remained unopened. A month later he learned that she had married her old love, the clerk in the Lands Department, transferred by request to Wagga, beyond the reach of Dad and his reputation. The following year Jonah married Miss Giltinan, chiefly on account of Ray, who was growing unmanageable; and on Monday morning it was one of the sights of Regent Street to see the second Mrs Jones step into her sulky to drive round and inspect the suburban branches of the Silver Shoe which Jonah had opened under her direction.

Chook and Pinkey did not need to stare at sixpence before spending it, but their fortune was long in the making. Meanwhile Chook consoled himself with the presence of a sturdy son, the image of Pinkey, with a mop of curls the colour of a new penny.

Text Classics

Dancing on Coral
Glenda Adams
Introduced by Susan Wyndham

The Commandant
Jessica Anderson
Introduced by Carmen Callil

Homesickness
Murray Bail
Introduced by Peter Conrad

Sydney Bridge Upside Down
David Ballantyne
Introduced by Kate De Goldi

Bush Studies
Barbara Baynton
Introduced by Helen Garner

The Cardboard Crown
Martin Boyd
Introduced by Brenda Niall

A Difficult Young Man
Martin Boyd
Introduced by Sonya Hartnett

Outbreak of Love
Martin Boyd
Introduced by Chris Womersley

The Australian Ugliness
Robin Boyd
Introduced by Christos Tsiolkas

All the Green Year
Don Charlwood
Introduced by Michael McGirr

They Found a Cave
Nan Chauncy
Introduced by John Marsden

The Even More Complete
Book of Australian Verse
John Clarke

Diary of a Bad Year
J. M. Coetzee
Introduced by Peter Goldsworthy

Wake in Fright
Kenneth Cook
Introduced by Peter Temple

The Dying Trade
Peter Corris
Introduced by Charles Waterstreet

They're a Weird Mob
Nino Culotta
Introduced by Jacinta Tynan

The Songs of a Sentimental Bloke
C. J. Dennis
Introduced by Jack Thompson

Careful, He Might Hear You
Sumner Locke Elliott
Introduced by Robyn Nevin

Fairyland
Sumner Locke Elliott
Introduced by Dennis Altman

Terra Australis
Matthew Flinders
Introduced by Tim Flannery

textclassics.com.au